A DiCarlo Brides Novel

Family Matters

Book 4

Heather Tullis

OTHER BOOKS BY HEATHER

A DiCarlo Brides Novel

FAMILY MATTERS

BOOK 4

JELLY BEAN PRESS
FILLMORE, UTAH

1430 W. Susquehanna Ave
Philadelphia, PA 19121
215-236-1760 | treehousebooks.org

Heather Tullis

Published by Jelly Bean Press, 90 S Main St. Ste #2, Fillmore, UT 84631
ISBN: 9780615806914
Cover design by Bill J. Justesen
Cover design © 2013 by Heather Justesen

CAST OF CHARACTERS

Camellia DiCarlo Talmadge (Cami)—the oldest of George DiCarlo's daughters, born to his wife, head of guest services. Married to Vince.

Sage Parker Watts—Second eldest, head of the resort Spa. Born to Darla Parker. Married to Joel.

Rosemary Keogh—Third eldest of George DiCarlo's daughters, born to Wanda Keogh, head of resort food services.

Lantana DiCarlo Bahlmann (Lana)—Fourth eldest, second daughter by George's wife, hotel manager. Married to Blake.

Delphinium Gifford (Delphi)—Fifth eldest daughter by Zelda Gifford, head of resort events.

Jonquil Chestnut—Sixth eldest daughter by Trudy Chestnut, head of the resort floral center.

Cleome Markham—Rosemary Keogh's daughter.

Vince Talmadge—Landscape architect, best friend of Jeremy and Gage. Married to Cami.

Jeremy Litster—local photographer, best friend of Vince and Gage.

Gage Mathews—head of Deer Mountain, the local ski resort. Best friend to Vince and Jeremy.

Harrison Forest—older half-brother to Sage by another father. Head of hotel HR.

Blake Bahlmann—regional manager of DiCarlo Resorts, stationed out of the Juniper Ridge resort. Married to Lana.

Joel Watts—former Navy SEAL, head of hotel security. Married to Sage.

CHAPTER 1

"Today's tragedy is going to change your life. For the better I think."

Rosemary looked up from the salmon she was deboning and saw Sage standing beside her at the restaurant kitchen counter. "Yeah? Thanks for the heads up, but I'm a little too busy for tragedy today." Still, she felt a little shiver go down her spine. Sage's predictions had a way of coming true, even if she sometimes couched them in vague enough terms that the average person might ignore the warnings. The word *tragedy* rang again in her mind—she was fairly certain Sage wasn't referring to a burned dish or dropped appetizer. "Not enough going on in your own department right now?"

Sage didn't react to the clipped words as her wide, brown eyes studied Rosemary calmly. Her olive skin and curling brown hair gave her the look of a gypsy—a not inapt comparison considering the random, always-accurate predictions. Though the half-sisters hadn't known each other long, Rosemary had seen enough of these predictions to believe in them.

"The spa is busy, but I had a few minutes' break and thought I should come warn you. It's been on my mind since I woke up this morning," Sage said. The chaos of breakfast preparation whirled around them, pans clattering, dishes clanking and staff calling back and forth to each other as they prepared for the convention, while feeding late breakfast patrons in the restaurant.

"Well, thanks for stopping by. I think." Rosemary didn't want to dwell on what the tragedy was going to be if there was no way to avert it. And how could a tragedy have a positive outcome?

Sage touched Rosemary's arm. "Just remember. Good things come out of bad sometimes too. And this will definitely be one of them." She gave her arm a little squeeze, and breezed out.

It was nice to no longer see evidence of the worry and stress that had plagued Sage through the summer and fall, but Rosemary wondered if it left too much time for her to worry about the rest of the sisters. She stretched her back muscles, forcing away the shiver of discomfort Sage's prediction had caused.

Maybe Sage had misunderstood her impressions. Rosemary caught on that, then put the whole conversation behind her. She didn't have time for cryptic messages.

Rosemary was dragging after a fourteen-hour day when she returned home, her feet sore, her muscles complaining, and with another long day ahead of her tomorrow. She took comfort in the fact that at least everything was ready for morning, even if *she* wasn't. Sage's warning had flitted into her thoughts several times through the day, but nothing she would consider tragic had happened, unless you counted the server who tripped over her own feet and dropped a table's meals just before she reached them.

That had been a mess, and the restaurant had to comp the meals—which had eventually made it to them, intact—but Rosemary would hardly consider it a tragedy. She tossed her keys on the kitchen counter and kicked off her shoes in the middle of the aisle, mostly with the hope of annoying Delphi who, in Rosemary's opinion, had a nearly OCD compulsion about orderliness. She poured herself some hot water from the espresso machine, grabbed one of Sage's secret tea blends and stepped into the sunken living room to join Delphi, who was watching the news.

"Anything interesting in your neck of the woods?" Rosemary asked as the newscasters droned on about some new legislation the Colorado House of Representatives was trying to push through.

"I dealt with a hysterical bride because the linens we ordered are a shade too pink for her reception, a CEO who decided to add an extra ten rooms for his convention *this* weekend, despite the fact that we're already at capacity, but I'm not having any trouble with my staff. You?" Delphi brushed the short, blond hair back from her face with perfectly manicured hands. She still wore the cream-colored blouse and navy skirt she'd put on for work that day and despite the fact that she had to have worked nearly as many hours as Rosemary, Delphi still looked perfectly pressed and presentable. Sometimes Rosemary could hate her for that.

A lot of people thought they were the two sisters who were the most alike, but Rosemary didn't agree. Sure, they were both strong willed and knew what they wanted, but Delphi had a way of telling you where to go without seeming the least impolite, while Rosemary wouldn't bother over the pretty words. They were both tall and blond, but Rosemary had long hair that she had to braid out of the way while she worked in the kitchen and she fought daily to keep the extra weight off. Delphi had a short cap of hair, was thin without exercise or paying attention to what she ate and totally uncoordinated, in opposition to the genteel, polished way she presented herself in every situation—at least when she was in public. Their histories were also total opposites, but that was another story.

Rosemary pushed the comparison away as it always made her feel a little inadequate. "Things ran mostly fine in the restaurant, the convention banquets went well—unless you've heard something I haven't—and I got my food order done. No major catastrophes—despite Sage saying a tragedy was going to change my life today." She tried to blow the warning off as if she didn't believe a word of it, but still felt an itch between her shoulder blades when she thought of it.

"Sage gave you a warning? That sounds ominous." Delphi took another sip from her teacup, the soft scent wafting over to Rosemary said it held chamomile. She was the only one of Rosemary's five step-sisters who was still unconvinced about Sage's abilities.

"New information regarding the bombing of a Washington DC café has just come in," a redheaded news anchor announced on the television. She stared into the camera with a serious expression.

"Senator Teremce Lampert of Minnesota is confirmed as having died in the blast, along with at least eight other people after a bomb was launched through a window during lunch hour. Authorities are still trying to track down suspects." She went on to discuss the controversial legislation the senator had been trying to pass and how it wasn't expected to get enough votes without his push behind it.

Delphi looked at Rosemary. "You're from DC; maybe that's your tragedy." She pointed to the television. There was a touch of sarcasm in her voice.

The camera panned back, showing the row of storefronts on the street. Rosemary recognized the café sign hanging crooked against the wall and sighed. She loved the little café and had been going there for decades. "It sure is. They make the best cannoli at that shop. It's even better than mine."

"Liar." Delphi picked up the remote and turned off the television. "No one's cannoli is better than yours, as much as I hate to admit that."

"Thank you." Though the loss of the café gave Rosemary wistful beats of nostalgia, Delphi's unusual compliment did make her feel a little better. "I'm off to bed. Tomorrow's going to be a bear." Rosemary carried her tea up to her room to sip on while she prepared for bed, wondering if she'd known anyone who'd been hurt in the bombing.

The morning zoomed by as the restaurant staff got the continental breakfast out for the finance conference, then turned their attention to preparing the lunches.

Rosemary was double-checking the croissants they had made that morning when there was a knock on the storage room door. "Come in," she called as she marked the number on her list.

"Hey, there's a guy out there who wants to talk to you." It was one of the servers. "I told him you were in the middle of something and tried to fob him off on Tate, but he said it was a personal matter and important."

Rosemary scowled, but set her clipboard on the shelf and responded coolly. "Thank you for letting me know." She wondered if it really was personal, or if that was just an excuse the salesman was using to see her.

He stood just outside the kitchen door, expectantly. First glance didn't say salesman, though. His suit was too nice, he held himself stiffly, and well, she couldn't put her finger on it, but his appearance put her a little on edge. "Hello, I'm Rosemary Keogh," she greeted him with a businesslike smile. "What can I do for you today?"

"I'm Thomas Sinclair, from Davis and Sinclair. I'm an attorney." The forty-something-year-old glanced at the people around them. "Is there somewhere quieter where we can talk?"

Rosemary felt the dread rise inside her. Was someone suing her? She decided to be very, very careful. She pointed to a private room a few feet away and he led her inside.

When the door shut behind them, she turned to him. "What's going on?"

He gestured to a chair. "Please have a seat."

"Do I *need* to sit?" When his expression softened a little, she sank into the one he'd pointed out, her bad feeling growing.

"A colleague of mine represents Don and Cecelia Markham in Washington, DC. He asked me to come speak with you, since he's unable to make the trip."

"Is something wrong? Did something happen to them?" Hard on her heels was worry about Cleome, their nine-year-old daughter.

He sat across from her and folded his hands on the tabletop. "Did you hear about the senator who was killed in that café bombing in DC yesterday?" When she nodded that she had, he continued. "It seems they were eating there at the time. I'm very sorry. They didn't make it."

Shock shuddered through her, stealing her breath and nearly stopping her heart. Grief was hard on its heels, with worry following right behind. Her mouth refused to follow directions as she tried to process the information. It took a couple of tries before she got out the words. "Their daughter, Cleo?"

He made a calming gesture with his hands. "She's fine. She was at school at the time. But," he pulled out some papers and passed them to her, "it seems the Markhams have appointed you as their daughter's guardian."

Her head spun and her hands clasped hard on her lap as she tried to put all of those pieces together. Cecelia was dead? She couldn't quite seem to pound that thought into her head. They'd spoken on the phone only a few days earlier, catching up as they did every couple of weeks. They had been planning for Rosemary's next visit to DC the following month—her bi-monthly trip to check up on the family in person and be part of Cleo's life. That brought home what he'd said a moment earlier.

"They want me to raise Cleo? Are you sure? I would have thought Cecelia's brother. Or Don's." She felt herself begin to hyperventilate. They were going to let her raise Cleo? Hope and terror filled her, though she could have sworn only a moment later that grief had filled her too much to allow any other emotions in, but they all seemed to squeeze inside her at the same time. Did Cleo know about the arrangement? Would she be okay with it? Could Rosemary bring her back home when there were two other women living in the house with her? What would they think?

Her lungs loosened slightly, though the pain of knowing that Don and Cecelia were gone was overwhelming. "Who's taking care of her?" She had to get to DC immediately. Her mind slowed to a crawl as she tried to make it compute. How could this happen?

"You'll have to contact the attorney for more details. He didn't tell me that much. Are you okay? Can I get you anything?" he asked. She saw the compassion in his eyes now, the worry that showed in the way his hands gripped the briefcase he'd been carrying.

"Just a second." Her daughter. Rosemary was going to get to raise her daughter, the one she'd given to Cecelia to raise. It was something she had never even dared to dream of and made her insides twist with excitement and pain all at once.

"I'm sure this must be quite a shock to you, considering they had family who could have raised the girl instead, but they wanted you to do it."

"Wow. I'm honored." She sucked in a deep breath and let it out. He didn't need to know the truth, that they had adopted her daughter and kept in touch. Cleo was the reason she'd gone home for visits—staying away for more than a year would have been too hard—the two-month gaps between visits now was harder than she had expected. "So I probably need to plan on being there for a while. What kind of arrangements do you think I should make?" Her head spun and she couldn't feel her fingertips anymore.

"That depends on if you decide to stay here or move back to DC."

She shook her head. "I don't have a choice. I have to stay here through the summer at least."

"All right, then. The attorney's number is on the top of the stack of papers."

"Thanks." Her hands trembled and she felt light-headed.

"Would you like me to get someone to be with you?" he asked. "If you have a friend or someone I can call, I'd be happy to do that."

"No. No, thanks." She shook her head, looked back at him and forced a smile while she tried to fit the pieces together in a comprehensive form. "I have several family members here. I'll go to one of their offices if I need to talk to someone." Obviously he wasn't from the area, or he'd have already known that—the whole town had talked about the twisted mess her father had made of their lives. She doubted her legs would hold her weight at the moment, but she didn't want to face anyone else right now anyway. How could Don and Cecelia be gone? And what kind of mother would she be with Wanda as her example of motherhood? "Their house and stuff?"

"Everything I know is in those papers. If you'd like to take a minute to read them, I'd be happy to explain anything you don't understand. Or you can have your own attorney look them over." He passed over a business card.

Rosemary flipped open the folder and tried to read the top page, but the words swirled in front of her eyes. She was still in shock. "Maybe when my brain clears. I'll have my attorney look them over, too."

Mr. Sinclair picked up his briefcase and coat and shook her hand. "I wish you lots of luck in the parenting adventures ahead."

"Thanks." Rosemary watched him leave, then returned her gaze to the papers in front of her. Shaking herself out of the fuzz that seemed to be taking over her brain, she pulled out her cell phone to call Alex, the attorney who had handled her father's estate. He was a pseudo relative—a cousin to two of her half-sisters, and probably already knew about her relationship to Cleo. It seemed her father had told him everything else about them. Family law wasn't his specialty, but he could help with the estate stuff and he had to know more about these things than she did.

She felt hot tears of grief roll onto her cheeks. Don and Cecelia were dead. It was like losing her father all over again. Maybe worse because the pain wasn't accompanied by the twist of resentment she hadn't been able to release about George. Cecelia had been the mother she'd wished she'd had and Don had filled in for the father who was gone most of the time. She thought of Cleo, of how alone *she* must be feeling. It made Rosemary want to drop everything and head straight for DC, but she had commitments and arrangements to make, so she'd have to stick it out, at least for a few more hours. She could check on flight times as soon as she had a chance to get her feet under herself.

Rosemary left a message with Alex's secretary and stared for a long moment at the folder, allowing herself to grieve for several minutes before wiping her face and forcing herself to focus on her job. Cleo was going to need her, so she'd be strong. Later, when Rosemary was alone, there would be time to fall apart.

She returned to the kitchen to find her assistant manager, Tate, scowling.

"What's wrong?" she asked.

"Dill. In the chicken sandwich filling."

She felt her blood pressure rise as she grabbed a spoon to taste the filling. When her sample confirmed what Tate had said, she turned to Rulon, who had been assigned to mix it. "You added dill?"

He rubbed a sweaty hand over his unshaven face. "It was an honest mistake. I'm sorry."

"You're sorry. The recipe calls for tarragon. They aren't even kept on the same shelf. How did you make the mistake?" Rage rose within her—much easier to deal with than her grief. She'd been on the edge of ready to fire him anyway. This was the last straw.

"Look, I'm sorry. It won't happen again." He didn't appear sorry though. His dark eyes were belligerent and he gestured angrily.

"You're right, it won't. You're done here." Rosemary's mind started whirling as she thought of everything they needed to do to fix the problem and still get lunch out on time.

"What do you mean?"

"I mean you're fired. I put up with a lot of things, but incompetence isn't one of them, and you've already used all of your freebies. Grab your things and get out of here."

His fists opened and closed and his arm muscles bunched. He was a couple of years younger than herself and he worked out often. For a moment she thought he might deck her, but instead, he used all of the gutter language his limited mind had absorbed and stormed out.

She sucked in a deep breath to center herself, then focused on what had to be done to salvage lunch. It was almost a relief to have something so comparatively minor to focus on instead of the emptiness inside her. "Do we have enough chicken to start over?" she asked Tate.

"No." He still wore his scowl.

"Fine." There was no choice; they had to have the filling for that afternoon's sandwiches. She turned to the others. "Who wants to get paid to drive to Denver for emergency supplies?"

She picked one of the five people who vied for the opportunity and did her best to put it out of her mind, but wasn't very successful.

CHAPTER 2

Rosemary was still fuming, working like mad to keep up with the restaurant demands and oversee preparations for the banquet that afternoon. She just couldn't catch a break, and she was tired. And hungry. But she wasn't going to indulge in anything until those sandwiches were made.

"Rosemary, can I talk to you for a minute?" It was Harrison, who always made her feel like a bumbling fool, though he never seemed to do it on purpose. He was using his calm, controlled voice—which meant they would probably be fighting in a few minutes, because that's what they usually did when they 'talked.'

"I'm a little busy here. Can it wait until after we get through the lunch rush?" She didn't even look at him.

"I think you can spare two minutes. How about if we go to your office?"

Her office? So it really *was* going to be a showdown. She clenched her teeth and turned the work over to Tate, her assistant, before whirling and heading for her office. Harrison followed along and after he shut the door to the kitchen, she turned to face him, "I'm running a little behind right now. I really can't spare the time, so try to keep it short, will you?"

"I just spoke with Rulon."

She knew it. "And he'd be the reason I'm behind. What, did he come whining that I yelled at him?" She put her hands on her hips and glared at Harrison, the gorgeous idiot. The way his brown hair fell over his eyes always got to her, but she could mostly ignore it when she was angry.

"He said you yelled at him in front of everyone." Harrison stood casually, his hands in his pockets. He always started out like this,

11

employing the take-it-easy approach, like his vegan, Mother Earth-type mother taught him, but it never lasted long. The muscle beside his eye twitched—a dead giveaway that he was already mad.

"Right, because he put dill in the chicken salad. Dill. Really? It was supposed to be tarragon, and he used twice what he should have in the first place, and it was totally unusable. I had to send Gillian to Denver to get more chicken because we're now short for the lunch we're catering this afternoon. That's several hundred dollars in ruined ingredients and over five man hours of wasted time that we have to make up because he's totally inept." That included the hour's drive to Denver, but Rosemary had to pay Gillian for the day and her gas, didn't she?

Harrison's lips pressed together. He never seemed to approve of her leadership tactics. "You should have brought him in here to fire him."

She knew she should have handled it better, had silently reprimanded herself for it several times already, but didn't appreciate Harrison telling her how to deal with her staff—even if he was the director of HR. "I didn't have the time or the patience. It's not like this is the first time he's done something stupid that's cost us. I was more than understanding on the previous three occasions." But today she had been primed to blow. Learning about the Markhams had honed the fine edge of her temper and she hadn't been in control of herself. She hated not being in control.

"Nevertheless."

She cut him off before he could continue. "Don't you *nevertheless* me. I don't have time to deal with this. Write me up if you want, whatever, I don't care. I have food to get out. If you'll excuse me." She tried to push past him, as tears started to prickle in her eyes, but he latched onto her upper arm.

"Whoa. You need to calm down if you're going back out there." His voice was low and even. "This is a problem waiting to happen."

"I can't calm down." She sucked in a breath and blinked rapidly, but a tear spilled over anyway.

His voice switched to worried. "Hold on. What's wrong?" His grip was loose, but secure, an odd combination. "It's not lunch that you're upset about, is it?"

She wiped at her cheek, flicking the tear away. "Don't be stupid. You think I can't deal with an employee? Everything isn't about this place, you know—even if you don't have a life outside the hotel." She yanked on her arm and he let go.

Steeling herself for the chaos of her kitchen, she pushed out of the office and went back to work. It was the best cure for grief, and a distraction from her worry.

Rosemary told herself that she ran her own kitchen and there was no reason to make a big deal out of taking off for a week or so, but after fixing the work schedule so she could take off, she headed upstairs to see Lana and Delphi.

Why had her father insisted in putting her in this position, anyway? She'd been happy in her downtown DC restaurant job, close to the Markhams and her daughter. He knew she just wanted to cook, but it hadn't been good enough for him, Instead he'd made it a condition of her inheritance that she spend the year in Juniper Ridge heading his latest resort's restaurant.

He'd strong-armed the rest of the sisters into working there as well, though a couple of them had been more than willing when the terms of the will had been read. And then there was the big house he'd bought for them to live in—six women in one house—even if it did have private bathrooms in every room—was asking a lot. Half of them were married now, including Cami and Lana, the two daughters by his long-deceased wife. None of them had known about the other girls. The fact that they had all been a secret had caused plenty of stress and trouble by itself but they were dealing.

They were a long way from being the happy family he'd apparently wanted for all of them, though, and she didn't look forward to explaining herself now. She smiled and greeted Gina, the executive office manager, and stuck her head in Lana's office. "You got a moment?"

"Sure, what's up?"

"Let me grab Delphi too so I can handle everything at once." She passed a few more offices, including Harrison's—it was empty—and knocked on Delphi's open door. "Got a minute for a quick meeting with Lana and me?"

Denial was on Delphi's face when she looked up, then her eyes narrowed and she nodded. No doubt she noticed Rosemary's red nose and eyes—she really needed to take a break to touch up her makeup. "Sure, no more than a minute, though." She stood and followed Rosemary out of the room.

Delphi entered Lana's office first and Rosemary closed the door behind them. "I have to make an emergency trip to DC. I just got a flight. It leaves first thing tomorrow. I could be gone for a week or more."

"But we have a big wedding this weekend," Delphi protested.

"It can't be helped." Rosemary steeled herself. "Some close friends of mine were killed in the café bombing yesterday. I need to get home for the funeral, and other things." She nearly mentioned Cleo, but decided to hold off a little while. She was still trying to grasp that.

"Surely the funeral isn't for a few days," Delphi protested.

"I don't know when it is," Rosemary admitted, "but there are other issues I need to handle that go along with it. I'll explain more later. Meanwhile, I've made some changes to the catering work schedule to make sure everything is covered." She filled them in on the adjustments so they would know who to contact in case anything came up.

When they finished, Delphi left, citing an appointment with a prospective client, but questions lingered in her eyes.

"This must be someone you're really close to," Lana said when they were alone.

Rosemary nodded. She'd grown closer to this half-sister over the past few months when Lana became pregnant. As the only one in the family—as far as she knew—who had ever been pregnant before, she'd done her best to support the slightly younger woman. Not that Lana or anyone else knew Rosemary had been pregnant before. Not yet, anyway. "They were more my parents than Wanda or George in a lot of ways. It throws some other wrenches in the works, but there will be time to discuss that later." She sighed, desperately wanting a hot bath full of bubbles and a glass of really excellent wine. "I need to get back to work. I'll see you later." She heaved herself from the chair.

"Tell me if you need anything. Really, Rosemary." Lana held her gaze for a long moment.

Rosemary nodded, though she didn't know if it was a lie or not.

Harrison was taking a stroll around the resort late that afternoon. He'd needed a moment to get out of his office and stretch his legs. He paused when he passed the restaurant entrance. He could see Rosemary standing in front of a table with a couple of octogenarian diners—they were locals, he knew because he'd seen them around enough to recognize them.

Rosemary smiled and covered the woman's withered old hand with hers, kindness and respect in her demeanor. She wasn't smiling as brightly as she often did when she interacted with happy guests and he wondered if the deal with Rulon still bothered her. She turned away from the table and nearly bumped into one of the servers, half-laughing as she said something that looked like 'such a klutz,' but since the server smiled as he continued to a family a few tables beyond the older couple, Rosemary must have been talking about herself and not him.

Harrison wondered why she seemed able to handle little things with grace and good humor, but wigged out on Rulon earlier. And what had caused her tears?

She pushed through the kitchen doors, the smile slipping from her face and sadness taking over a moment before she disappeared from view.

He turned and continued on down the hall, then ducked in to see Sage, his half-sister by their mom. She was half-sister to the rest of George's daughters as well, including Rosemary, and always seemed to have insights.

"What's up?" Sage looked up from her computer monitor when he stopped in her office doorway. Her wild dark curls were pulled back as they always were while she worked.

"You got a minute?" he asked.

"For you? Sure."

He shut the door behind him. "So what's up with Rosemary? She looks like death warmed over." The two weren't particularly close, but Sage had a way of knowing things, often even if people didn't tell her.

Sage shot him a surprised look. "You haven't heard? Some people she was close to back home were killed in that bombing that killed that senator."

He'd heard about the bombing on the news the previous night, and earlier, when Rosemary was upset and at the point of tears, she must have already known about her friends. It made Harrison feel like such a jerk. But she made him feel that way on a regular basis, so that was hardly unusual. "No wonder she's... off."

"Yeah. So go easy on her, will you?" Sage's voice was light, but he could tell from the worry lines around her eyes that she was worked up about it. "She'll be heading to DC first thing in the morning."

He nodded. "That explains a few things."

"Aren't you going to DC next week to work with their new HR director?" Sage asked him speculatively.

The thought had occurred to him, too. He'd made the appointment a couple of weeks earlier. "I have meetings. She might be back by then if she's leaving already." He wasn't sure if he *wanted* her to be back or if he wanted a chance to talk with her away from work—away from everything that made crossing the line into friendship so difficult here. It was something to think about.

There was a pile of work on his desk, which he needed to get back to, but he knew he would have trouble focusing on it now. The blond woman he had brought to tears that morning, however, was very much on his mind. She always was, seldom leaving him alone for long, but this was something more. If only he'd known earlier, he would have handled it differently.

Too late for that, though. Too late for a lot of things. Considering the way she never let her guard down around him, even for a second, he doubted that would change.

Still, a few overtures of friendship might not hurt.

CHAPTER 3

Rosemary was going for broke on the elliptical when Harrison walked into the exercise room downstairs in the sisters' house that evening. He watched her. She could feel him even though he hadn't announced himself and he stood behind her. It sounded crazy to say it, but the tone of any room seemed to change when he entered it.

"What?" she asked, a little breathless when he didn't speak.

"Are you trying to kill yourself?"

That made her chuckle breathlessly. "No, it's everyone else who is giving me heart attacks. Don't they know they should give a body a little warning? Huh? What's with people leaving me bequests I'm totally unprepared to deal with?" Joy, terror and grief still warred inside her. What was she going to do? How could she possibly explain to Cleo why she didn't keep her originally? And what did you do with kids anyway? It was one thing to visit and play in the yard with her, it was another thing to be a full-time parent. There would be homework and play groups and soccer practice, rules to make and punishments to mete out when rules were broken. Not always great at following other people's rules, she knew it would be difficult to set and follow them for her daughter.

She worked so much, and she shared a house with, well, only two other women now out of the original five. So there were a few extra rooms. But how would *they* feel about it? She hadn't talked to anyone about the guardianship, but she would have to have a chat with Delphi and Jonquil tonight.

The terms of their father's will made it impossible for her to move out—unless Alex found some freaky legal loophole he could twist. That would almost be freakier though, because it would mean her father anticipated something like this, which he totally couldn't have.

"If you don't want the bequest, turn it down," Harrison suggested. "You don't have to accept something just because someone wanted you to have it."

"I can't. You don't turn down a kid." There it was, in the open. Out loud.

"Whoa." He grabbed one of the elliptical's handles, forcing her to slow down. "A kid? Someone died and left you their *kid*?"

"Yeah. Though I guess she's technically my kid." Giving up on fighting him—or was it herself?—she slowed her steps until they stopped. She closed her eyes for a moment to gather strength before turning to Harrison. This was the last thing she wanted to admit to him—of all people, why did it have to be him? Why was he always the one to show up when she felt the most vulnerable?

"She's yours because they left her to you?" The tentative expression on his face made it clear he was trying not to presume, but sensed it was more than a legality. "And who left you a child? I knew something happened to friends in DC, but I didn't realize you were *that* close."

"My old neighbors. They were like family to me." She grabbed a towel and mopped at her face. She hadn't eaten enough dinner to have worked out that hard, and she knew it. She dismissed the thought with the idea that maybe there was some sliced turkey in the fridge—protein, low fat. It would be perfect. "Their daughter's name is Cleo. Short for Cleome."

It took Harrison a couple of seconds to answer. "Wait. Isn't that a kind of flower?" he asked. All of the sisters' names were some kind of flower or herb as horticulture had been one of her father's passions—hotels and women being the other two. Apparently.

"Yeah. They let me pick the name and I chose that because it gave her a little piece of family history." She should just come out with it, but had been keeping this a secret for so long, she was surprised at how hard it was to share.

His eyes narrowed and his words were careful. "Why did they let you pick their baby's name?"

Rosemary sat on the nearby weight bench. "Because she was my baby. They adopted her." Her voice was low and the words were painful to speak, but it was almost a relief when she got them out.

He sat beside her. "How old is she?"

"She'll be ten in April." Tears threatened, but Rosemary pushed them back. She couldn't deal with them right now. "I don't know what to do." She covered her face with her hands. "I can't believe they're gone."

His arm came around her, holding her close. "Hey, I know it's rough. But you'll be okay. You and Cleo. You're one of the toughest people I know and you obviously love her."

"How can I raise my daughter?" Words started tumbling out of her mouth without thought. "I work insane hours and share a house and we live in the middle of nowhere. She's used to the city and this, my irritating friend, is not the city, in case you've never noticed. I don't know anything about being a parent and what if child protective services looks at me and says no way? What happens to her then?"

He pulled her against his warm side, his voice was low and soothing. "Shh, one step at a time. When do you go to DC?"

"In the wee hours of the morning. The funeral's the following day, just got word about it." Her voice caught on a sob. "So fast. It's all happening so fast. How do I... What am I doing? That girl deserves better than me. Cecelia was like the perfect mother, and I'm... not. Why do you think I let the Markhams adopt her in the first place?"

"Hey, a lot has happened for you in the past ten years. You're going to be fine. You have a ton of family support here, and I bet Vince's mom would love to add one more granddaughter to the mix—Hannah is about the same age, isn't she—so you'll have a grandma figure. And the rest of us will pull around you." Hannah was Cami's niece by marriage, and seriously adorable.

20

"Do you just come and go here as you please?" she asked, feeling awkward about him seeing her fall apart, and just now realizing that he didn't belong.

"Delphi let me in. She directed me to the fridge, then told me you were down here if I wanted to harass you into something that resembled your own personality. She was worried."

"Sure she was." Rosemary chuckled. "You can always count on Delphi to make sure the most irritating person is directed straight to my side." She softened the words by leaning her head against his shoulder for a few seconds. It was odd talking to him like this. Comforting, and taking comfort from guys hadn't been on her to-do list since Cleo's birth dad split. "Thank you for listening. I guess I better break it to the others that they're getting a new roommate, and I have no idea when I'll be back. I'm going to wake up from nightmares that the restaurant kitchen is going to fall apart without me."

He laughed. "You probably need to pack if you're going to make it onto the plane on time. And take a shower first." He wrinkled his nose.

She balled up her fist and smacked him in the shoulder, though she didn't put much effort behind it. "You're such a jerk sometimes." But she felt oddly better.

"If you need some support in DC—"

"Thanks, but I'll be fine," she cut him off. "Alex will help me through the paperwork and I need to put all of my focus on Cleo." But she wanted someone to hold her hand. Someone besides Alex—who was in Chicago anyway, though he came to Juniper Ridge for visits at least once per month. The thought of facing her mother alone was enough to give her indigestion, but it was almost a guarantee considering she lived in the same neighborhood as the Markhams. Not that Rosemary would stop by when she was in DC, but she couldn't completely ignore Wanda if she was in town for the better part of a week. Wanda wouldn't allow that.

Settling things for Cleo was bound to be a messy, lengthy process. What did she tell the girl, anyway?

Harrison didn't push, but he didn't look very happy about her refusal, either.

Harrison left the bright, warm DiCarlo home to return to his quiet, dark, chilly cottage. He flipped on several lights, knowing Sage would get after him for wasting electricity, and turned on the television for company. Most of the time his empty place didn't bother him much. He worked long hours, liked his privacy, and headed over to see Sage when he got lonely. It was one of the reasons he'd taken this job—because he wanted to be close to his sister.

He opened his fridge and pulled out bread, cold cuts and cheese. It had been a difficult day and he didn't have the energy for cooking anything. He thought again of Rosemary coming out of Lana's office earlier, of the warmth that radiated between them. He thought of Sage and Joel and how happy and content they seemed now. And then he looked at his empty house and felt alone.

It wasn't a new feeling, so he refused to dwell on it. He'd made choices. There had been a woman a few year earlier who wanted to marry him, make a family, and he'd broken things off with her. He hadn't wanted to—he'd been very tempted to propose and make that perfect nuclear family—mom, dad, kids. But it hadn't been right and he hadn't been able to convince himself otherwise.

Sometimes he thought he was still that sad little boy whose father ran off and who had watched his sister be loved and nurtured by two parents—even if George hadn't been around much. He thought he'd gotten past it, but seeing Rosemary again, seeing her with her sisters and the way Lana and Blake were anticipating their baby's birth seemed to increase his urge for family, to be connected and part of something more.

Tonight, when Rosemary talked about her daughter and becoming a parent, he'd felt that tug stronger than ever. Felt it for her.

Had he been crazy to offer her his support? He layered on the smoked ham and pushed it from his mind. That way lay madness—as he'd already found since his arrival in Juniper Ridge.

"Okay, what's with the emergency meeting?" Jonquil asked as she set popcorn and chips on the coffee table in their sunken great room an hour later. The last of the sisters arrived only moments before and Rosemary refused to speak without them present, even if three no longer lived in the house. She didn't want to have to go over any of this again, so handling all of their questions now was a must.

She was anxious about how everyone would take her news—especially Jonquil and Delphi. Harrison was the first person she'd told about Cleome in years—and she never would have mentioned her to any of them if it weren't for her chance to regain custody now. Some things were best kept to oneself.

"Are you going to tell us why we're here?" Delphi asked as she pulled out her earrings. "Not that losing your friends isn't a big deal, but you didn't call us all here to bare you soul."

Rosemary had been lifting a glass of water to her mouth and was glad she hadn't been drinking when she heard that—she might have inhaled a mouthful. As it was, it took a moment to answer. "You're not as far off as you think."

Sage patted Rosemary's knee. "It's okay, no one will give you trouble about what you're going to say."

"You sure about that?" Delphi asked, but the words were mild, more a tease than a real challenge. Sometimes it was hard to tell with her, though.

"Pretty sure." Sage smiled, her dark gypsy features calm and supportive.

23

Rosemary nodded and plunged ahead. "I got pregnant when I was nineteen."

Eyes bugged, breaths of surprise were drawn in and the room became quiet enough to hear Delphi's earring hit the carpet. She scrambled to pull the pearl stud out of the deep pile and Rosemary couldn't help but feel a little satisfaction that her announcement had thrown her cool-headed sister off-balance.

She continued. "There was this couple in my neighborhood—really sweet, friendly, let me come over all of the time. Cecelia taught me to cook. They couldn't have kids of their own, so I offered to let them adopt my little girl. They were thrilled. Now they're," she had been planning to say *dead* in that matter-of-fact voice she had been using for the whole story, but couldn't get it to come out of her throat. She changed her word choice and still had a waver in her voice when she spoke, "gone. It leaves my daughter, who is nine now, an orphan. This morning when the lawyer came to tell about them, he said the Markhams wanted me to become her guardian if something happened to them."

More gasps, but Sage was right—no one gave her a hard time. Not yet, anyway.

"So you have to bring her back here, to live in our house." Delphi's face was blank, not giving away any hint of how she felt about it.

"I'd get a place of my own if it were an option, but thanks to Dad's will, it's not, so yeah, I'm going to have to bring her back here. I know that means you and Jonquil are going to be inconvenienced with the noise and mess, and giggling voices, but until September—"

"Right," Jonquil said with a firm nod. "There are three empty bedrooms now. They all have private bathrooms and desks in them, so it's not like she's going to be taking over our private spaces. If we can deal with Lana the hot-water hog here for the first part of the year," she paused to grin when Lana protested, "we can manage a nine-year-old."

Rosemary nodded, feeling relief, even though she expected nothing less from Jonquil. She turned toward Delphi—the one who was more likely to object.

"I don't see that there's much choice." The words were a little harsh, but the tone wasn't. She spoke low and looked more sad than mad. "It's not like you can turn down your kid. If you wanted to do that, you already would have and we wouldn't have heard a word about it."

"You don't want Cleo here?" Rosemary asked, her heart clenching at the thought that Delphi might make it hard for Cleo.

"I don't have a problem with it. And I'll try not to be too big of a pain about it." When Rosemary's brows lifted high enough they must have been encroaching on her hairline, Delphi scowled. "She's your little girl, which makes her every bit as much a part of this mess as the rest of us. You think I'm some monster that I can't see she needs someone who cares about her? You do, right? Want her to move here? You never said it, but I've learned to read you a little."

"Of course I want her! You think I would have given her up at all if I'd felt like I had another reasonable option—or if the Markhams hadn't been there, waiting with open arms to treat my baby the way every kid deserves?" Anger blasted through her at the insinuation that she might not be thrilled at this second chance.

"What about the father?" Cami asked. "Where was he through all of this?"

"He took off the minute he found out I was pregnant," Rosemary said, crossing her arms over her chest in a defiant gesture. There was only a twinge of regret now, after so many years, though it had been painful at the time. "I couldn't even find him to have him sign the papers. Never heard a word from him again."

"Lovely taste in men, you have," Delphi said.

"Yeah. Tell me about it. Me and men are such a bad mix. It's too bad they have to be so appealing." Rosemary sighed heavily, thinking of Harrison and the way he came to talk to her earlier. He was so confusing.

"So what do you want us to tell everyone?" Cami asked.

Rosemary considered, still not clear on how she felt about everything. "Nothing for now. I'll talk with the attorneys and Cleo, see what's going on, and we'll figure it out when I get back." The next words were hard to speak, but despite their differences and their petty squabbles, they'd all managed to pull together when needed for the public eye. "I've never told anyone about this, not any of the guys I've dated or any new friends. I just don't talk about it, so I'd prefer it if we keep things quiet for now. If the media catches wind of it, just say... I don't know. Just say that I've gone to a funeral and we have no comment at this time. I guess."

"We can do that. We're excellent at the 'no comment' line," Lana said. "And getting more expert with every passing day."

"That's just sad," Rosemary said, but she felt better now she'd gotten it all out.

Harrison couldn't get Rosemary's worried face out of his mind. She was in DC now, dealing with everything on her own. She was grieving and worried—he'd noticed how rarely she showed what she really felt so it had to be bad. Usually she just put on a touchy exterior, said something outrageous and let everyone else blow up around her. But she didn't do that this time. No, this time she'd crumbled.

He rubbed his eyes when he had trouble focusing on the insurance paperwork sitting in front of him.

"You okay? You look tired." Sage entered the room carrying two hot-drink cups—the reusable kind, of course. "I had a feeling you could use this."

She set a cup in front of him, and from the scent of it, she'd made her favorite wake-up tea blend.

"Thank you. You always know." He took a sip and noticed it was the perfect temperature.

"You're worried about Rosemary." She took a sip of her own drink. "I'm worried too. Something, I don't know. Something's bothering me." She twisted her necklace, making the green and blue polished rocks shimmer in the florescent lights.

He felt a tight ball form in his stomach. "You mean a *feeling* feeling, or just a general feeling?" Sage had always had precognition. She claimed she could never use it for herself, but randomly she would make very specific predictions that always came true. The general feeling thing was less reliable, but he was more likely to heed her warnings anyway.

"I'm not sure. I tried focusing on her during my meditation this morning, but I couldn't get anything clear. It wasn't specific like sometimes, just this feeling that she shouldn't be out there alone." She took a sip of her tea. "You leave for DC tomorrow. You should stop in to see her, just to check on her. For me." She looked at him over the rim of her cup, a glint of mischief in her eyes.

The temptation to go with his sister's suggestion was strong. He wanted to be there for Rosemary, wanted to check on her, but would she even let him in the door? "I'm not sure that's a good idea."

She watched him over the top of her cup as she took a long swallow. "Hmmm. I think it's a very good idea. You need to start making amends with her if you're going to get her to see you differently, you know."

Harrison didn't respond to that. There was no point arguing with her about his feelings. She'd always been able to read him. "I don't know if that's possible. Things started out bad a decade ago, and they haven't gotten much better, even after months of working together." He considered their chat at her house the previous night to be a fluke even though it was definitely an improvement over their usual arguments. He could see what she really was, under all of the veneer, but unless he could get her to look at him as something more than the pain in her rear, it would make no difference.

She smiled. "The whole ordeal on the ship would almost have been funny now if she didn't hold a grudge for so long."

"Yeah. Who knew?" He tried to smile back, but he'd never regretted anything he'd done more than he regretted the words he'd said that day. "You better get back to work."

"Right. You, too." Unoffended, she stood, but came around his desk and squeezed his shoulder. "See her while you're in DC, Harrison. She needs you there."

He watched her go and considered her suggestion, wondering if he was crazy for even thinking about it.

CHAPTER 4

The funeral was the pits. Rosemary had known it would be, but she didn't expect it to be quite so difficult. She gave Cleo a hug at the viewing, the blond girl's face was wan, scared and sad. Rosemary thought she must be dying a little inside, trying to figure out what came next and how to go on without the people who had been everything to her. Rosemary had felt much the same way when her dad died, and she'd been an adult, grown and on her own.

Don's brother, Mike, gave the eulogy, and Cecilia's cousin sang. The double caskets brought the whole thing home for Rosemary. There was no viewing, thanks to the bomb blast. Rosemary was just as glad. She'd rather remember them as they had been a few weeks ago when she'd visited.

After the interment, Rosemary went back to Cecelia's brother's house for refreshments and talk. Cleo rode there with the neighbors she'd been staying with, but found her when she had been there less than two minutes. She latched onto Rosemary's hand. "I don't know many of these people," she whispered.

"Yeah. I don't recognize very many of them, either. Maybe we should get something to eat and sit in the corner there." She wasn't hungry, but hadn't eaten anything since the airline food the previous day—her appetite was non-existent. She knew she needed to eat something, even if it was just a little bit. And Cleo would need to eat. She was too thin already.

"I'm not hungry," Cleo said.

Like mother, like daughter. And that was a strange thought. "Just a little bit. I bet you're hungrier than you think."

Cleo shrugged and went along with Rosemary to fill up their plates from the fruit and veggie trays, cold cuts and cheese, bread and rolls in several varieties, and Cleo grabbed a slice of cake. They got glasses of water and found spots away from the main traffic.

"How are you doing?" Rosemary asked when they were seated.

"I miss you." Cleo leaned slightly against Rosemary. "You used to come over all the time."

It had been one of the reasons she hadn't wanted to take the job in Colorado. Though 'all the time' was a bit of an exaggeration. A couple of times a month was more accurate. Though Cecilia and Don had both kept Rosemary's connection to the girl a secret, they had encouraged the two of them to spend time together. Rosemary had been grateful, as giving up Cleo had been the hardest thing she'd ever done. Going to Europe for two years to study with master chefs had been agonizing—she'd only made three visits home the whole time. Thank goodness for email.

"My Uncle Mike doesn't really want me. But he thinks I should live with him anyway. My other uncle says it's because he wants my parents' money." She looked at Rosemary quizzically. "We weren't rich."

"No, sweetie, you weren't." *You will be now.* "But there's often money set aside in case one of your parents dies, to protect you and take care of your needs while you're growing up. Your uncle must think whomever takes care of you will get that money." Don and Cecelia had been frugal, but he didn't make more than enough for a comfortable life, and court costs for the 'estate' would probably eat up most of what was left.

"I don't like Mike much. I don't want to live with him." Cleo's brow furrowed and her jaw set.

So no one had seen fit to tell her the truth. Rosemary nearly did, but decided she better wait until after everyone left and she had a chance to talk to the attorney. "I don't think that will be a problem, sweetie. Now eat some more. It's been a crazy few days for you."

Cleo ate, quietly, wearing her thinking face. "I miss my parents."

Rosemary put her arm around the little girl and pressed her cheek to Cleo's hair. "Oh, sweetie. So do I."

People milled around. A few stopped in to say hello, talked to Cleo—or talked down to her, which was more often the case. Her uncle Mike made a show of being solicitous, but Rosemary could smell insincerity a mile away. Cleo was right about them. Rosemary could see it. She'd been through it with half a dozen of her mother's live-in boyfriends over the years.

She was happier than ever that Don and Cecelia had thought to make her the guardian instead of either uncle.

When they met afterward for the reading of the will—a term which made Rosemary want to laugh because they couldn't have had much besides their daughter and their home to settle—only the two brothers, Cleo and herself were in the room. Rosemary was glad she'd had the heads up about the will stipulations regarding guardianship, because finding out about their wishes in front of these people would have been disastrous.

"I know you're all here today because you're concerned about Cleome's welfare," the attorney began.

"Cleo. Just call me Cleo," she said in a low voice. "Cleome's a stupid name."

"Sorry, Cleo," he said. "This must be a very scary time for you. But your parents wanted to make sure you had the best person to take care of you."

"I want Rosemary."

The room went quiet.

"But, honey," Mike interjected. "Why would you want to live with her? She's practically a stranger. We're family."

"Back less than a day and you're already sinking your fingers into things," the other uncle, Scott, said.

"I never talked to her about staying with me," Rosemary objected. "But I'd love to have her if that's what's best for her."

"That's what I want. I don't want to live with them." Cleo pointed to both uncles in turn. "Mike doesn't like kids and Scott treats me like a baby who is too stupid to figure anything out."

Mike glared at Rosemary as if she were responsible for the ruination of all his hopes and dreams. He put his hands on his hips and narrowed his eyes. "She didn't want you before. What makes you think she wants you now? She's probably just after the money."

Rosemary felt all the blood drain from her face at his words. How had he known about her? She hadn't thought the Markhams had told anyone. "Money doesn't matter to me."

"Sure." He sneered.

"We're getting off topic here," the attorney stated, a little exasperated. "The point is what Cleo's parents had in mind for her."

"But the state will have the final say, of course," Mike said.

"Unless there's a solid reason for Cleo to go elsewhere, her parents have named Rosemary as her guardian."

Cleo threw her arms around Rosemary and buried her face in Rosemary's torso. "Good. Can we go home now?"

Rosemary realized Cleo thought they were going to live in her family home, where she'd grown up. Her heart sank. "What else does the will say?"

"All assets go to Cleo through a trust that can't be touched until she's eighteen except for expenses related to extra educational opportunities, which have to be signed off by the firm. After that, she will need two signatures to get money out, hers and yours until she's twenty-five. They did this to ensure that she'd use the money for college or something similarly sensible. At age twenty-five, the balance is hers to do with as she pleases." His lips lifted slightly. "It's not a huge amount, but with appropriate investments should ensure her education and something to start her adult life with."

"Good." Not that it mattered, Rosemary would be well able to provide for Cleo on her own, but it would be good for her daughter to know her parents loved her and made sure she was taken care of.

"You really don't care about the money? You have to raise her on your own dime," Scott stated.

"I have a few to go around." Seeing the glint in his eye, Rosemary clarified, "Even without my inheritance—which was substantial—I could name my price in any of two dozen cities and get a job. I don't need anyone's financial assistance to raise Cleo."

"So *now* you want a kid. Now she's half grown," Mike said. "Are you just not into babies?"

Rosemary didn't want Cleo to learn about their relationship like this, but didn't know what to say except the truth. And she didn't want her daughter to think she hadn't been wanted. "I've always loved Cleo. I haven't always been in a position to be a parent. I am now."

If Cleo understood, she didn't react.

He seemed unimpressed. "*Right.*"

"You'll probably need to stay in town for a week or so," the attorney interrupted. "It'll take that long to get everything in order and have her school records transferred."

That made Cleo lift her head, puzzlement on her face. "School records. Why do I need to move them?"

Rosemary wrapped her arms around the girl. Her daughter. "Because I live in Colorado, honey."

"But I have a house here. We can live here." Panic showed on Cleo's face. "I don't want to move. I want to stay with my friends. You just said you can work anywhere."

It broke her heart. "Sweetie, I have a job there. Responsibilities. I can't just leave them."

"You left here without any trouble," she accused.

Rosemary felt her heart breaking. She didn't want to upset Cleo any more than she had to, but she had to live in Colorado, it was the terms of her contract, and the will. And there was no way Rosemary could ever live in her old neighborhood again, no matter how nice it was. Especially not with her mother still living nearby.

"I have to go back to Colorado. At least until the end of August. Then we can talk about coming back out here, if that's what you want." *Please, no.*

"But that means I'll spend school and summer and my birthday away from my friends." Tears overflowed onto her cheeks.

"You'll make new friends and have a lot of chances to learn new things, like how to ski and stuff." Rosemary felt lame even suggesting it. She hated skiing, but if Cleo wanted to go, she'd suck it up and deal with it. "And in the summer there are lots of mountain bike trails and hiking and um, other cool things." She'd have to look into those things, since she hadn't really paid any attention to them before.

"But I want to stay here." Cleo pulled away and ran to the door, yanking on the knob until she got it open.

Rosemary was a step behind her as she entered the hall and snatched Cleo into her arms, though she was way too big to lift. "Sweetie. Hey, come here. I'm sorry. I know this isn't what you want. This is a bad time for you. I was way older when I lost my dad, but it was really hard for me. It must be really tough even for a strong kid like you to deal with."

Cleo turned and wrapped her arms around Rosemary's shoulders, holding on tight, her tears dripping onto Rosemary's black dress. "I just don't want anything else to change. Too much is changing. I just want to stay here. Where it's the same."

Rosemary held her close, snuggled up against her and felt her throat tighten with emotions. "It's never going to be the same again. I'm sorry, Cleo, but sometimes when things change, they change forever. And I don't just mean losing your parents. Other things won't ever feel the same, no matter how hard you try to make them be."

Her throat clogged up as she thought of how she'd felt when she learned she was pregnant, feeling her baby grow inside her, then having to give her up. She went back to school and did her best to act as if nothing had changed, but really, everything was different. "I bet you'll like it in Colorado, though. It's beautiful, and the hotel is really cool and my sister Sage is building a big house with a huge indoor pool."

Cleo sniffed, pulling back and wiping at her face. "Really? A pool in their home? Is she rich?"

Rosemary smiled. "Something like that. Her husband really likes to swim. He used to be a Navy SEAL, so he's this super-tough military dude. And my sister Lana is having a baby around the first of May. And Cami's husband has lots of nieces and nephews and I bet they'd love to do stuff with you."

She had Cleo's attention, so she pushed on, talking about everyone in Colorado. "Vince is Cami's husband; he's a landscaper, so he knows everything about growing plants, and Jonquil plays with flowers in her shop and makes bouquets and stuff all day long. And I just know everyone is going to love you." She pressed the hair back from Cleo's face, glad to see her calming down.

"So I'll have a whole bunch of aunts and uncles?" She looked doubtful.

"Yeah. But I promise, they're nothing like those guys." She hitched her thumb toward the office. "They're way nicer, even Delphi and she's a bit of a poop head."

Cleo smiled a little at the comment. "I still don't want to leave my friends."

"I know. But there's always email, and Skype. I bet we could set up a time you could video conference with them to catch up." Rosemary was stretching now, trying to find a way to make Cleo accept the inevitable. And Skype would be a reasonable option—much better than running her cell phone usage into the ten-thousands.

Cleo looked intrigued. "Is it hard?"

"Nope. Really easy. We do it all the time with the guys from the main office."

Cleo sniffed. "Well, maybe it would be okay. Until the end of the summer."

Step one, Rosemary thought with relief. "Good girl. Now, let's go inside and see what else we need to know before we go back to your home, okay?" Cleo had been staying with neighbors, but that was only until Rosemary could take over.

The two uncles stalked out before Cleo had done more than put her hand in Rosemary's.

Mike stopped on his way out to glared at Rosemary. "You aren't a fit mother. If you were, you wouldn't have given her up in the first place."

Rosemary felt Cleo's hand tighten in hers and she froze as the men disappeared.

"What did he mean?" Cleo asked.

Rosemary closed her eyes for a couple of seconds. Cleo knew she had been adopted, just not who her birth mom was, until now. "How about if we talk about that when we get back to your home?"

"You promise?"

"Cross my heart." Rosemary did the actions as she spoke.

Cleo studied her for a moment, then nodded. They went in and sat again, though this time Rosemary pulled Cleo onto her lap so she could wrap her up tight in a hug.

"Are things okay?" the attorney asked.

"Yeah. We're fine. Or we will be fine," Rosemary amended. Maybe not anytime soon, but eventually. "Is there anything else you need to tell us?"

"I've been in contact with your attorney." His brow lifted. "Family law isn't exactly his specialty."

She chuckled. "No, but I want him involved even if he passes the bulk of it off to someone in his office. He understands the unusual dynamics of my situation better than anyone."

"That's understandable. It looks like the house still has a balance owing, and there are a few bills that will need to be discharged out of the insurance."

"No problem. Tell me where to send a check and how much and I'll make sure the bills get paid until things are settled."

He nodded. "I'll send that all along in an email."

"Thanks." Rosemary accepted the rest of the papers and stood. They put on their coats, then Rosemary took Cleo's hand again and led her out to the front where they caught a cab. She just had to remember to take one step at a time and she'd be okay. And if that didn't work, there was always the elliptical.

CHAPTER 5

They had been back at her home for only a few minutes when Cleo looked up at her. "What did Uncle Mike mean, you gave me up already?"

Rosemary had hoped to have more time to consider this. She wanted to strangle Mike. She sat on the sofa and patted the spot beside her. "You know I met your parents when I was about your age."

Cleo squinted at Rosemary. "You're not really going to tell me, are you? Are you my birth mother?"

She felt her chin muscle twitch. "Yes. I am."

"Why did you give me to my parents?" Cleo's forehead wrinkled.

"I thought that was what I was explaining when you interrupted me." Rosemary forced a little smile to show she wasn't mad.

"But, you weren't talking about that. You were trying to distract me with stuff that's... irrelevant."

Rosemary smiled in delight. She loved how precocious Cleo was. A big reader, the little girl had always used words far beyond most kids her age. "Nope. But it might have sounded like it. Just sit back and listen."

When Cleo was settled, Rosemary began again. "Your parents moved here when I was ten. I remember it was Thanksgiving the first time I met them, so it was right after my birthday. Your mom was really sweet and always had something nice to say to me. I lived around the corner."

"Your mom still lives there. She's not very nice to me." Cleo pulled a face.

Rosemary debated for a moment, then leaned in so she was almost nose to nose with the girl. "Do you want to know a secret? She's not always very nice to me, either. But *your* mom was. She always made me feel welcome and she taught me to cook. My mom was gone from home a lot with her boyfriends, and when they were there, the guys never seemed to like me much."

"She had more than one boyfriend?" Cleo's eye were wide as pies.

"Not at a time, silly." Rosemary tapped her nose, though she had wondered sometimes if her mom *had* strung more than one guy on the line at a time. She was deceptively sweet and she was beautiful, so it often took guys longer than you'd expect to look below the shallow exterior and realize the person beneath wasn't nice. Not nice at all.

"Oh, okay. Go on."

"I didn't like being at home, so I was here a lot. I think your mom liked that because she wanted to have children so bad, and they tried everything, but it wasn't working." Rosemary remembered catching Cecilia crying one afternoon. She had said she was sad she couldn't have kids of her own, but then brushed it off as if it wasn't a big deal. Rosemary had known better, and watched when they were around little kids, seeing the pain and wistfulness in her face.

"I sometimes make bad decisions," Rosemary admitted, not sure how else to explain. "And when I was in college, I got pregnant. I was still really young and I loved my baby almost from the first moment I found out I was pregnant." She kept careful watch on Cleo's gaze, making sure she understood this was the truth.

"I wanted to keep her, but I was still in school and I knew if I became a mom then, that I wouldn't be able to finish school. Then I would end up in a really bad job where my little girl would be in daycare all day long and we wouldn't have anything. I would probably be really stressed and ornery all the time and that would make me a terrible mom."

She brushed a lock of hair back from Cleo's face. "I saw your mom. She wanted a baby so badly, and I knew she would be the most awesome mom ever and that she would let me watch my baby grow up and be part of her life so I didn't have to wonder what happened to her. Then I could be a sort of big sister to her." There were tears in her eyes now, though she managed to keep them from falling.

"It was the hardest thing I ever did," Rosemary admitted, "deciding to let your parents adopt you, but I knew you would be happier with them."

Cleo looked as though she wasn't sure if she believed it. "So you did want me?"

"Always. I always wanted you." Rosemary wiped tears from her eyes. "I love you so much."

Cleo started to cry and leaned against Rosemary. "I miss them. I want my mommy back."

"Me too, honey. Me too." She held Cleo tight, just letting her cry and soak in the changes in her life.

"What do I call you?" Cleo asked after a while.

"Rosemary, just like you always have. I know Cecilia and Don will always be your parents, and I'm so grateful they were so awesome. You can call me anything you want. Even Queen Rosemary, if you want."

That made Cleo giggle, as it was an old joke between them. "You're not a queen."

"I'm the queen in the kitchen. And you better believe it." She sucked in a breath. "Now, did you want to visit your friends or anything? We won't have much longer before we have to move to Colorado, so you better see them while you still have time."

Rosemary was surprised at how well Cleo took the news, but then little kids did have a way of bouncing back. On the other hand, issues tended to resurface. She ought to know.

Harrison rubbed his sweaty hands on his pant legs and pulled the key from the ignition. He'd taken the excuse to visit Rosemary as Sage suggested.

He and Rosemary may not always see eye to eye, but she often pretended nothing was bothering her even when she was upset about something.

Now he worried that showing up on her doorstep would make the gulf in their relationship worse, though. Funny how that possibility hadn't seemed so real until he had arrived in DC and turned the car toward the address Sage had tracked down for him.

He stared at the white stuccoed rambler, well maintained and inviting in a neighborhood that was starting to show evidence of neglect, but had obviously been quite nice a decade or two before. Would she even let him in?

He grabbed his keys, the pizza he'd picked up on the way there, and the bag with the cookies he'd bought at a nearby bakery. If he was going to show up on Rosemary's doorstep to check up on her—risking her wrath—it was best if he came with a peace offering. Not that she was likely to eat much of the food, but maybe Cleo would like it, anyway. There was a rental car in the driveway, so he knew Rosemary had to be there.

His stomach felt tight and a little unsettled as he walked to the front door, switching the bag to the hand with the pizza so he could knock.

"Who is it?" a young girl's voice asked through the door.

"My name is Harrison. I know Rosemary," he said in return.

Little feet pounded on the floor and then the girl's voice called down the hall, her mother's name the only word that was distinguishable.

A long moment passed as he felt himself starting to sweat and then the door opened. Rosemary pushed the fall of blond hair over her shoulder and stared at him in surprise. "Cleo said you were here. I thought I heard wrong."

A cute blond head poked out from behind Rosemary. "You know him?"

"Yeah, he's Sage's brother," Rosemary said, guardedly. She looked at the pizza and bakery bag. "What are you doing here?" she asked him.

"I had to come in to the local resort and thought I'd pop by to see how things are going. I figured you probably haven't eaten dinner yet."

Her eyes narrowed. "You came to check up on me?"

He braved her possible wrath and smiled. "Sage worries. I knew she would feel better if I could reassure her that you're still eating and seem to be holding it all together."

She stared at him for a long moment, as if unsure whether to believe him or not, then opened the door wider and gestured for him to enter. "Right, because I'm so delicate."

He flashed her a grin and pushed through.

Cleo stood out of the way, watching him, as she had the whole time. She looked over at Rosemary thoughtfully, then back at him again. "You're Sage's brother, but not Rosemary's?"

"That's right. Sage and I have the same mom, and Rosemary and Sage have the same dad. I'm kind of part of the family, but not really."

"Like me," Cleo said.

"Oh, no, you're really part of the family. All the way. I hope you like pizza." He set the box on the dining room table.

Cleo ran over. "I love pizza! It's my favorite." Her nose wrinkled. "You didn't get anchovies did you? My Uncle Mike always gets them and they smell yucky."

She was a doll. "Nope, no anchovies. I don't like them much, either." He opened the box and gestured inside so they could see it. "Just pepperoni and olives this time. What's your favorite?"

He kept his eyes on the little girl as Rosemary moved to the cupboard and pulled out plates and glasses. He knew where she was every moment, acutely aware of the wariness in her eyes and the way she seemed off kilter. He kept up a steady stream of chatter with Cleo though, finding that easier than facing Rosemary—and it gave her a chance to get her bearings again. The longer he was there, the less likely that she'd kick him out.

She brought over the stack of plates and handed one to him. "How are things at home?"

She'd only been gone two days, but he understood that she was nervous, more than concerned. "Great. Lana and Blake are unbearably happy and Jonquil is scarfing down Ho-Hos again." He met Rosemary's eyes, well aware of her on-going battle against Jonquil's love of preservative-filled snack cakes.

"Sounds about right." She touched her daughter's head, smoothing the hair down in back. "Eat your pizza, bug."

Harrison changed the subject to something funny that happened at the hotel. He stayed through dinner and the cookies, drawn to both mother and daughter, and impressed with how Rosemary handled things, but concerned by the worry lines on her forehead and how tired she looked. She ate some pizza, but not even a full slice. He hung around as long as he dared, then decided it was time to make his excuses before she kicked him out. He turned to Cleo. "You probably need to get Rosemary to bed. It's getting late and she gets a little cranky when she doesn't get enough sleep." He stood and grabbed his coat.

Cleo giggled.

"I'm never cranky. I have no idea what you're talking about," Rosemary said, though her butter-will-not-melt expression said she knew better.

Cleo giggled again. "She doesn't go to bed early. She sends me to bed, then stays up late doing things around the house."

"Adults can be like that," he said with an understanding nod. "When she wakes up in the morning, does she head straight for the coffee pot and grumble about how she misses her espresso maker?"

Cleo's eyes grew wide and she grinned. "Yes! How did you know?"

He looked at Rosemary's scowl and managed to keep his expression mostly even. "Just a good guess."

"Cleo does need to get ready for bed," Rosemary said, interrupting the conversation. "We have a lot to finish up before we head back to Colorado."

"I'll be busy tomorrow and then have to head back myself the next morning, but I'll see you soon." He turned to Cleo and held out his hand for a shake. "It was nice to meet you, Cleo."

"It was nice to meet you too," she said formally, giving his hand a firm shake.

"All right, bug. Go put on your pajamas." Rosemary gave her daughter a little push toward the back hall.

"But—"

"No buts, just bed." She pointed away, a no-nonsense look on her face.

Cleo heaved a sigh. "Fine. Goodnight!" She said this last over her shoulder and then headed down the hall.

Harrison shrugged into his coat. "It was good to see you. She's a cute kid. You should be proud."

"Of course I am." She folded her arms and stared at him. Her voice was quiet and a little confused when she spoke again. "Why did you come?"

Just when he had been thinking he might avoid the inquisition. "I thought you could use a friendly face."

Her eyes narrowed and her shoulders shifted. "We're not friends, Harrison. Why have you been so nice lately? Are you feeling sorry for me? I don't like pity."

As if he wasn't fully aware of that. "I don't pity you. Besides, you called me your friend the other day."

Her face crinkled at the edges. "I did not."

"Of course you did." He gestured a little. "So it was off handed and you added the word *irritating* in front of it, but I definitely heard the word *friend*." How could he explain that his feelings went way beyond that without her kicking him into the snow and telling him never to darken her door again? "I'm concerned, but it's not pity."

She studied him. "I don't get you, Harrison."

He smiled. "That's okay. There's plenty of time for that later." He held her gaze for several seconds before she pulled away and opened the front door for him.

"See you soon," he said, then walked out into the cold.

She shut the door behind him and he strolled out to his rental car. They had a long way to go before she would move past the hard feelings they'd been nurturing, but the confusion and uncertainty on her face told him that maybe he had a chance with her after all—if he could put her off balance now and then.

Rosemary closed the door behind Harrison and wondered what that was all about. He's been oddly nice to her in the past few weeks—the cussing out in her office about Rulon being an exception. She'd completely forgotten about him coming out to DC for meetings and wondered why no one else had mentioned it before she left Colorado.

She remembered the first time they ever met—seeing him across the deck of the cruise ship her father had booked her onto. She had given birth to Cleo only a few months before and still had most of her baby fat—and some she'd packed on during her teen years with comfort eating.

She'd seen Harrison and felt an immediate zing of attraction, she'd even moved across the deck toward him, then saw him get two plates of pizza and take one back to his companion—the sweet looking girl with the wild brown curls. They talked like they'd known each other for ages and she'd felt a punch to her gut. Of course he wasn't interested in her. Of course anyone she was that attracted to would have a girlfriend. She was just the mousy nobody Jamie had been able to dismiss and walk away from when he learned about the baby.

She hadn't been attracted to anyone since Jamie—Cleo's dad—and he had been an indifferent boyfriend and took off the moment he'd learned she was pregnant. She hadn't seen him since, and didn't really care anymore. It hadn't been love. She'd wanted it to be, willed it to be, stupidly slept with him in the hopes that it would become love for both of them. But it hadn't been.

She turned away from the couple and picked up some food for herself, taking her plate to another part of the ship where she wouldn't have to see the cute couple laughing together.

That night she had met with the director for their singles cruise and Rosemary had been surprised to find the other couple was part of their group. Harrison—she hadn't known his name then—looked at her and stared. It made her self-conscious and she patted her short blond hair and felt a good thirty pounds heavier than she already was. The girl touched his arm, drawing his attention away and Rosemary tried to focus on what the director was saying.

When one of the other girls had commented on how good-looking Harrison was later that night, she hadn't realized he was close enough to hear and shot back something about how plain and mousy his girlfriend was. It had been a lie—Sage was as exotic as a gypsy and Rosemary was jealous, feeling like a big, awkward lump.

Harrison said something nasty about Rosemary's weight and stalked off. They ignored or snipped at each other for the rest of the cruise.

When Rosemary met Sage again at the reading of the will and heard her name, she'd realized immediately who she was and wondered what happened between Sage and Harrison. They'd had different last names, so she hadn't realized the two of them were siblings. Not until later.

46

She remembered now how the pain had come back to her, layering on the pain of losing her father, and the attorney's announcement that the six women in the meeting were all sisters. Her father's demand that they move to Colorado to open the resort only worsened the pain. She'd seriously considered walking away from her inheritance, even if her part of the inheritance would go to some stupid yacht club for rich kids to have more pampered lives than ever. And a cheerleading camp of all things. But she'd caved when she read her father's personalized letter to her. Learning that she'd been wrong about Harrison all of those years ago, that he had been Sage's brother, not her boyfriend, made her feel like a fool.

"Rosemary, are you going to read to me?" Cleo's voice broke her from her reverie, bringing her back to the present.

"Yeah, bug. I'll be right there." She just needed a minute to compose herself and finish the train of thought in hopes that it would help her put it in perspective.

She wondered if Harrison had recognized her right off, or if Sage had to remind him about who she was, but she'd recognized him the moment he showed up in Juniper Ridge. He had a stack of files under his arm as he prepared for the whirlwind interviews they were going to do for employees and his dark hair had been wind-blown.

She didn't realize until the next day that he and Sage were half siblings, just like Sage and herself, but she knew him, felt the same longing as before. When he met her gaze, the breath backed up in her lungs and she forced all of the bravado she could manage when they were introduced. "Oh, HR director. A necessary evil, I suppose when you have this many employees." She looked him over as if he were an insect and walked away, proud that she had lost so much weight, but somehow still feeling like that borderline-obese young adult.

It had felt good at first, getting her dig in, but later she'd been sick about it. Why had she been so nasty when they could have started over without the hard feelings between them? She'd regretted that comment every day for the past six months.

Now she wondered if his appearance on her doorstep meant they were finally past that, and why she was still fighting him when the attraction had only grown as she'd gotten to know him a little.

She shook it off as she pushed into Cleo's room, making herself smile because there was no reason to let her little girl know how messed up she was.

CHAPTER 6

It was Rosemary's third day in DC and she stretched her back in agony. The couch was not comfortable, but she wasn't about to take Cleo's bed, and the only other bed in the house was Cecilia's and Don's and there was no way Rosemary could handle sleeping there. Not at this point anyway. There was a hotel room with her name on it at the DC resort, but she couldn't pull Cleo away from her home any sooner than absolutely necessary.

She walked around the perimeter of the house and decided to check into the detached garage. There was a lot of stuff in there that would need to be dealt with. Later. Maybe in the spring or fall when skiing ended and summer activities hadn't started yet. By then Cleo might be ready to handle seeing her parents' house cleaned out. Or they might be getting ready to stay there, if Rosemary decided she could stand to live in the neighborhood after all. Or if her mom moved somewhere else.

As if conjured there by Rosemary's thoughts, her mother's voice called from the street. "Rosie, there you are. I heard you were in town."

She turned toward her mother and forced a tight smile. "Hello. I intended to stop by before we head back to Juniper Ridge." A blatant lie. "How are things with you, Mother?"

"We? So the rumors I hear about you taking in that girl are true? After you managed to get rid of her once." Wanda Keogh sauntered up the driveway.

"I never wanted to get rid of her. I love her, and she knows it. How are you?" Rosemary was determined to keep the topic of conversation off herself.

"Fine. Not as fine as you with your big inheritance. Though now you have a brat to raise, you won't have nearly as much time on your hands to play around. Of course, you can afford the best childcare available. If you wish. Unlike me."

"Give me a break. I know what Dad paid you every month. You could have sent me to boarding school if you liked and still lived fine. Unlike *some* people, I'm bringing my daughter home with me because I want to be part of her life." She caught herself a little too late and bit back the rest of the things she'd love to say to her mother. Instead she changed the conversation. "How are things with Larry?"

Wanda put her hands on her hips. "We split up last month. Didn't you hear? Oh, right. You don't call, you don't write. You ignore me because of all of the things you've got going on with hot ski instructors."

Rosemary managed not to roll her eyes. She hadn't been on a date since she moved to Colorado. Her job didn't exactly leave time for relationships, and with Harrison around, no one else looked even remotely interesting. Idiot man drove her crazy. "No. I don't call or write because we're both happier when we're not part of each other's lives. Now, did you want something, or can I get back to what I was doing?"

Wanda's eyes narrowed on her daughter. "You always had a mouth on you. Your father spoiled you, made you think you were worth his time and money, even though neither were true. But I suppose you deserve each other. He wasn't so great, either."

"You didn't always think so," Rosemary called after her mom as she walked away.

"Everyone's entitled to their evening of stupidity. At least I cashed in because of mine."

Rosemary clenched her teeth and told herself not to react. That's all she had been to her mother—a paycheck. George had been very generous with his financial support, but it was never enough for Wanda. Even knowing her mother never loved her, it still hurt to hear it now.

Rosemary went into the garage, thinking that she would give herself five minutes to stew and then she would move on. Worrying about her mother only stressed Rosemary, and didn't fix anything. The shelves were full—fuller than she remembered, but she hadn't been in there for years. The walls were full of shelves and pegboard organizing garden tools, half-empty paint cans and camping gear.

The car was still parked there—it was a new mid-sized sedan, a Honda in midnight blue and still had the dealer-printed plate in the back window. That meant the real plate was probably in the pile of mail on the hall table. Since the car wasn't going anywhere for a while, Rosemary opted to ignore it for now.

Don and Cecelia had taken the nearby subway tunnel into downtown DC for their lunch date, leaving the car parked—a not uncommon event considering how hard it could be to find parking downtown.

Rosemary ran her hand over the glossy paint and remembered the faded Geo Metro they'd been driving since before Cleo was born. They had taken her to the hospital in that car, had brought her and Cleo home again a couple of days later. She had remembered sitting behind Cecelia and looking over at her baby's face, the sweet way she puckered her lips in sleep, the few bare inches of skin they allowed to show between her soft pink sleepers and the blankets.

Rosemary had reached over and brushed her knuckle down Cleo's cheek, knowing she wouldn't have too many more chances. She'd made arrangements to miss a few weeks of classes, but she needed to go back the following Monday if she didn't want to be hopelessly behind everyone else. The last thing she wanted to do was face everyone's questions about the baby, what she'd done with it, the speculation and whispers. But for that few minutes as the car returned to the warm house filled with love and laughter, Rosemary was able to just stare at her child and know Cleo's life would be good because she would have a mother who wouldn't treat her like she was a burden and a father who was closer than a phone call away.

Rosemary blinked away the memory and the tears that welled in her eyes. It had been almost a decade, but the memory of that day was so strong, she could feel the pain still clawing inside her. Only now it was joined by the pain of losing the best parents she or Cleo could ever have.

She sighed, then turned back toward the exit, brushed the handle of something with her leg and heard a creaking sound. She looked up in time to see the shelf of camping equipment wobble, then break, dumping the contents, which poured down on her. She stopped the camp stove before it knocked her against the car, but it slid down and bruised her leg. The tent tumbled after it, beaning her on the shoulder as the Dutch ovens clattered to the ground and the big blue-enameled coffee pot hit her in the face. Several other items banged against her on their way to the cement floor and she thought for a second that the whole wall might collapse on her.

The crashes continued for a moment and then settled as almost everything along that wall ended up piled on the ground around her. When it all came to rest except for the clanging sound of a can rolling across the cement, she realized that she'd been holding her breath. Her heart raced and her hands shook. Her cheekbone hurt, and she would probably have bruises on her arms and legs.

She wondered why Don had piled everything up like that—he had a little girl, why hadn't he made sure it was secure? The thought of Cleo getting caught in the fallout sickened her—she might have been killed. Rosemary looked at the gear filling the floor on either side of her and rested her head back on the top of the car. This wasn't going to be fun to wade through, but she had to get out of this mess. She'd have to come back and sort through all of it later.

Maybe in June.

After stepping on, over and between equipment, she finally made it out. She checked her watch again and saw that it was after lunch and she ought to go start the process of checking Cleo out of school. It broke her heart to have to tear the little girl away from her friends, but it couldn't be helped.

Rosemary grabbed her court documents, granting temporary guardianship, her ID and information for the school where Cleo would be attending, and headed for her rental car.

Rosemary checked Cleo out of school and they ran some of the dozens of errands that had to be handled before they left for Colorado. Her phone rang as she walked through the door, exhausted and achy from the earlier accident. She recognized the number on the caller ID as belonging to Juniper Ridge, but in her muddled state, wasn't sure to whom it belonged. She answered it, thinking that if it was one of her staff and it wasn't a true emergency, heads were going to roll. "This is Rosemary."

"Hey, are you at home?" The voice was Harrison's.

"Yes. Are you still in town? I thought you'd be gone by now." She wasn't sure if she wanted him to be gone, or if she just didn't care.

"I leave in the morning, but for tonight I thought I could take you two out for dinner, maybe we could catch a show. I'm sure you could both use a change of scene."

"Harrison, that's sweet of you, really. But we don't want to go out tonight." She didn't want to see anyone today—especially him. Though she'd used cover-up on her cheek, it was swollen and turning purple. And she really needed to veg for a while

"Yes we do!" Cleo said, scrambling over to her. "We want to go out tonight. Really. I want a shake."

The doorbell rang and Rosemary touched her forehead, wondering if her headache was going to get better or worse.

Cleo whooped, running to the door. She stopped and asked who it was, but opened the door almost immediately, revealing Harrison on the other side, still holding his phone to his ear.

Rosemary slumped a little—now he was here, Cleo wouldn't back off and let her stay home for a quiet evening. She ended the call and stuck her phone back in her pocket. "Really, Harrison, tonight is not the night to go out."

His brow furrowed as he drew closer. He hunched down so their faces were on the same level. "What happened? You have a bruise." His fingers ghosted just above it, tickling the fine hairs on her skin.

"I have several bruises," she said, not wanting to explain. "There was a little accident in the garage today. Nothing serious." She was not going to mention how very serious it *could* have been, not now. Not in front of Cleo. Besides, if she said anything about that to Harrison, he'd tell Sage, who would tell the others, and then she'd be smothered with concern.

"And that would be why you don't want to go do something tonight. I was really thinking maybe we could head out to Chuck E Cheese." He turned to Cleo, who jumped up and down.

"I want to go there, Rosemary! Please say we can go. Please?" She clasped her hands together and fluttered her big eyes and hopeful grin.

Rosemary sighed. There was no way she could turn Cleo down when she looked like that—not without a good reason. "I have the funniest feeling I'm going to lose, even if I argue."

"Yay!" Cleo wrapped her arms around Rosemary's neck, yanking her to the side and making her head pound a little more.

"I need some pain medication first. Give me a minute." Rosemary moved to stand, and Harrison held out a hand to help her up.

"Are you sure you're okay?" His eyes seemed to peer right through her.

"Really. I have a little headache. Nothing serious. Just give me a second. And I ought to change my blouse." It was still covered in dust and debris from the accident. "Go get your shoes," she told Cleo.

Before she knew it, they were pulling in front of Chuck E Cheese. "How did I not realize how far we drove?" Rosemary asked, looking over at Harrison. They had talked about things to do in DC all the way to Virginia, and Cleo had sung them belated Christmas carols from her school program.

"I don't know. I don't recall Scotty beaming us across the distance," he teased.

Rosemary smiled despite herself.

They ordered a big pizza with *almost* everything on it—just like Cleo liked—and they competed in games, tried to bonk weasel heads and fill water balloons first. Rosemary found Harrison was surprisingly competitive, which she met head-on. "Come on, you think you can take me?" she asked as they stood in front of Spy Hunter, an old arcade game she played often as a kid.

"You better believe it. I was the pro at this game when I was her age," he gestured to Cleo.

"That game is so lame, it's not even cool like the Wii or anything," Cleo announced. "You had stupid games when you were kids."

"Oh, we did, did we?" Rosemary asked as she grabbed her daughter and tickled her. Cleo shrieked with laughter and Rosemary tipped her unbruised cheek onto the little girl's head, so happy in that single moment. "I was the world champion of this game—I bet I can beat Harrison's score. Don't you think so?"

Cleo looked around Rosemary's shoulder to studying Harrison. "He looks pretty tough."

"Tougher than me? No way. You know I'm tougher than anyone."

"Hey, you talk big," Harrison said. "Care to put your money where your mouth is?"

She laughed despite herself. "Loser pays for the winner's next game?"

"You're on."

She didn't even feel bad when she had to ante up the quarters for the next round.

CHAPTER 7

"There's a lot of snow here." Cleo said as they wound around the mountain roads near Rosemary's house two days later. It was a relief to be reaching home as Rosemary was exhausted from the crazy week. Her aches and pains were getting better, but she had to use serious stage makeup to cover the bruise on her cheek.

"Yep. The skiers like it that way. Snow keeps them from hitting bushes and rocks."

"I want to learn to ski. And to snowboard. And to drive a snowmobile. Does anyone you know snowshoe?" Cleo asked.

"Fine to the skiing and snowboarding, the snowmobile is out of luck for a few more years—though maybe we can find someone to take you for a ride—and I'm sure someone around here snowshoes, but I don't know who." She made a mental note to ask the resort concierge. If anyone in the area took people out, they would probably know.

"This road is really windy."

"Are you getting sick?" Rosemary wondered if she had anything the girl could puke into. She didn't think Cleo had been prone to car sickness in the past.

"No. It's just really windy. And the trees are tall. There are a lot of them. Are they like this everywhere?" She stared out the window, watching the world flash past her.

"Pretty much." Rosemary nearly sighed in relief that the barrage of questions was at an end. She pulled up to her house and clicked the garage remote.

Cleo's eyes widened. "Cool. This is where you live? It's so huge."

"Yep. It had to fit six of us, so there's lots of space. Try to keep out of other people's rooms unless they invite you in, okay?"

"I'm not stupid. I know how to respect other people's space." Cleo sent her a dirty glare.

Cleo was growing uncharacteristically snippy, but though Rosemary's own temper was being tested by it, she understood the fear of the unknown. Cleo would be living with two total strangers in a new town and making new friends. They had been traveling all day and spent the previous day packing up the things Cleo felt she couldn't live without.

They were both exhausted. Rosemary just hoped the meeting with everyone went smoothly tonight. She had tried to talk Jonquil out of doing a big shindig with the whole family—that was a sure-fire way to overwhelm the kid—but she would not be put off. As usual.

The garage was full of cars, and there had been a couple of vehicles out front, including Harrison's, so this would be a big group.

"Cool, who drives the motorcycle?" Cleo asked when they passed it on the way to the kitchen door.

"Delphi. No, you may not ride with her. Not until the snow clears up enough the roads are decent anyway, and even then, only if she's willing. If not her, maybe Jeremy will take you out." Rosemary wished she'd kept that part to herself, she wasn't really a big fan of motorcycles, and the thought of her daughter on one was scary.

"Jeremy?" Cleo had been asking questions, and Rosemary had shown her dozens of photos of everyone, but Jeremy wasn't a relative, so he probably hadn't come up in the discussions.

"He's the photographer who does most of the weddings and things at the resort. He's also Vince's best friend." Rosemary pushed opened the kitchen door and was faced with a roomful of people, which included Alex. When had he gotten to town? Wow, they really had gotten everyone onboard. "This hoard of people is your new family. Of sorts," she said when she looked at Harrison.

"Not to be confused with the sane people who raised you." She looked at Cleo and said in a voice loud enough to be heard by everyone. "You won't get confused though, because sanity isn't really in big supply here. Except for Sage, who knows the difference between butter and margarine."

Cleo's brow furrowed. "Um, isn't one plant fat and the other animal fat?"

"Yes, that's true, but it goes so much deeper than that. I have a lot to teach you." She looked back at the ten pair of eyes. "Let's start with the smart one."

"Wait, wait. Let's see if I can do it. I've been looking at the pictures." Cleo had gotten her enthusiasm back, though Rosemary didn't expect it to last for long. She started on the right. "That's Delphi. She's the one with the cool motorbike, right?" She looked to Rosemary for confirmation.

"Sure thing. She's even more of a bossy pants than I am."

"She's the fifth sister," Cleo continued from memory. "And next to her is Jonquil. She works with flowers and she's number six. She's really athletic and skis."

"So right," Jonquil answered. "Rosemary is a slacker, she doesn't like to ski–how is it possible that anyone doesn't like skiing?" Jonquil shook her blond curls. "I'll take you out sometime if you want. I do lots of fun things because unlike *some* of my sisters, I'm not married to my job."

"Says the woman who wouldn't go home after breaking her leg," Cami muttered.

"Cool!" Cleo said, brightening. "Okay, then you're Cami and Vince, right? You just got married a few weeks ago. And she bosses around the desk clerks and bell boys and he works in people's yards."

"Yep. He's the grunt man, and I'm the third most bossypants person here," Cami said. She looked pleased that Cleo remembered, and not at all irritated by her job description.

"Wrong. I'm the bossiest of them all. That puts you in fourth place," Lana said. She was standing slightly in front of Blake in a cute maternity blouse and he had a hand on her hip.

"Actually," Rosemary said, "I think Cami's bossier than I am, so that puts her in third place."

"Wrong. You're firmly right behind Delphi," Harrison said. "And Lana is only bossiest because she's, well, the boss. I don't think she's naturally that bossy."

"And now *you're* the one who's wrong," Cami said. "Trust me, for the younger sister she's always been seriously bossy."

Cleo giggled at the silliness and moved on. "And Sage is there. She does massages on people's feet," she pulled a face at this. "And the big dude behind her is the security guard. You guys were married a couple months ago. You're a military guy and like to swim. Joel." Cleo looked at Alex and shook her head. "I don't know who you are."

Rosemary introduced Alex. "But he's not around much. He's important though, because he's going to make sure that you get to stay with me forever. And he's sort of family through the two redheads."

"Good to meet you." Cleo looked around the room and back at Rosemary. "Can we eat now? I'm starved!"

Rosemary smiled, relieved that Cleo didn't seem cowed by all of the new faces. "As soon as you pick out your room. There are plenty of bags out in my car still, guys. If any of you are man enough to help." She headed for the stairs leading to the open second story. "I'm the only person still sleeping upstairs, the rest have all defected to live with their husbands. They said you can have your pick of the rooms."

"All right." Cleo raced for the stairs and all of the guys headed into the garage.

Predictably, Cleo picked Lana's room with the ocean-themed mural and comforter that looked like ocean waves. When they came back downstairs, everyone was getting food or already eating.

"Young ladies first," Lana said when Cleo approached. "Go ahead and get into line."

Everyone had contributed something from Sage's humus and organic rice chips, to Jonquil's chocolate cream cake rolls—a recipe

Rosemary had taught her that summer—to a goulash Vince must have made because Cami was hopeless in the kitchen.

Cleo ate, but didn't last long after that, worn out from her trip. "It was all really good. Thanks." She had turned suddenly shy, so Rosemary took her upstairs.

"Get into your jams while I put some of these clothes away. Tomorrow we'll take you to the school and get your enrolled."

Worry filled Cleo's eyes. "Do I have to? Already? I'm tired."

"That's why you're going to bed now." Rosemary waited while she changed, then sat on the edge of the bed. "Look. I know this is really scary. It's been rough, and it's not exactly going to get easy overnight. But all of those people out there care and want to make sure that things are okay for you, and hopefully things will even be good before too long."

Cleo played with the stuffed cat she'd had since she was a toddler. "They aren't my parents."

"Nope. No one will ever be Cecilia and Don. They were super special people. But so are you and you're going to be okay. You know I love you?"

"Yeah. I do." Cleo hugged her tight. "I love you too."

"All right, get some sleep. I'll try to keep the riffraff from making too much noise." She dropped a kiss on Cleo's head.

Cleo giggled again as she settled under the blankets.

Rosemary felt incredibly unprepared for what lay ahead. She came back down the stairs to sit with the others.

"She seems to be doing pretty well," Joel said when Rosemary sat across from him.

"Yes, she sure does *seem* to be." She wanted to say more, but wasn't sure how much to say.

"Do you think she'll settle in okay?" Sage asked.

"Who knows?" Rosemary touched the back of her neck, slumping into her seat. "She's been keeping it together by sheer force of will, but she starts in a new school tomorrow, and everything is different. It could be nightmarishly emotional tomorrow, or we may have a couple weeks of smooth sailing, but eventually that little girl's pain is going to come out, claws extended." Rosemary knew all about pain-induced claws. It was a miracle she'd not turned to alcohol or drugs to get through some of the rough times.

"It doesn't have to be like that," Jonquil said.

"Nope, I could get lucky, but let's face it, she's my daughter, so she's going to wig eventually. Sooner is better than later. She's lost something massive. You don't get over that fast." She stared at the empty fireplace. "Sometimes you never get over it."

"So what'll you do?" Delphi asked, her eyes wary.

"Just love her to pieces. What else can you do? She's mine." She smiled after she said it, pleased to hear the words tripping off her tongue. "And for the first time I actually get to admit that. It doesn't matter what happens, I'll just love her and hope for some kind of miracle that I don't screw up too badly. And if I do screw up, I know you'll set me straight." She looked at Delphi.

"You better believe it," Delphi said.

"Are you afraid of messing up?" Lana asked. "I'm terrified of making mistakes." She touched her growing stomach. "And my baby didn't just come out of a major trauma."

"Everyone messes up." Rosemary looked at Lana. "You nearly threw away Blake, and he's made you disgustingly happy. Cami almost kicked Vince to the curb, and Sage and Joel were nearly killed by a stalker for heaven sakes. We're all damaged—and that's not counting stuff before we met last spring."

"Then it's good she has all of us. Because one of us is going to be there for her, even if the rest of us are clueless," Sage said with a firm nod.

Yeah, that worked for now, but if Rosemary took Cleo back to DC at the end of her contract, who would be there for her then?

"I wonder," Cami said tentatively. "Do you think maybe you shouldn't announce to the world that she's your daughter?"

Rosemary glared at her. "Right, because I want her to think I'm ashamed of her? Not a chance."

"I don't mean that," Cami said.

"No, but you don't know what you're saying," Delphi said. "You've never felt like a second-class citizen because Dad wouldn't acknowledge you in public. You never had to be his dirty little secret, and have visits with him, but not be allowed to go places with him where someone might know you, because then someone might find out and ruin his life."

"You weren't..." Cami seemed to reconsider what she was saying. "You felt like that?" She looked at the four half-sisters. As one of George DiCarlo's legitimate offspring, she hadn't dealt with the same issues as the rest of the girls.

"Not often," Sage said, "but sometimes."

"A lot." Rosemary nodded.

"All the time," Delphi said.

"I knew he loved me, but yeah, I felt it. I couldn't tell anyone, couldn't tell my friends about my fun trips with him and had to make excuses when he came to town for why I couldn't do stuff with them. Everyone else just said they were hanging with their dads for the weekend," Jonquil said. "If I'd said that, people would have wanted to meet him, so... lie, lie, lie."

Cami and Lana looked at each other in dismay. Apparently this hadn't occurred to them at all. They hadn't known any of the others existed until the reading of George's will and definitely hadn't experienced any of it themselves.

"Wow, now I feel like an obtuse idiot," Lana muttered.

"Serve me up some of that." Cami leaned back in Vince's arm. "And then he announced it to the world after he was dead so he wouldn't have to face the questions."

"Yeah." Rosemary shifted in her seat. It had been a weak and selfish thing to do, but as much as Rosemary resented that fact, she still loved him.

"That said, Cami's not entirely wrong, either," Delphi said.

Rosemary glared at her. "What do you mean?"

"Cleo just lost her parents—the only ones she's known. She's always known you, but it's not like she's had time to adjust to the fact that you're her birth mom, and you moved her halfway—more than halfway—across the country to start a new school. Maybe she doesn't want to tell anyone yet. You should let her decide whether or not to spread the word."

Rosemary couldn't believe what she was hearing. "But I've spent the past nine years having to keep this secret and I don't want her to feel like I don't care, like I don't want her." How could Delphi say that?

"This isn't about you. This is about her." Delphi's gaze was direct, her voice low. "Let her decide. Tell her you want to be open about your relationship, but that she gets to control who knows and when. You've had choices in this, Rosemary. They may have been really awful options, and the situation was crap, but you were an adult and you had options when you gave her up. Dad would have helped you out if you decided to keep her, we both know he would have. She needs options now so she can feel in control of something."

Rosemary felt her jaw twitch as she held her tongue, trying not to spew her anger. Trying to take a moment to consider what Delphi was saying. She thought of how devastated Cleo was, and how she would feel if it were her—could she even guess how Cleo would feel? Finally she nodded. "Okay. I'll make it her choice."

It grated on her to agree with Delphi about anything, but Cleo did need some control, and this one wouldn't kill Rosemary—she'd still get to have her daughter living in the house with her full time. That's what mattered, right?

Cleo listened from the balcony that overlooked the open kitchen, dining and great rooms. She'd thought from the way they joked earlier that they were all good friends; she didn't realize they had arguments and fights too. And they were fighting about her. She was relieved that Rosemary would let her tell people when she was ready, but was afraid they would get sick of her and send her away. Her Uncle Mike said she was a pain—would Rosemary think so too? She got rid of her once before, even if she *said* she didn't want to. What if Cleo never wanted people to know and Rosemary got sick of keeping the secret?

When the subject changed to something about the hotel, Cleo returned to her bed, sliding in soundlessly. She liked it here—not as much as home, but it was better than living with one of her uncles. These people seemed nice, mostly. She decided to be extra good so they would let her stay.

CHAPTER 8

Cleo looked nervous as they sat at the island the next morning eating muffins and orange juice. Well, Cleo was eating muffins and orange juice, Rosemary was having a cup of coffee, black, and half a wheat English muffin. She hated them, but it was fewer calories and she had to stick to her diet.

Sage came breezing in the door to the garage, her dark curls springing out all over her head. "Hello, I hoped I'd catch you before you left for school." She helped herself to one of the muffins and poured hot water for tea.

"No food at your place?" Rosemary asked, amused. This was why Harrison thought he could still just drop into the house randomly, even though his sister hadn't lived here in over two months. They did tend to have an open-door policy for family and friends.

Had he been right? Were they some sort of friends? After their dinners together in DC, she thought they might be and wasn't sure how to feel about that.

"No, actually, I came to give Cleo a bit of good news." She filled the tea ball full of her favorite tea mix—which she blended herself—making them wait while she fiddled with everything.

"Yes," Rosemary said to Cleo's questioning look. "She's always like this. You get used to it. Give her a minute to finish playing with her drink and then maybe she'll have enough attention left over to share with us."

"Oh, yes, sorry." Sage set the cup of tea beside her plate and looked at Cleo. "I have the strongest feeling that today is a day of change for you, but that good things are coming your way. I know you're going to make a super friend today." She beamed at them both as if that said it all, then took a bite of muffin.

"Well, then, you're bound to have a great start at your school, just like I was saying," Rosemary said to Cleo.

Cleo wore a look of total disbelief. Not surprising seeing as how she'd never been exposed to Sage's astrology readings—which weren't actually astrological, but some other thing she attributed to the stars. "What about Rosemary? What's her day going to be like?"

"Oh, I don't know about her. Sometimes things come to me, and I know stuff, but not for her, not today. You're the one the stars have aligned for." Sage took a sip of her tea, then checked her watch. "Shouldn't you be heading out by now?"

"Yes. You're right." Rosemary downed the end of her coffee and wished the English muffin had been a little bit bigger. "Grab your backpack and off we go."

Cleo dragged herself from the island after finishing her juice. She slid into her coat, grabbed her bag and snatched the end of her muffin to finish in the car. When they were on the road, she turned to Rosemary. "Sage's what you were talking about when you said everyone is insane, right? Who really believes in the stars?"

"Almost everyone, when Sage tells us things. I have no idea where she gets it all from, but she's right a lot, like a real-life fortune teller." Sage used to hide her predictions by mixing them into horoscope readings from the newspaper, but she'd given up on that before Christmas.

"How much is a lot?"

"Always. She is so accurate it's spooky. I don't mean like once in a while she's right, or most of the time you can *twist* it to be right, I mean every single time she says something like that, she's right on target. The day of the bombing, she came to the kitchen to tell me that there was going to be a tragedy, but that it would bring amazing opportunities too. And here you are."

Cleo looked uncertain at best. "You think I'm an amazing opportunity?"

"Yeah, I do. I'm not saying that being in charge of you doesn't scare the beejeebees out of me, because it does, but even though I would way rather have your parents alive," Rosemary fought to keep her voice level, but heard it crack, "I'm really glad that you were able to live with me, since you had to live with someone."

"I'm a problem to you," Cleo said solemnly. "Someone to worry about getting from one thing to the next. I heard you talking about it with the others this morning, trying to figure out who would pick me up and where I would go after school today."

Rosemary hadn't realized Cleo had been able to hear. "You're not a problem. Circumstances could be easier, but you're never a problem. It'll be all good, and Jonquil will pick you up from school this afternoon." She wanted to shift the focus of the subject. "So, Sage has blessed your day with smiles and new friends. All will be well."

"Right." Cleo still looked doubtful.

Harrison glanced out in the parking lot at the end of the workday and noticed Rosemary's car was still parked out there. He was surprised, considering this was Cleo's first day of school. Why wasn't Rosemary home with her daughter?

He walked to the kitchen and stuck his head into the office where Rosemary was bent over her desk, her blond hair braided down her back and a cup of coffee sitting beside her. He wondered if she had totally forgotten that it was there and if it was cold. When she reached out absent-mindedly and picked it up, sipped, then pulled a face and put it down again, he knew his guess was correct.

A shuffling noise to his right had him peeking around the door to see Cleo huddled over a book at a make-shift desk, an annoyed expression on her face.

"Hey, kiddo."

Rosemary didn't react at all to his voice, as if she'd known he was there, but Cleo smiled in greeting. "Harrison, what are you doing here?" She glared at Rosemary. "She keeps saying we're going home soon. But she never leaves the computer. She keeps flipping through papers and swearing, then typing like crazy." A dimple appeared in one cheek and her lips quirked when she lifted her voice. "When we got here, she said everyone was insane. Was she talking about herself, too?"

Rosemary whipped around and glared at Cleo, but it was only half serious.

Harrison nodded. "Yeah, she's as crazy as the rest of them. I'm sorry you have to live there, but it'll never be boring."

"Well *this* is boring. I finished my homework a long time ago, and the book I got at school is for babies. I read it in second grade."

"I'm almost done. I promise. I just have to catch up on paperwork after being gone all week," Rosemary said. She looked at Harrison with impatience. "What are you doing here? Did I forget some paperwork?"

"No. I just popped in to see what was going on. How about if I take Cleo around the hotel and show her the cool stuff while you finish that up? Then you can take her home." He tried to keep the censure out of his voice, but her scowl said she'd caught it.

"Please?" Cleo stood quickly, sticking a bookmark between the pages of her chapter book.

"That's fine. I'm sorry, bug. I didn't mean to be here so long." Rosemary sighed, then explained to Harrison. "Jonquil was supposed to take her home, but this afternoon they rented the presidential suite for tonight, so she's been doing all new flower arrangements for it." She shifted her attention back to Cleo. "I promise, when Harrison brings you back, no matter what I'm in the middle of, we'll go, okay?"

"Okay." Cleo tucked the book in her backpack, then looked at Harrison. "I'm ready. Where're we going?"

Seeing the hotel through the eyes of a nine-year-old who had never been anywhere this fancy was a revelation. Harrison vaguely remembered his own first encounter with one of George DiCarlo's luxury resorts, but he had been quite young at the time—several years younger than Cleo—and it hadn't meant as much to him.

Cleo was bright and full of questions, asking about how they cleaned the pool, and why there were trees inside the solarium, and who took care of them, and if she could study there some time. She was eager to try the cup of cocoa the girl working at the café offered her, and was disappointed when Harrison told her it was too close to dinner for a cinnamon roll or cupcake.

"We never have anything good, except when other people are around. Rosemary hardly eats anything and it's always healthy—which must mean *yucky* because English muffins are *gross*."

Harrison had noticed Rosemary's eating habits as well, and had hoped that she ate more at other times, since their dinner schedules didn't mesh often. But from the fact that she looked as emaciated as a model for Cosmo, he doubted she indulged much. He was sure she hadn't been that thin when they met again that summer. "Maybe she'll do better now that you're here, and she's home again. Being away from home can be hard for some people." But he knew he was just placating her.

She made a non-committal noise in response.

"How was school today?" he asked eventually.

"Fine. Your sister—Sage is your sister, right?" When he nodded, she continued, "She came by this morning to tell me that I was going to have a good day and make a friend." Her face was bright with excitement.

He smiled. "Yeah? I bet you did too, because she's amazing like that."

"Yeah, Hannah is so cool and we're going to get together and hang out. Is Sage always right? Rosemary says she is but my mom said psychics are like magicians and none of it's real."

"Most of the time I think you're right, but if Sage says the stars have a message for you, she's not making it up." He leaned in and lowered his voice conspiratorially. "I don't think she really gets it from the stars. She's just got a gift for knowing things, and I've never known her to be wrong."

Cleo's eyes were bright with curiosity. "Weird."

"Yup."

"So if I asked her if I was going to pass my test in school..."

He laughed. "It doesn't work that way, kiddo. Sorry. She can't control what information she gets. You'll just have to take it as she gives it to you and be happy about it. And study for your tests so Rosemary doesn't have to go all bossypants on you."

They walked along in silence for a while longer on their way back to the kitchen when Cleo spoke. "Do you think Rosemary is sorry my parents made her take me now?"

He looked at her in surprise. "What? No. Why would you think that?"

She shrugged. "I don't know, it's just that she seems really stressed out all the time, and it's only been a week. And, well, she gave me up for adoption, so she must not have wanted me." She bit her lip and looked at him from the corner of her eye, like she was afraid to look at him straight on.

His heart went out to her—to both of them. It was a rough situation. He stopped in the middle of the hall and crouched down, so he faced her nose-to-nose, then lowered his voice again. "You know what she told me when she found out she was going to get to bring you home?"

"What?"

"That you deserved someone better to raise you than her. She's worried. She wants to be a great mom, but she doesn't feel like she'll do a good job."

Cleo's hand slid into his, giving it a squeeze. "That's silly. How could she be a bad mom?"

He smiled and straightened. "I don't know, especially with someone like you helping her out."

Cleo smiled as they entered the kitchen a few seconds later. She headed straight for the office. "You said we could go now."

Rosemary looked at her computer a little wistfully, as if she didn't want to leave it yet, but nodded. She saved her file and shut down the computer. "The rest can wait. What do you want for dinner tonight?"

"Pizza!"

Rosemary reached out and pressed the hair back from Cleo's face. "You always say that."

"I always *want* it."

"All right, I'll make French bread pizzas tonight. We'll stop by the store and get some bread."

"Sounds good. You don't think you'll have extra, do you?" Harrison asked. He could always go for dinner if Rosemary was cooking, and he wanted to talk to her about what Cleo had said.

Rosemary eyed him. "I suppose, if you promise to behave."

He felt a tug of attraction at her smile, as he always did. "I can try."

"Close enough." She grabbed her coat and purse and they headed for the door.

He decided to consider that a good sign.

CHAPTER 9

There was only one regular grocery store in Juniper Ridge and the organic store closed early, so Rosemary wasn't surprised to see the place packed. The clientele ran from harried housewives to glamorous spa visitors and snow bunnies to families with young children. She smiled as they moved through the crowds, Cleo's hand in hers. She was here with her daughter for the first time. This wouldn't be the last, either. As they made their way to the bakery, she waved to several people she had met in the past six months. If she'd been thinking ahead, she would have mixed up some dough that morning so she could bake it when she arrived home. She would have to start thinking about regular meals now her daughter was around.

"Rosemary, how nice to see you. You too, Harrison." Etta eyed them speculatively, but if she was making two plus two equal five, she didn't say so.

Rosemary looked up into the friendly blue eyes of Vince's mother. "Hello. How is the winter treating you? Vince said the ice has been a hassle for you to get in and out of your driveway."

"Yes, we shouldn't have put it on such an incline, but we weren't thinking at the time." Etta tipped her head in acknowledgment and turned her gaze to Cleo. "You must be Cleo. Cami said you were going to be living here from now on. Hannah said she met you at school today. What do you think of your new house?"

Cleo shrugged. "It's nice. I wish we had a pool, but Rosemary said Sage is building one."

"She sure is. It probably won't be done for a while yet, but I bet if you begged nicely, they'd let you use the one at the hotel."

Cleo turned to Rosemary and fluttered her eyelashes ridiculously. "Could I, Rosemary?"

She laughed. "Yes. But not without making arrangements with us first. You can't be in there alone. Not ever."

Cleo put her hands on her hips. "I'm not a baby."

"No, you're not." She squeezed her daughter's hand. "But swim safety is important. And hotel rules say no one under fourteen without adult supervision."

Cleo harrumphed a little. "I bet you don't make the Navy guy have someone babysit him when he swims."

Harrison set a hand on Cleo's shoulder. "When you finish SEAL training, we'll let you swim unsupervised too."

Cleo didn't appear amused, but Rosemary had to smile.

"Lana's having a baby," Cleo said, apparently deciding a change of topic was in order. "Do you think Cami will have one too? It would be cool to have cousins. My parents each had a brother, but neither of them got married. And they don't like kids much." Her nose wrinkled.

"I hope she does," Etta said, "but I guess we'll have to wait and see. Vince has lots of nieces and nephews—and not just Hannah. She comes to my house sometimes. You should join us one afternoon." Etta shifted her basket from one hand to another.

"That sounds good," Rosemary said. "Call me when you have Hannah over again and I'll see if we can work it out."

Etta made excuses about needing to get home to start dinner and they waved goodbye, before continuing into the bakery area.

"She's nice," Cleo said.

"Yes, she's very nice. I've met Hannah, she's a lot of fun." They picked out French bread and continued to the meat and cheese aisle. "So, was Sage right? Did you make a good friend today like Sage said you would?"

"Yes. Hannah!" She giggled a little. "She's going to have her mom ask if I can sleep over this weekend."

Rosemary felt her gut clench at the thought of her baby staying over at someone's house overnight—even if it was Vince's sister. "I guess I'll have to talk to her mom and see what we come up with."

"A sleepover already?" Harrison asked as he picked up a bag of shredded mozzarella.

Wrinkling her nose at his choice, Rosemary grabbed the bag and put it back on the shelf. "We're not using that. Who do you think you're shopping with, anyway?" She grabbed a package of fresh mozzarella to shred at home. "Pre-shredded mozzarella. Always dried out and subpar." She let the sentence fall into little more than a mutter, teasing him as much as anything.

He grinned. "My mistake." He tugged a small package of Canadian bacon from the display. "Is this okay for your majesty?"

"Yes. That's fine." Rosemary was pleased that he'd understood the tease. She considered the vegetables in the fridge at home and decided they still needed some fresh peppers and a can of olives.

Cleo eyed Harrison. "Are you psychic like your sister?" Her tone showed curiosity mingled with disbelief.

"Nope. Sometimes I get itchy feelings about things, but only once, no, twice, actually, I had an impression strong enough to count, and I messed it up. Sage gets impressions all the time, though." He grabbed a bag of chips from an end cap. "Are the kids here further along in math and stuff than you, or behind you?"

"About the same." Cleo shrugged. "Can we get Twinkies for dessert?"

Rosemary turned and glared at her in mock horror. "I cannot believe you are my daughter. How could you possibly eat that trash?" She laid on the drama and huffed loudly, pleased when it make Cleo giggle. "Just ask Jonquil what happened when she tried eating Ho-Hos around me. Seriously, you're both such neophytes."

Cleo looked around them, reminding Rosemary that they'd told her it was *her* decision when to tell others they were related, and she'd totally forgotten. When no one was close, though, Cleo turned to Harrison and asked in a stage whisper, "What's a neophyte?"

"Someone who's new to something—specifically someone who doesn't know enough to be aware that only Rosemary is capable of making anything worth eating."

Rosemary elbowed him, though it was mostly for show. "There are plenty of people who can cook fine, but Hostess isn't one of them. Don't worry, Cleo, I'm going to teach you and then everyone will bow to your amazing powers in the kitchen."

Harrison sent her a commiserating look. "She uses a lot of long words considering she's always pretending to be some tough street kid, doesn't she?"

"What makes you think it's an act?" Rosemary stuck red and green peppers into a bag. She looked up to see Rulon coming toward them, a scowl on his face. She did not need a confrontation with a former employee, but she couldn't avoid him now.

"What do you think you're doing here?" he asked her.

"It's a grocery store. I'm buying groceries." Rosemary straightened.

"You probably think you own the place, don't you? You own the whole world—you're one of the mighty DiCarlos. Guess what, most of us don't care. And you might run that hotel, but it doesn't make you the only game in town, you know? You think you're all big and important, but you're nothing. And you're going to pay for causing me trouble." He walked forward and pointed his finger in her face. His breath smelled of beer and he reeked of cigarette smoke.

"You better back off, Rulon." Harrison pushed between the two of them, and Rosemary shifted Cleo behind her.

"Oh, you and her, huh? Is that why you let her get away with anything at the hotel? I should have known." His face twisted with anger. "You're both going to be sorry."

The grocery store manager walked over. "Is there a problem, sir?"

"No. I'm leaving." Rulon sneered at them and pivoted, stalking away.

Rosemary gave Cleo's hand a squeeze, hoping her daughter couldn't tell she was shaking. "Thank you, Jeff. It's always hard when you have to fire someone. He wasn't very happy about it."

"No problem. We're sorry he bothered you. Let me know if you need anything." He nodded to them and walked away down the drink aisle.

"That was interesting." Harrison's gaze held a modicum of censure. He hadn't approved of how she'd handled Rulon, and after she had time to calm down, she wished she'd handled it better as well. It didn't make it okay for Rulon to get in her face, though.

"Who's that guy?" Cleo still watched in the direction he had disappeared, biting her lip.

"Someone who used to work for me. He doesn't anymore. Come on, he won't bother you again." Rosemary hoped it was true.

CHAPTER 10

Cleo liked to watch the birds flitting through the trees. She liked to hear their song even more. It was so cold here, but birds and squirrels were everywhere outside the house, and she loved that there was a tree next to her window.

She looked down at her homework and scowled. She hated math; why did they even have to study it? They had calculators didn't they? A bird started to sing outside, making Cleo smile. She couldn't hear it very well, so she walked over and opened the window just a few inches to make it easier to hear.

A cold breeze blew into the room and she yanked the blanket from her bed to wrap up in while she finished long division.

There was a loud noise from downstairs and Cleo jumped up, anxious for any excuse to get away from her desk. She found Delphi standing up at the top of the stairs—she'd fallen over as she came up from the basement.

"Are you okay?" Jonquil asked, her lips twitching like she was holding back a laugh.

"Fine."

"Could you be any less coordinated and still be able to walk around?" Rosemary asked from the kitchen. "Then again."

"Shut it." Delphi snagged a soda from the fridge. Glancing up, she smiled. "There you are, kiddo. How was school?"

"It was okay." It had snowed over the weekend, so she and Hannah had stomped out the outlines of a house in the snow during recess. They were going to play in it during the next break, but some of the younger boys messed it up when they got out for their recess period. Stupid boys.

"Good."

"Is your homework done?" Rosemary asked, barely glancing up from her laptop.

"Um, almost." It was a stretch, there was still most of the page left, but she deserved a break, right?

"Then you can *almost* come out of your room. Go back and finish. Let me know if you have trouble and need help." She returned her attention to her laptop. She was always on the computer in the afternoon—her mom had spent time with her after school, not been wrapped up in a job. At least they were home instead of at the hotel—her office there was so *boring*. There wasn't even a window. Of course, Harrison was at the resort and she really liked him—he was nice and treated her as if she was smart instead of like a dumb kid.

"Do you need a snack?" Jonquil asked.

"No," Rosemary answered before Cleo could accept. "She already had two cookies and some carrot sticks. She can wait until dinner."

"You're such a slave driver," Delphi grabbed a cookie from the jar and flipped through some papers she'd brought up with her.

"You betcha. It's what you all love about me." Rosemary didn't even look up from her laptop.

Cleo huffed a little, but went into her room, grabbed her blanket and wrapped in it again, before sitting at her desk. The math wasn't that hard, it was just so boring and she hated doing it.

She was finishing up the last row of problems when Rosemary came in.

"How's it going, short stuff?" She rubbed her arms. "You opened the window? Why?"

"I wanted to hear the birds." Cleo protested when Rosemary started to close the window.

"It's freezing out there. You're going to have to save your bird loving for when you're outside until it gets warmer out there." She twisted the window lock.

"You never let me have any fun," Cleo grumbled.

Rosemary sat on the edge of the bed. "How's the homework?"

"Almost done."

"Great. You want to make a snowman after you finish up?"

Cleo's head whipped around to look at Rosemary. She wasn't sure if she believed it because it had been so long since they did anything just for fun. Rosemary used to do crazy fun things with her all the time. Before her parents died. "Really?"

"Yeah. Really. Hurry up."

Cleo returned to her work with renewed determination, zipping through the problems in record time. She was going to build snowmen with her—well, sort of her mom.

She thought about that word, mom, in relation to Rosemary. She wasn't sure how she felt about that, now that she knew, but she would think about it. Now she would get to go out and play.

Harrison stood in the driveway and watched Rosemary and Cleo rolling giant snowballs in the yard. They must be making a snowman. He thought about joining them, but wasn't sure if he should intrude in their mother-daughter time. It was nice seeing them play together, Rosemary teasing and carefree.

Jonquil came onto the front porch and looked at him. "Sage called. She said to tell you today is the day. Seize your chance at love and ask out the girl of your dreams."

Harrison turned to her, not believing a word of it. "Really?"

She pursed her lips. "No, but she should. It's good advice, so go do it."

He chuckled. "I didn't bring my boots."

"Wimp. I've just lost all respect for you. You're wearing running shoes instead of your shiny executive loafers. Weren't you raised on an organic farm? I thought farmers were tough."

"Yeah, we were tough in Southern California, where it never snowed." Still, he was tempted to insert himself in their fun.

Her gaze bored into him. "I'm not going to invite you for family gatherings with food—which is all of them—if you can't ask her out by the end of the week. It's not that hard, just ask her for dinner."

"You think she'd go with me?" He turned his gaze back to Rosemary. The blond hair that hung down nearly to her derriere stuck out of the knitted cap and kept getting in her face. He thought it was funny that she kept brushing it out of the way instead of doing a braid like she wore at work.

"If you asked her right. She doesn't scowl at you nearly as much as she used to."

He smiled. "That's hardly comforting. But I'll think about it."

"Good. Don't think too long." She went back inside.

Harrison decided a little time in the snow wouldn't hurt anything, so he waded out in the two-foot drifts, and sucked in a breath at the flash of cold snow against his leg. "Hey, could you use another hand? It looks like you're making a monster snowman."

"Snow-woman," Cleo clarified. "But you can help."

When Rosemary just looked at her daughter and got an adoring look on her face, he took that for a yes and started another snowball.

The girls finished the body for the snow-woman while he rolled a big ball for the head.

"Let me help you with that," Rosemary said when he carried it over.

"You think I can't handle it on my own?" he asked.

"Well, I don't know how many snow-women you've made, living in So-Cal and all. I figured a little supervision might be in order." The edges of her lips twisted with fun.

He lifted the ball onto the body and she grabbed it from the other side, helping to slide it into place. His fingers—totally frozen through his thin gloves—brushed hers as she shifted it slightly and he looked up at her.

She met his gaze and he felt a zing of electricity flash between them. The moment seemed to freeze and he brushed his fingertips across her knuckles. He thought she swallowed reflexively before she pulled her hand away, turning toward her daughter.

His heart pounded and he sucked in a deep breath of cold mountain air.

Maybe she wouldn't shoot him down after all.

CHAPTER 11

"Good job on the homework," Rosemary said as she put it back in Cleo's folder. The girl had time to work on it in Rosemary's office—again—but hadn't seemed to be paying too much attention to it.

"So I can go to Hannah's tomorrow night for the sleepover?" Cleo asked, clasping her hands and putting a pleading expression on her face.

Rosemary rolled her eyes, though she thought it was adorable. She looked at Harrison who had stopped in with ice cream at dinnertime and begged some food off them. He grinned.

"Sure, you can go tomorrow night," she said. "That was the deal." She'd already had a long chat with Hannah's mom about which adults would be there and the other girls who were invited.

"All right!" Cleo jumped up and danced in a circle. "We're going to stay up all night watching movies."

"Terrific. That will make Saturday *so much fun*," Rosemary said under her breath as she put away the pan from dinner. "It's time for you to head to bed, bug. Come give me a kiss." She poked out her cheek and pulled a face, making Cleo giggle. Still, her daughter gamely came over and kissed her cheek.

"Good night, Rosemary. Good night, Harrison."

"Good night, bug. And don't come down for a drink of water three times, okay?" Rosemary said.

"Fine." Cleo sighed heavily as if she were being asked to do a really difficult task, but she went upstairs to her room.

Rosemary was exhausted. The day had been endless and she wanted nothing so much as to go to bed and sleep for ten hours, but she had paperwork to finish tonight and had to be up early tomorrow to check the food order when it was delivered. A couple of times they had sent the wrong things and she'd had to send it back—that was much easier to do if she caught it when the delivery man was still there.

She put her hands at the small of her back and stretched. A hot soak wouldn't go amiss, either.

"You look all done in," Harrison said, studying her. "Are you getting enough sleep?"

"I'll live." Rosemary rubbed her eyes. "You didn't have anything better to do than to come hang out here tonight?" She kept her voice light, not wanting him to think she minded his presence. It had been fun—a fact that still surprised her when she thought about it.

"Some of my favorite people live here." He shifted closer, his gaze steady on hers.

She wasn't sure how to take his comment. He hadn't visited this often when Sage lived with them.

A scream pierced the air, and Rosemary ran for the stairs on instinct, headed for the sound—Cleo. Harrison was hard on her heels. The second scream was not quite as ear-splitting, but contained a word that made Rosemary's heart nearly stop.

"Snake!"

Rosemary came to a skidding halt in the doorway when she saw Cleo on the bed and the snake swirling around on the floor between her and the door. Cleo looked at Rosemary, her face white with panic.

"Hold on, sweetie. Just stay there." Rosemary looked at Harrison. "Do something." She was frozen with fear and didn't think she could make her feet move again.

He was down the stairs in a flash, taking the last three in one leap and bounding into the garage.

"What's going on?" Jonquil asked from the bottom of the stairs.

"There's a rattle snake in Cleo's room." Rosemary looked at her daughter and realized her reaction was freaking Cleo out even worse.

Right. Calm. She took two deep breaths and looked at the snake again. It wasn't being threatening at the moment—if you discounted its existence in the room as a threat, which she didn't exactly. "Okay, I'm calmer. It doesn't look poised to strike or anything, but I can't get to Cleo because it's between the two of us."

"A rattler, at this time of year?" Jonquil froze. "Did you block it in the room? Because it might feel threatened if it has nowhere to go." She set one foot on the bottom stair, then hesitated as if she was worried about becoming snake bait.

"Um, yeah, I guess, but it isn't—" She stopped talking when the snake turned to her and started shifting in her direction. "Oh, crap. Now it's headed for me."

"Back away slowly and keep an eye on it," Jonquil directed. "Just, I don't know, don't let it get too close."

"How do you know about snakes?" Rosemary asked.

"I rock climb. I decided knowing my predators was a good idea."

"Right." She shifted back into the hall, keeping her eyes on the rattler, while listening to her daughter sob hysterically. "It's okay, kiddo, it's not interested in you. See?"

"It's going to bite you and then you'll die, just like mom and dad," Cleo wailed.

"Not if I can help it." The words were barely more than a mutter as terror gripped her. The rattler grew closer and she stumbled back into the railing that overlooked the living area.

"How can you stop it?" Cleo asked, sobbing.

Harrison exploded back into the house from the garage and took the stairs two at a time, a shovel in his hand. "Good thing Vince left this behind."

Relief trickled through Rosemary, though she didn't know if Harrison had any idea how to use the weapon, now he had one. "He left one for Jonquil when she wanted to plant bulbs a few months ago. Never took it back with him."

"Lucky for us." He paused to study the situation, then approached the snake.

It reared back and he jabbed, hard and fast, severing the head about six inches back from the jaw.

Cleo screamed, Rosemary shuddered, and the rattler slithered and jerked in its death throes, splashing blood everywhere.

Harrison put the scoop of the shovel upside down over the head as it continued to twitch, then stepped through the doorway to the bed, reaching out to Cleo. "Come on, bug. It's okay, the snake is dead now."

Cleo jumped into his arms, sobbing into his shoulder.

He brought her out. "Let's go down to the basement. I'll clean it up while you get her calmed down."

Rosemary was glad he carried Cleo down because her knees felt like jelly. She was shaky and a little queasy. "Thanks."

"No problem. You owe me a special treat, don't you think?" he asked, already acting as if it had been nothing, but his hand shook a little as he lifted it from the railing when they reached the dining area.

"Anything you want. You name it; we'll make it for you. Anytime." Rosemary followed him down to the sitting area in the basement and sat on the sofa. He set Cleo on her lap and the little girl happily latched onto Rosemary instead.

Jonquil knelt beside them and Delphi came out of her bedroom, sliding her earbuds out so she could hear. "What's going on?"

Rosemary rested her head back on the sofa, feeling about ten years older than she had fifteen minutes earlier. The whole tableau only took two or three minutes, but it seemed like so much longer. She was glad when Jonquil filled Delphi in.

They all soothed Cleo, Rosemary grateful to have her close, to be able to calm her. She'd never been so terrified in her life.

Footsteps came down the stairs and she looked up to thank Harrison again, but he spoke first. "Everything's cleared away. You'll probably need to get someone in to clean the carpet."

"I was so scared," Cleo said. Her breathing had almost returned to normal, though tears still ran down her cheeks. "I thought it was going to get me. Then I thought it would get Rosemary." Her hold tightened even more on Rosemary.

"It's all right, bug. Everything's fine." Except now that she had time to think, Rosemary couldn't figure out how the snake had gotten into her daughter's room. Snakes were supposed to hibernate at this time of year. They shouldn't be around to slide into people's locked houses and under beds... or wherever it had been hiding. The house didn't even have mice, so how had a snake gotten in?

Harrison knelt down beside them. "You'll want to call Joel to have him copy the recording from the cameras so he can figure out how it got in. I checked behind and under all of the rest of the furniture up there, so we're clear."

"No! I don't want to sleep alone. Let me sleep with you tonight," Cleo looked at Rosemary, her eyes pleading. "Please. I won't be able to sleep by myself."

Her bed was queen-sized, so it was big enough to share. Rosemary knew some expert would probably say she was enabling or something, but she couldn't say no. Not this time. "All right, bug. You can sleep with me tonight."

"I'm going to check in my bedroom too," Delphi shivered as if her skin were crawling. "We ought to check the whole place."

"Seconded," Jonquil said. "I'll call Joel now to check the cameras and help us poke around."

"Good idea." Rosemary considered. "I think we need to talk about how to keep this from happening again. How does tomorrow night sound?"

"Sure, that's fine. I'll let everyone know," Jonquil said.

She and Delphi went upstairs, saying they were going to dig through the main rooms before hitting their own.

Harrison moved to sit beside Rosemary. He looked at Cleo. "That must have been pretty scary, huh?"

"Yeah, I thought I would die." Her eyes were red and puffy and new tears were making tracks on her cheek, though her breathing had calmed.

"Good thing you have so many people who love you to take care of you, isn't it?" he asked.

Cleo considered his words for a minute, then nodded. "Yeah." This time she rested her head on Rosemary's shoulder, but she didn't bury her face. "Will you stay with us tonight?"

Harrison's face registered surprise, but Rosemary was the one to speak first. "Honey, he needs to go home. We'll be all right here. You're going to sleep with me."

"I want him to stay. He can sleep in Sage's old room. He's her brother, right? It'll be okay. And then I'll feel better."

Rosemary looked at him and he smiled, tapping Cleo's nose. "I can do that. Then I can take you to school in the morning before I go to work since Rosemary has to go in really early."

Cleo's body relaxed, making it impossible for Rosemary to protest.

"Come on, let's go upstairs," Rosemary said.

"Carry me," Cleo asked.

"I can't, honey, you're almost as big as I am."

Cleo pouted.

Harrison stood and reached out to her. "I'll carry you up. Come on, short stuff."

She went into his arms willingly and Rosemary rose to her feet, still feeling shaky. Using the wall to support her, she made it up the stairs behind them, then up the second flight to her room.

Harrison set Cleo on the bed, and glanced around the room. "Italy."

"It's the best place on the planet," Rosemary said. She loved her room and the way it made her think of her internship in Florence.

He looked at her. "It seems there are a few things about you I still don't know."

"That's the understatement of the year." She managed not to snort.

"Then maybe it's time I did something about it. Have dinner with me next week?"

Rosemary felt her heart catch. He was asking her out? She wanted to and she didn't want to, all at the same time. They had just started to be friends; would dating ruin that? "Oh, I don't know, I have Cleo—"

"No, you have to go with him. I'll hang out here with Jonquil," Cleo insisted. "We'll have fun. She can show me how to make those chocolate pinwheel things you taught her. And you never go out and do things. You should."

Harrison lifted a brow. "See, you have to go with me, otherwise she won't get one-on-one time to bond with Auntie Jonquil."

Feeling a little railroaded, but not particularly unhappy about it, Rosemary nodded. "Well, then. I guess that would be fine. I'll check with Jonquil to see if she's free." Jonquil actually dated now and then, unlike herself and Delphi, so it was possible she had plans.

"Good." Harrison backed out of her room. "I'll let you two settle in for the night."

Rosemary wondered if that meant he could tell how tired she was. It wasn't worth thinking about, so she said goodnight and shut the door, then grabbed some PJs and went into the bathroom to change.

The paperwork would wait until tomorrow.

CHAPTER 12

Rosemary got Cleo off to Hannah's before dinnertime on Friday and was grateful she wouldn't have to share the bed again that night. Cleo was not a calm sleeper.

She returned to the kitchen at home and finished putting the enchiladas together, then slid them into the oven. Delphi was on call at the resort that evening, so she wouldn't be there to discuss the snake, but the rest of them would arrive with healthy appetites. Rosemary wished she could have gotten out of making this a dinner meeting. It was always harder to eat light when the whole group was together. She pushed the thought away, not wanting to think about what the meal would do to the scales the next day.

Soon everyone started to trickle in.

They all talked and laughed, the married couples cuddled, and Harrison showing up with a cake he'd bought at a local bakery. It was a little disconcerting having him there, part of the group all of the time when she was trying to figure out how she felt about him. The thought of going out with him on a date was exciting and unnerving. What if they fought the whole time? They didn't exactly have a great track record for having calm and rational conversations. She reconsidered, realizing that had changed, mostly, in the past few weeks.

When everyone arrived, Rosemary called them to get some dinner and they all scattered across the great room, their plates overflowing.

She picked at her food, eating a bite now and then, not intending to eat half of it, but trying to fit in. She waited for most of the food to be gone before she turned to Joel. "So did you see anything interesting on the tapes?"

"Yeah." His face looked grim. "Someone was here yesterday. He sneaked in and placed the snake in Cleo's room."

Rosemary felt her stomach clench. "Why? Why would someone do that? She's just a little kid."

"I couldn't get a shot of his face. He covered it with a ski mask, and I think there may have been padding under his clothes as well. I don't know. But he went into several rooms first, so he was looking for hers."

Rosemary thought she was going to be sick. She set her plate aside. "Someone wants to hurt my baby? Or at least to scare us?"

"I can't believe they got past the alarm codes. Did someone forget to lock up?" Jonquil asked.

Rosemary thought back, then swore under her breath. "I don't think I set it. I ran out to pick up a couple of things at the store. Now that everything has been calming down, I didn't think I needed to worry about it for quick trips. Obviously I'm an idiot."

"But that doesn't answer why," Harrison said. "Was it just a scare tactic for one of you?" He looked at Rosemary, "Especially you, considering she's yours."

"No one knows that except you guys," she protested. "And I don't know why they would want to get at me, either."

"Maybe someone you fired?" he asked.

"Like Rulon, you mean?" When had she known it would come back to being her fault?

He shrugged. "Or one of the other half-dozen people you've fired since September."

She hated when he got after her for being too picky with employees. He had no idea what incompetence she had to deal with sometimes. "I didn't fire them all."

"No, some of them you chased off with your sweet personality," he said.

She glared at him. "I didn't chase off anyone who was pulling their weight. I can tolerate an awful lot of bad behavior, but that doesn't mean I'll put up with everything."

"Right, because you're so tolerant and understanding," Joel said, but he was grinning. It was amazing how much more often he smiled since he and Sage got together.

They were ganging up on her, though it never bothered her as bad when Joel teased her as when Harrison did it. "Bagging on my temper isn't getting us anywhere and I'm not that bad anyway. Often. We need to figure out why someone tried to hurt my little girl. She's way more important than your entertainment."

They started compiling a list of anyone who might want to get back at her, or the other sisters still living in the house.

"You need to eat more," Harrison said when the others started clearing away their plates.

"I'm not hungry anymore. The discussion stole my appetite." It wasn't entirely untrue.

"Harrison's right," Jonquil said. "You work too hard to eat so little, and chasing Cleo around is more exhausting than you expected. I know it is."

"And you've lost too much weight since you moved here," Cami added. "You were pretty thin before, but now you're like a wraith."

"I am not. It's only a few pounds, and I don't have much appetite," Rosemary protested. What was this, bag on Rosemary day? Did they want her to get fat again?

"Eat some more, then. Make me feel better," Cami said, staring at her.

Rosemary scowled, but finished up the veggies and a couple bites of the enchiladas. "Happy now?"

"I will be after a few more bites."

"Leave off. I'll pay closer attention to what I eat, okay?"

"I don't think paying attention is the problem," Delphi said under her breath.

Rosemary didn't dignify the comment with a response, feeling defensive. "I cooked; you all get to clean up. I expect the kitchen to sparkle when I get up in the morning." She stormed up the stairs feeling like that teenage girl again who couldn't do anything right.

Rosemary rubbed her sweaty hands on her dress pants and checked her watch again. The caseworker from Child Protection Services had said she'd be here ten minutes ago. She crossed from the great room into the kitchen area. Cleo was eating her after-school granola bar, kicking the legs of the bar stool where she sat.

"So what's going to happen when the lady gets here?" Cleo asked.

Rosemary wasn't entirely sure, and hoped the woman had been honest when she said it wasn't a big deal. "She'll take a look around the house to make sure it's safe for you, ask about our routine, and talk to you for a little bit. It's not a big deal." But it felt like a very big deal.

"Then why are you so nervous? You keep checking your watch. And you keep walking between here and the living room."

"Right. Well, maybe I'm a little nervous. Everyone says it's not a big deal though." She made herself stop pacing.

The doorbell rang and Rosemary hurried over to it.

A middle-aged woman with a very good dye job and penciled brows stood on the other side. "Hello, I'm Lena Carpenter. I'm with CPS."

"Of course, I'm Rosemary. Please come in."

Lena looked around the open spaces as she entered. "Nice house. I remember when it was being built."

"Yes, we're lucky my father was so forward thinking." If he hadn't been, they would surely have killed each other before now. "We have an exercise room and a sitting room downstairs along with a couple more bedrooms. Each of the bedrooms has a private bath."

Lena's gaze caught in a corner of the room. "You have cameras?"

"Yes, it's part of the security system. They cover the yard as well. My sister Sage's husband installed them when we moved into the house as extra security. You can never be too careful." She really hoped Lena didn't ask why they needed the extra security—talking about Sage's stalker, or any of the other things that had happened since their arrival—wouldn't impress Lena. Though every time they'd called the sheriff's office was on record somewhere, so she supposed it wouldn't be hard to find out.

"No, careful is good."

Rosemary showed her the garage and other public spaces and Cleo took Lena into her room and showed her the private bathroom. They stayed in her room and talked for a while. Rosemary stayed in the kitchen as directed and pulled out vegetables for dinner that night, cutting them nervously, wishing she knew what they were discussing. What if the caseworker didn't like her, didn't think she was a fit parent? She couldn't stand to lose Cleo again—especially not to one of the uncles. She told herself she was being ridiculous, of course they would let her keep Cleo, but it was hard to believe sometimes.

They came back down the stairs, Cleo talking about how much fun she had with Jonquil.

"Sounds like you have a helpful family," Lena said. "I'll need you and your sisters—the ones who live here—to come in for fingerprinting for background checks. If everything clears, I don't anticipate there being any problem with you getting permanent custody. You might want to consider officially adopting Cleo, though."

Cleo's face scrunched up. "But I told you, she's my birth mom. Why would she need to adopt me?"

Lena turned to her. "Because when your adoptive parents signed the paperwork, that made them your legal parents, and Rosemary didn't have any more rights to you. If you want to make it all official again, then she should adopt you so the courts see her as your mom, all nice and legal."

Cleo looked worried about this. "I don't know if I want to be adopted again. Would I have to change my name?"

Rosemary's throat grew tight. "That's okay, bug. We can talk about it later, if you decide you want to. Until then, we'll just worry about permanent guardianship so you can stay with me."

Cleo nodded, but she looked troubled.

"Where do we get the fingerprinting done?" Rosemary asked.

"The sheriff's office can handle it. Let me leave these forms for you. You and your sisters will have to have them notarized and there are directions for getting me the fingerprints. Since you're from out of state, the reports can take a few months to come back, but the initial background checks look good for now."

"Thank you." Rosemary felt one of the knots inside her release.

Lena gave them a few more directions and then left.

"Are they going to take me away?" Cleo asked when Rosemary had closed the door behind the caseworker.

Rosemary forced a smile. "No way, bug. You're here to stay. How about pulling out your homework?"

Cleo sighed heavily. "Do I hafta? Can't I help you cook instead?"

Pleased, Rosemary relented. "Fine. I'll help you with the homework later. Can you grab the chicken out of the fridge?" She pretended that she wasn't worried, but deep inside she couldn't shake the feeling that they would find her lacking.

"Good. Just like that." Rosemary encouraged one of her new hires as they rolled croissants for the next morning's breakfast. "You're a natural."

"It's not hard like I expected," Julie said, grinning.

"Nope. Just another two hundred to go and we're golden."

She felt more than heard Harrison enter the room. "What's going on, Harrison?"

"Did you lose track of time? Cleo's getting out of school in a few minutes," he said from behind her.

She glanced up at the clock and frowned. "What happened to the past two hours?"

"Work would be my guess. You get distracted sometimes."

She glanced over her shoulder at him and saw the smile teasing the edges of his mouth. "True enough." She pulled off her gloves. "I gotta head out, but you're really doing great. Just keep going."

"Thanks!" Julie beamed and bent back to work again.

Harrison moved out of the way so she could get to her office. She collected her purse and coat and they headed toward the front doors.

"Just out for a stroll?" she asked.

"Something like that. How is Julie working out?"

"So much better than Rulon. She's a peach."

"She seemed to like working with you," he said.

"Who wouldn't?" She snuck a peek at him in time to see him shake his head slightly.

"I do, so I guess anyone would," he answered. "I guess I mostly see when things aren't going well with your employees, but most of them seem happy enough."

"Glad to hear it." They bundled out into the back parking lot and she stopped and stared at her car. Then swore vociferously as she rushed over to it. All of the windows had been smashed out—even the windshield was mostly missing. "How? Who? When?"

Harrison already had his phone in his hands. "I don't know, but I'm going to find out." When he started talking to the person on the other end of the line, it was clear he had called Joel. He pulled keys from his pocket and handed them to Rosemary. "You better go. Take my car. I'll catch up with you later to get it back."

She wanted to protest, but school would be out any second. And Joel could catch up to her at home. "Thanks." She crossed a few cars over to Harrison's and slid inside—then pounded on the steering wheel a couple of times with her fist. Rulon was behind this, and she was going to prove it.

When Harrison came into her house a couple of hours later with Delphi he looked terrific—all tousled and a little tired. He shook his head and answered before she could ask. "There are no cameras in that part of the lot and the cops aren't hopeful about being able to prove who did it."

Rosemary gritted her teeth and passed back his keys. "Perfect. Now I have to get the windows all replaced. What's that going to run me?"

"We had it towed to the shop for repair. They'll work it out with your insurance company. You should just have your deductible." He leaned against the counter, watching her chop veggies for dinner. "Are you going to have extra of that?"

She wanted to growl, but smiled instead. "Since you handled all of the hassle with my car, it's the least I can do, isn't it?"

"I think so." He smiled, which would have turned her knees to gelatin—if they hadn't already headed that way when he walked in the door.

"Think you can get the runt from her room to help you set the table? She's probably ready for a break from ignoring her homework."

"Yeah, I can do that." He sauntered off, leaving Rosemary torn between wanting to smile and wanting to smack herself for even thinking about him like that.

"Hear anything about my car?" Rosemary asked Joel the next afternoon.

Joel sat at his desk scowling at the computer. He shifted away from it to look at her, relief sliding onto his face, as if he was glad to have an excuse to take a break. "They're looking for Rulon. His mom said he's visiting some friends for a few days, but either she doesn't

96

know where he is or she isn't telling. When they track him down, they'll bring him in for questioning."

Frustration poured through her. "Why can't this just be easier? Why can't something go right?" She balled her hand into a fist.

"I know," he soothed. "We'll find the answers. Don't worry, they'll bring him in." He nudged the chair near his with his foot. "Sit down."

She shook her head and rubbed her lower back. "I need to get back to work. I just wanted to take a break and see what you know. I'm sure it's Rulon."

He steepled his fingers. "You're probably right. Let me handle it. You've got your hands full."

Rosemary nodded, knowing he was right. "Let me know when you hear something."

"I will."

She headed back to the restaurant. Her date with Harrison was that night. She was going to put this out of her head and enjoy a night out.

CHAPTER 13

Three days passed before Rosemary and Harrison were able to coordinate their schedules with Jonquil's so they could have their date. Harrison's schedule was the standard eight-to-five, but Rosemary's was all over the map, and a wedding that weekend had Jonquil working until her eyes started to bleed—or so she'd said.

When the night finally arrived, Rosemary stood in front of the long cheval mirror in her room and studied her clingy black tea-length dress. She wondered if she should have worn something else. Did it show that pudge of fat on her hip? Ever since Harrison had come back into her life, the weight consciousness had increased ten-fold. Now he had become such a big part of her life, she wondered all the time whether he still thought she was fat—even though she had slimmed down after the cruise where they first met.

"You look beautiful," Cleo said as she sat on the bed, watching Rosemary pick through her jewelry.

"Thank you." She pulled out the diamond studs her father had given her when she turned eighteen. She didn't own much jewelry and hardly wore it, but tonight, her first date with Harrison, felt like the kind of night where she should wear something that glittered. It would give her a little boost of confidence that she needed when her stomach quaked and her nerves stretched.

"You don't usually wear so much makeup." Cleo tipped her head and studied Rosemary. "Are you wearing a lot so he'll kiss you?"

Rosemary felt her stomach clench a little more. "I just want to look nice tonight, that's all. I don't know if he'll kiss me or not. Or if I'll want him to." She winked at Cleo. She and Harrison had barely held a non-hostile conversation until a few weeks before the bombing. She was confused by the change in their relationship, led mostly by Harrison letting her irritability flow over him with barely a ripple. She hadn't figured out why things had changed. Not that she was complaining. "Do you want to try my lipstick?" It was the kind of thing Cecelia would have done—had done when Rosemary was still a teen.

Cleo's face crumpled a little. "Yeah. Mom let me test her lipstick sometimes too." A tear slid down her cheek and she wiped it away. "I miss her."

Rosemary sat beside her on the edge of the bed and slid her arm around Cleo's shoulder. "I know you do. Me too. She was the best mom, ever, wasn't she?"

"Yeah." Cleo rested her cheek against Rosemary. "And Dad, he was really great too. They loved me a lot. Didn't they?"

"They sure did, bug." Tears rose to Rosemary's eyes and she wanted to retort with one of her off-the-cuff comments that focused the attention away from her pain, but this wasn't the time. Cleo needed her. "You have no idea how excited they were when they got to bring you home. They actually brought us both home from the hospital together and took care of us until I went back to school. Your mom just wanted to cuddle and hold you every minute of every day. She'd wanted a baby for so long."

"But they couldn't, so they adopted me."

"That's right. She used to say you were her best thing." Rosemary used her thumb to brush away a wet trail from her cheek. "I had to agree."

The doorbell rang and Jonquil called up the stairs, "Rosemary, it's Mr. Wonderful."

Rosemary laughed. "Tell him to take a seat. I'll be a few minutes."

"No, you should go down. Don't make him wait," Cleo said, tugging on Rosemary's hand.

"Hey, I'm talking with my girl about the mother we both love. Harrison can wait." She straightened and looked at herself in the mirror again. Her eyes were red and her nose practically glowed. "Perfect. If I put on this lipstick then my whole face will be red."

Cleo giggled even as she wiped fresh tears.

Rosemary leaned over and kissed Cleo's forehead. "Come here and I'll help you with the makeup."

She powdered her face and put on the lipstick. She glided some on Cleo's skinny little lips and walked her through blotting, then packed her clutch. Rosemary frowned at her reflection in the mirror, thinking she looked terrible, but it wouldn't exactly be the worst Harrison had ever seen her. Cleo ran ahead down the stairs and wrapped her arms around Harrison so enthusiastically that he took a step back to keep from falling over.

Rosemary chuckled when she saw it, glad Cleo had bonded so readily to people here, but a little unsure how she felt that one of those people was Harrison.

"That's some welcome you've got there," she said to him from the top of the stairs.

He chuckled. "Best ever." He looked up at her and the smile widened. "You look terrific." A furrow grew between his brows as she came closer. "Is something wrong?"

"No, Cleo and I were just reminiscing. We're fine. You ready?" She didn't think she'd be able to eat anything tonight, not with her nerves firing at his nearness, but she'd do her best.

His eyes held understanding. He picked up Cleo and gave her a smacking kiss on the cheek. "You have fun with Jonquil and make sure she leaves Rosemary's kitchen in the same order as when she starts."

"It's not her kitchen. It belongs to all of us." Jonquil crossed her arms over her chest and glowered a little, though the little twitch at the corners of her mouth belied her angry tone.

Rosemary returned the attitude. "Leave it a mess and you'll find out whose kitchen it really is."

Cleo giggled. She could always see through Rosemary's shields. "She'll put you in time out!"

"That would be a real shame. Jonquil might shrivel up and die if she couldn't go in to work or slap on a pair of skis," Rosemary agreed.

Harrison took her hand. "Are you ready to go?"

"Sure." She put her free hand on Cleo's shoulder, but talked to Jonquil. "Be nice to my girl here so I'll let you hang out again, but don't let her get away with anything."

"Awwww!" Cleo protested.

"Love your guts."

Rosemary allowed Harrison to help her with her coat and accompanied him out to his car.

"Is everything really all right?" he asked as soon as the door closed behind them.

"Yeah, just remembering Cecelia. It hits at odd moments, doesn't it?"

He nodded, but didn't answer.

"Have you ever lost someone you loved, besides Dad?" It seemed odd sometimes, to remember how important her father had been to Harrison, but the way Sage described it, he had been the son her father never had. That made her wonder about his father, but Sage hadn't been willing to divulge and Rosemary hadn't wanted to push, knowing it could end up with her having to talk about Wanda. Now things were different.

He helped her into the passenger seat, then came around to his side without answering. When his seatbelt was on, he turned the key. "No. I haven't lost anyone else I really loved. George was the first, and he wasn't my parent. Not really. More like a favorite uncle. I've never been close to grandparents or anything."

Rosemary hesitated. "What happened to your dad? Your real dad, I mean. Sage said your mom was married to him, but things went south and he booked before she met our dad."

His lips thinned. "This is a heavy conversation for the beginning of a first date. How about if we save it for dessert?"

Rosemary hesitated, wanting to push the subject, but not wanting to start things on the wrong foot. "Okay. So how, 'bout them Nuggets?"

He shook his head, relaxing at the change of topic. "They're having a terrible season. You'd think with Curtis Werner on the team they'd be doing better, but they don't use him enough."

She settled back in the seat and they talked basketball. Easily taxing the extent of her sports knowledge in only five minutes. "Where are we going?" She'd noticed he wore a suit—with the jacket—which he hardly ever did at work.

"A special place. Just wait." They drove down the mountainside to a little lodge next to a lake. "I hear they have a nice little restaurant and that we won't be interrupted by business associates a dozen times."

She liked that idea. She really needed to get away from the hotel more often.

"Who told you about this place?" She asked once they were seated and their drinks had been poured. The place was intimate, with cushy booths and dimmed lights. The logs that formed the wall were exposed on the inside and there was a huge fireplace in the middle of the room, providing light, heat and ambiance.

"One of the concierges. There's no point having a resource like that at my fingertips if I don't use it." His eyes caught on hers and the teasing expression in them made her heart race.

"Absolutely." She opted for sparkling water—fewer calories—and tipped her glass against his. "Did you always want to work in human resources?"

He laughed. "No, not at all. It just happens that I ended up being good at it. George pulled me into it."

She smiled, thinking about her dad. "He had a talent for seeing things like that, didn't he? And what does your Mother Earth, nature-loving mom think about you going all three-piece-suit on her?"

He chuckled. "She hates it. At least Sage is working with natural healing techniques, but I'm the rebel—going against the grain, giving into social pressures." He smiled, but there was an edge of wistfulness in it.

She understood that perfectly. "It sucks to let a parent we love down, even when we know we're making the best decision for us. Dad always wanted me to head up a kitchen, like I do now. I didn't want to—I liked just spending my days cooking without all the hassles of ordering and being in charge of everything. So he came up with this crazy scheme to make all of his daughters live up to their potentials." She shook her head.

"You're a good manager, Rosemary."

She shot him a look of disbelief. "Yeah, you say that now because you're hoping for a goodnight kiss, but I remember the way we've argued about the way I handle my employees." Those criticisms had hurt more than they should have.

He slid his hand over hers. "Hey, I mean it. You can be a little rough on incompetence, granted, but you handle the rest really well. You shuffle your schedule, handle problems as they arise, and handle complaints from guests with surprising diplomacy considering how unreasonable some of them are."

"That's an understatement." She knew her shortcomings, even if she didn't like having them pointed out.

"But you handle it most of the time. You offer praise where it's earned and prod them to do better, to stretch for your praise. Most of them meet the challenge. I like that."

She felt warmed by the acknowledgment. "So I'm doing fine, and Rulon was nothing to worry about?"

He snorted a little. "I'm still going to call you on your crap when you need me to, but most of the time I think you do good, great even."

Rosemary couldn't help but feel good about that. "I thought you thoroughly disapproved of me until not so long ago," she admitted.

"I didn't." He reached across the table and took her hand. "I just didn't know how to talk to you. We kept crossing swords every time we talked. I don't know why and I couldn't seem to change things."

As long as they were being painfully honest. "I know why, and it goes back to my tremendously appealing character traits. I'm not the easiest person to get along with." When he didn't argue, she ignored the niggle of pain and pushed him a little. "So why did you ask me out? Why are you here when you know how, um, poorly I deal with disappointment?"

He watched her for a long moment. "If I told you the truth, you wouldn't believe me."

"Try me."

Harrison didn't speak for a moment, though it was obvious he was considering it. "I had a feeling about us the first time we met. It gets stronger all the time."

She remembered her own instant attraction, but didn't think that was what he meant. "You mean the kind of feeling Sage gets sometimes?"

His lips quirked. "You're good at reading between the lines."

She considered that, unsettled by the statement. "That's kind of freaky. But you *are* Sage's brother."

"I noticed that."

She pulled a face at him. "You ever have any of those woo-woo things happen before? I mean, you mentioned to Cleo that you did, once, but I have to wonder. I mean, really. I don't believe in that crap—except for Sage because she's freaky accurate. So you really felt that?"

"Yeah, just that once, or rather twice, I guess. Like I said." He sipped at his wine, allowing the moment to stretch. "It was when I met you."

She froze. Was that just a smooth line, or was he for real? "You didn't act like you even remembered me when we met again last summer, and you definitely didn't treat me any different than you did the others. Until I popped off at you, which didn't take long." She touched her neck in a defensive gesture. "Everything from the cruise just flooded back to me and I had this immature knee-jerk reaction."

"I know. And I didn't see you for the first time when we met last summer. I walked into the dining room earlier that day, saw you again and knew that you were the same person I'd met on the cruise."

She stared at him. "You recognized me that fast?" She'd thought about asking Sage about him before that, remembered how attracted she'd been to him the moment their eyes met on the ship, but it had been water under the bridge—or the prow—so she'd let it go. If she hadn't seen him being so careful of his sister when she'd gotten hurt, hadn't reacted so badly, things could have been much different.

"I felt it on the ship. I felt it again when I saw you this summer, poring over the list of kitchen supplies."

Now she really did doubt whether she could eat anything. Her heart pounded like crazy and she felt more than a little unsettled. This was so much pressure—he thought there was something real going on here, more serious than she'd ever considered. She pushed back from the table a little.

Regret pulled at his mouth. "I'm sorry, I freaked you out. I didn't mean to."

She took a gulp of water, then nearly coughed up a lung when some of the carbonation went down the wrong windpipe.

"Are you okay?" He was at her side in a flash.

She sucked in air. "Yeah, I'll be fine. Really." Not really. What was she doing on a date with him? He was a totally picket fence sort of guy, and she wasn't getting serious about anyone, no matter how much she liked him. She'd been hurt before, seen her mother date and split with dozens of guys, and knew what a hound dog her father was with women. She kept coughing, wishing she'd gotten regular water instead of the carbonated kind.

A moment later it seemed most of the restaurant staff was clustered around the table and the other patrons were watching, their eyes studying her as if they hoped they were seeing a heart attack in progress.

She sucked in a breath. "I'm fine, really. I just swallowed the water down the wrong pipe. I'm okay." She waved them away with a few more reassurances and pointed to Harrison's chair when he stayed standing beside her. "Sit, please. This has been enough of a spectacle already." She was grateful they hadn't eaten at the resort restaurant, imagining the fuss everyone would have made.

And she was still wigging about his comment.

"So, how about those Nuggets," he asked as he took his seat, though they'd already canvassed that thoroughly.

"Don't worry about it, really Harrison. I'm fine." She considered. "But I don't think I want to talk about your one or two, I guess, psychic experiences in any more depth. Not right now."

He nodded, but disappointment hung around his mouth. "Then how about if we talk about your time in Italy? You said it's your favorite place in the world. Where did you train?"

That was a much more comfortable topic, so she settled back, forcing the other thought to the back of her mind. Italy was much safer. Her salad and his pasta arrived a few minutes later and she sprinkled vinegar on the mix of leaves and veggies.

"Taste this," he said, holding up a bite of cannelloni for her.

It looked decadent, like the cannelloni she'd eaten in Italy. "I don't think that's a good idea. It looks terrific and I might be tempted into stealing your whole plate."

"Then I'll order another one," he said, shrugging it off.

She took the offered bite and nearly swooned it was so good. She chewed it slowly, enjoying every nuance and trying to figure out what was in it that her recipe lacked. "That's seriously amazing."

"Good, have another bite then," he offered it to her.

"I can't. You'll be hungry if I eat half of your food."

"Then I'll have room for dessert. I hear they make excellent tiramisu."

That was an inducement she couldn't turn down. She'd spend more time on the elliptical in the morning.

CHAPTER 14

Harrison loved watching Rosemary eat, and persuading her to do it when she was so reluctant to risk the calories was pure pleasure. She enjoyed food more than any woman he'd ever met—and yet she was rail thin. Much thinner than she'd been the previous summer. At first he'd thought it was his imagination—she was beautiful at any size, and when they met on the cruise eight years earlier, she hadn't been thin, but he'd been instantly smitten anyway.

From time to time over the years since, he'd wondered if his strong impression that she was the woman for him had been his imagination. And if it wasn't, then would he get another chance, because he hadn't known who she was or how to find her. He'd dated other women, moved on and made a life, but he hadn't been able to completely forget her. Finding her there in the hotel kitchen that day had nearly sent his heart into hyper drive. Over the past six months, he'd grown more certain that the impression had been right, though he hadn't known how he was going to break through their disagreements to see if they could have the relationship he hoped for.

As he stood from the table after dinner, though, he worried that he had totally freaked her out. If he lost her now because he had been more honest than she was ready for, he would regret it for the rest of his life. "If the weather wasn't so cold, I'd suggest a walk outside in the moonlight."

"I'd take you up on it, if I weren't worried about becoming a Popsicle." She accepted his hand, swinging it a little between them. "We've been here over two hours."

"Yes. I wish it could have lasted longer." They picked up their coats and he took advantage of the chance to help her on with hers to brush his fingers over the sensitive skin along her neck. She shifted her shoulder, indicating that it might have affected her a little. It made him happy. She really wasn't immune to him. Sage had suggested to him once that his and Rosemary's arguments had been caused by sexual tension and pure bull-headedness. She'd insinuated that he was equally as bull-headed. He could admit to himself that maybe she was right.

He opened the door, leading her back toward the car. "So how are you finding motherhood now that you've had ten days or so to adjust?"

"Yeah, because it's like getting a goldfish—the adjustment period is no big deal, and you hardly have to change your life for them."

"So, not used to it yet?" he teased.

"Not even close. But it's nice. I love having her here, and yet it's really hard for her, too. At least we can talk about her mom and dad, share memories. Can you imagine if she'd ended up with strangers?" She shook her head. There was a moment of pensive silence before she added, "And then I worry I'm going to turn into my mother."

Snow crunched under their feet on the blacktop and a night owl hooted. "Tell me about her. You never talk about what it was like growing up," he prodded. He was unendingly curious about her as a kid and how her past made her into what she was now.

She shook her head, frowning. "You don't want to hear. Trust me."

He turned to face her in front of the passenger-side door. "That bad?"

"I don't talk about this with anyone. Ever."

He considered her words, but he didn't think she was telling him no, just that she was nervous about it. "You can trust me."

She nodded toward the car door and he opened it, letting her inside. He figured she wasn't going to share, but once he had started the car, she began slowly. "When I was twelve I begged Dad to take me to live with him. I was so mad that Lana and Cami got to live with him, but he wouldn't take me. Being at my mom's was... pretty horrible sometimes. She kept me around because she wanted the child support checks, but that was about it."

"Come on, that can't be it. She must love you." He couldn't imagine it being any other way, even if they didn't see eye to eye.

Her fingers twisted together on her lap. "No, I really don't think she does. Or that she ever did." She looked out the window, her face turned away from him. "She saw me as a meal ticket, and someone to blame things on. I started to cook in self-preservation; you know—cook or starve. And her boyfriends were useless most of the time. And that was when they were okay."

It hurt to hear her talk about her childhood like that, made him swallow hard to try to dislodge the lump in his throat. "Did George know how bad it was?"

"I thought he'd figure it out when I begged him to let me live with him or go to a boarding school or something." Her voice was quiet, matter of fact. "I think he didn't want to see it, so he didn't. I don't think he really understood what was going on, though, or he'd have shipped me somewhere to get me away. As long as the checks kept coming, Wanda wouldn't have cared."

"And now we've wandered into the same kind of painful territory that had me putting you off earlier." He took her hand, wanting to reassure and encourage her while his heart broke a little for the girl she used to be. "I'm honored that you told me so much."

She was quiet for a moment. "Whatever this is between us, you obviously have strong feelings. I thought you deserved to know."

"Are you trying to scare me away?"

A smile flit across her face and then disappeared again. "Maybe. I'm not sure how I feel yet."

He ran his thumb across her knuckles. "I'm sorry if I put you on the spot. I want to know when you want to tell me, but I won't pry. Well," he reconsidered, "I'll try not to pry. I can't promise I'll succeed."

Her fingers brushed his cheek. "Maybe another time. I know I missed my dessert conversation window, but if you want to bring that other stuff up, I'm all ears."

He sighed a little. He hated talking about this, but he couldn't expect her to open up if he wasn't willing to reciprocate and their stories weren't that far apart. "We were talking about my dad," he said. "I don't know anything about him, really. Some, here and there. Mom didn't like to talk about him so I didn't ask much. He left when I was still an infant, decided he didn't want the responsibility. She got the divorce, though I'm not sure if he initiated it, or if she did. We never heard from him again, as far as I know. I don't think he ever sent child support, either. She dated on and off, but never fell in love enough to marry again. She always said she was gun shy, but I think she was worried about protecting us, me and Sage. And protecting the secret about George being Sage's father. Sometimes I wonder why she bothered to hide it, if it wouldn't have been much easier just to tell the truth, but she respected his wishes. Last summer after everything came out someone accused her of keeping the secret because she was afraid the child support would go down, but she's barely spent any of it. Money's not really that important to her and the organic farm does well enough."

Rosemary nodded. "Did your mother know, do you think, who Dad was, or that he was married when they dated?"

"No. Considering her rather hippie beliefs, Mom's never gone for married men. I don't think he told her, and she wasn't the type to ask questions people didn't want to answer—unless it was me or Sage. When we were growing up she would pry until she peeled back every secret, she prods for information now, but not like she used to. She claims we're adults and deserve some privacy, but I know it's killing her to let us live our lives without interference. She's a good mom that way." He shrugged a little, though the topic made him uncomfortable. "How about your mom?"

"I'll never know if she knew who Dad was, or that he was married at first, but I doubt that would have bothered her. The sanctity of marriage has never been a concern for her." Rosemary's voice was bitter. "I talked to her the day you came to DC, the first day. She referred to my birth as *cashing in.* Dad enabled her to live very well for the past thirty or so years. She wasn't happy when he died and left nothing to her."

Harrison let that thought linger for a moment, sickened by her mother's cruelty. "What happened with you and Cleo's dad?" he asked, giving in to the burning question that had been nagging at him since he learned about Cleo.

Her face hardened a little. "He split when he found out I was pregnant. He didn't want a kid, didn't want to be tied down."

Harrison couldn't imagine not wanting Rosemary's child. "Would you have married him and tried to make it work if he'd stuck around?"

She shook her head. "I don't think so. I wanted to love him, but I didn't. Wanted him to give me something I couldn't get at home, but he wasn't ready, and I don't think I was either." She picked at her skirt. "It was a mistake from the beginning. I don't think I'm really built for relationships."

Harrison wondered how much of that was true, and how much a way to protect herself from being hurt. "Bad place to find yourself in at that age."

"Yep, but it worked out great for everyone in the end. The Markhams were like parents to me. They taught me about gardening and baking and let me come play in their fairy cottage anytime I wanted." She smiled. "I think we need a fairy cottage this summer for Cleo—she loved the one at home as much as I did at her age."

That was such a magical thought he couldn't imagine the Rosemary he knew now giving in to her fancies. "What's a fairy cottage?"

"Just a spot in the back yard where the vines created a sheltered area. They had the most amazing blooms. It smelled like heaven in there."

"Maybe you'll need to talk to Vince about setting something up," Harrison suggested, though he was thinking about his own property more than the girls' home. He could just see Cleo tucked away, having a fairy tea party with friends while he and Rosemary made out on the couch inside. Or making out with her in the fairy house while the girls played inside. He wasn't picky.

He was reluctant for the evening to end, but Rosemary had to work early, so he took her back home after dinner. He walked her to the front door, wondering if he should take that kiss he so desperately wanted. Maybe he shouldn't. He didn't want to put her off a second date, but he'd been trying not to stare at her mouth all evening—for six months of meetings, parties and encounters—and wanted to taste it. As they stopped on the front porch, she took the question out of his hands. She leaned in, slid her hands around his waist inside his coat and pressed her lips to his.

Harrison had already feared she was his everything, that there would never be anyone else who really mattered the way she did. But the moment their lips connected, he could see visions of their wedding, of her holding a dark-haired baby and a toddler running through the house, nearly bumping into Rosemary and her precious cargo, then falling on his diapered rump. He saw them exchanging rings at the altar and growing old together.

It all struck him in a blinding instant, so much stronger than he'd ever expected that it made him dizzy. He yanked back in surprise and stared at her for three labored breaths.

"What?" Confusion entered her eyes and she started to move away.

"Nothing." He pulled her close and covered her mouth with his, wanting that future more than anything he could imagine, knowing it could happen for them, but only if he made it.

She wrapped her arms around him again.

He tipped her head to the side and trailed kisses down her neck, inhaling the perfume she'd dabbed at her pulse points. "Another date, soon. Tomorrow."

She laughed and he felt the movement along her neck as he pressed his lips to her skin.

"Skiing Saturday with Jonquil and Cleo. You up for it?" she asked.

Anything. Everything. "Yes." It was only a day and a half, he could wait that long.

"Great. See you at eight. Earlier if you want to have breakfast with us first." With reluctance, she pulled back from his arms and slid inside.

Harrison watched her go, saw through the window when she greeted Jonquil then glanced up the stairs to where Cleo would be sleeping. He turned and walked to his car. He really had to talk to Sage about his weird vision. But not tonight. There were a few things to sort out in his head first.

After spending the night and morning mulling over the images and impressions he had experienced the previous night, Harrison decided he should have lunch with his sister. Sage had been dealing with her precognition for decades and he hoped she'd have some insight for him.

When he arrived at the spa at lunchtime she was in a treatment, but her assistant manager said she'd be out soon. He grabbed a magazine on natural healing and flipped through it, not really interested in the text, but needing something to do so he didn't fidget too much.

Sage came out of her treatment room a few minutes later and walked over, stopping in front of him. "What's going on? You need a deep muscle massage? Someone probably has an opening."

He shook his head. "I wondered if you'd like to grab some lunch. Or are you planning on eating with Joel?"

She looked at him for a moment and nodded. "I'll let Joel know we're doing a brother-sister lunch today. He'll be okay with it."

"I don't want to be in the way," Harrison protested, knowing it wouldn't stop her and glad for it.

"Don't worry about it. He understands sometimes you're going to need me around too." She flashed him a smile. "Besides, I want to hear about your date." She waggled her eyebrows at him.

He felt his face heat a little and saw curiosity on her assistant's face. "That's kind of what I wanted to discuss. In a manner of speaking."

"Good. Give me a few minutes to clean up my treatment room and call Joel." She turned on her heel and headed off again.

She was fast and soon they were walking into the hotel's snack bar. He preferred the main restaurant, but he didn't want to take the chance that Rosemary would come out to say hello.

When he picked a booth on the far end, Sage lifted her brows. "Privacy?"

"Yes." He felt like an idiot. He'd never discussed his dates with Sage before—but none of them had been The One, or her sister. And it was really the visions he needed to talk about and no guy friend would understand what that was like—even if he were close to anyone out here.

They ordered and she opened her bottled water while he sipped on his soda.

"So what's going on?" she asked. "You said this was about your date—was there a problem? Because when I asked Rosemary about it, she was smiling."

"It was fun. I think I might have freaked her out a little, so I'm glad she's smiling." He played with the straw in his cup. "I never told you what happened the first time I saw her, way back on that cruise, and again when we met here."

"You didn't have to," Sage said. "I could see that there was an affinity there. I never noticed it with you and anyone else you dated."

Harrison sucked in some air. "The first time I saw her I knew. Somehow I knew she was going to mean something to me. When she was nasty to you I wrote it off as a crazy thought. But she kept popping back into my mind at odd random moments—nine years passed and I couldn't completely forget her. So when I saw her again, I recognized her immediately. I recognized that moment of connection and knew I had to get to know her, to give things a chance to go somewhere. For some small part of me, it's always been her."

Sage's brows lifted. "You think any of this is a revelation for me?"

He laughed nervously, both relieved and embarrassed at once. "No, of course not. What was I thinking?" He brushed the hair out of his eyes and recentered his thoughts. "The thing is, it's never been like that with anyone else—I don't just mean that feeling of connection to her—I know I'll never feel that with anyone else. I mean, feeling anything in that way—that freaky precog thing you do all of the time. I've never done that except with her."

"Now my precog is freaky?" she asked, her lips twisting up a little at the edges.

"What do you mean, *now*? It's always been freaky," he shot back.

She laughed. "Fair enough. So what do you see when you're with her."

He closed his eyes, seeing the flash of images again. "Everything. Always. When I kissed her last night, it was like being slammed with my whole future." He shook his head. "It freaked *me* out, no way was I going to tell her about it.

The waitress brought their food and he smiled and waited until she moved far away enough not to hear them. "I saw her holding our child in her arms, an older little boy toddling around. It threw me for a loop."

Sage folded her arms on the table, leaned forward and studied him. "That's a pretty incredible gift. And what you need, isn't it?" She squirted lemon on her salad. "Rosemary's, hmmm, a little prickly. She can be hard to get to know and she tends to put up walls to keep people out. You've seen your future with her—and don't think I don't envy that. It sucks never being able to use my gift to learn things about myself. Anyway, you know you can have that, and that it'll be good. Not necessarily easy, but worth it."

He nodded, reassured that she didn't think he was crazy, that she supported his feelings when his relationship with Rosemary, at first glance, would seem doomed.

She reached across the table and touched his hand. "The next few weeks are going to be rough, rougher than you think possible. Hold on and don't let it get to you. Things will turn out for the best, one way or another."

He was surprised. "What do you know?"

She shook her head, her brows furrowing. "Nothing concrete, but there's definitely something brewing. Keep her close, her and Cleo—and talk to Cleo about you and Rosemary. It'll make things easier."

He picked up his sandwich. "I can do that. Now, how are things coming with the house plans?" He needed a change of subject.

She picked up her fork and stabbed at some lettuce leaves. "We start digging the pool house the second the weather permits. We're still finalizing details for the actual house."

"But that comes secondary to the pool?" he teased.

"You know it does." She talked about their house plans with a happy smile.

Harrison couldn't help but hope Sage was right. When he spoke to Rosemary he downplayed the way his father's rejection had affected him, the fact that George's lies had hurt him almost as much as they hurt Sage, but there was part of him that wondered if the problem was partly him.

Intellectually, he knew better, but in those years between first meeting Rosemary and his move to Colorado, he'd wondered if he was the reason none of his relationships made it more than a few months. Now he knew it wasn't him—it was because those women hadn't been *her*. He just needed to remind himself of that when things got rough—and Sage was right, it wasn't going to be easy.

CHAPTER 15

The workday was almost over and Rosemary still pored over order forms. She really needed to delegate this to one of her assistants—Tate would be happy to handle it—but she was too big of a control freak and she knew it.

"Are we going soon?" Cleo grumbled from where she sat at the make-shift desk nearby, doing her homework.

"Soon. I promise."

"That's what you said twenty minutes ago," Cleo grumbled. "I have all weekend to do homework, why do I have to do it all right now?"

"Then I guess how long it takes will depend on your definition of *soon*."

"I wish you'd let me go see Harrison. He takes time to talk to me, at least."

At his name, Rosemary's mind automatically detoured to their kiss the night before. He had kind of freaked her out when he insinuated that his one psychic experience had something to do with her. By the time he said goodnight though, she'd pushed it from her mind—or the thought of kissing him, something she'd wanted to do for quite a while, did. She wondered if she'd been hoping the chemistry just wouldn't be there so she'd have an excuse to walk away. But apparently chemistry really wasn't one of their problems.

Thoughts of his revelation wouldn't stay gone. As soon as her head had hit the pillow, it had been uppermost in her head again. She should end things now, right now, before they went anywhere. But then she thought of their kiss and how perfect, how right it felt when he held her, how much she wanted to feel that again, and she couldn't make herself walk away. Maybe in a little while, when they ran out of things to talk about and the novelty of their relationship had worn off. She'd just been thinking about him for too long to look at it sensibly. "Give me five minutes of quiet and I promise we can go."

"Five minutes?" Cleo sounded doubtful, but she stopped complaining.

A moment later the phone on Rosemary's desk rang and Cleo groaned. Rosemary wanted to groan too—she wanted to go home—but she held it in. "Kitchen, this is Rosemary, how can I help you?"

"Rosie, I knew I would find you there. You're such a workaholic." Wanda's voice snapped Rosemary's thoughts away from the numbers that had been running through her head.

"Mom." She sent her voice several degrees cooler than for most people and sat back in her chair.

"How are things in Colorado? I bet they have wonderful skiing there. One of my friends went to Park City last month, is that near you?"

"No, it's in Utah, not near me. What do you want?" When her mother took on that wheedling tone and tried to make small talk, Rosemary knew she wanted something. It used to be that she wanted Rosemary to ask George for more money, an advance or something, but now George was gone and rumor was out about how much Rosemary and the others would be worth, it was her turn, apparently.

"Why are you so mean to me? You know I'm not very healthy. I'm fragile."

She was as healthy as she wanted to be, and always had been. "Your point?"

"I need to go to a specialist to see what's going on with my lungs. They hurt, Rosie, and I need the doctor."

Rosemary felt the desire to give in. She'd always craved her mother's approval, but she'd learned years earlier that it was fleeting, melting away moments after the favor had been granted. She steeled herself to be firm. "Then go. I'm not stopping you."

"He's really expensive, honey. I know you want me to get the treatments I need, don't you?"

Rosemary sighed. She'd seen it coming, but she was past giving in—she wasn't going to bankroll her mother's fancies any more than George had in his last few years. "Yes. And I bet if you go get yourself a job, you could afford your special treatment."

"But I'm too sickly for a job. Who would hire me? You have to help me, Rosie."

"Who indeed." Rosemary said the words quietly so she hoped they wouldn't be understood over the line. "Do you remember when I was in DC and you gave me that line about cashing in on your mistake, Mother? Well, the bank is closed. You'll have to go find another source of income."

This time when she spoke, Wanda's voice was no longer wheedling, but angry. "You owe me, Rosemary. You're going to pay or you'll be sorry."

"Take it up with my lawyer." She hung up without saying goodbye.

"I don't like your mom very much." Cleo bit her lip.

"Me neither."

"That makes three of us," Harrison's voice added from the doorway.

Rosemary's head pulled toward him like it was being controlled by a rubber band. "When did you get there?" She usually sensed him, but she was so focused on the call she hadn't noticed his arrival.

"I heard the phone ring while I was walking up," he admitted.

"Great." So he'd heard the whole thing.

Cleo looked at him hopefully. "Can you take me for a walk and show me housekeeping? You said you would last time but we had to come back first."

"You want to see where they do laundry?" His brows V-ed over his eyes.

120

"She's bored stiff and I'm trying to finish this order," Rosemary explained. "It really has to go in today."

"Ah, in that case, my little friend, let us go seek the secrets of the laundry machines." He held out a hand for her.

"Clean up your books first," Rosemary said as Cleo stood.

"Of course," she grumbled, but complied.

Harrison winked at Rosemary. "Ten minutes, fifteen tops. Will that be enough?"

"Plenty. Thanks." She watched them go, then turned back to her forms. She didn't know if she would be able to concentrate enough to finish the order before he got back, though. Not with Wanda's whining voice in her head. She'd been firm, but it still twisted her up inside. The last thing she needed was for Wanda to start harassing her at work. It was why she had added Wanda's number to her cell phone's blocked call list—no messages. Rosemary wondered if there was a way to block her calls on the main hotel lines.

She pushed the thought away and forced herself to focus on what she needed to do so she could take Cleo home.

CHAPTER 16

The next morning Jonquil got Cleo and Rosemary suited up to go skiing. Rosemary was definitely not looking forward to the ordeal, but Cleo was so excited she couldn't say no. After what happened with the snake, she didn't want to chance her little girl being out of sight when she wasn't in school. When Harrison showed up for breakfast, she decided the advantages of sticking out the ski day might outweigh the pitfalls. If she didn't break anything falling on the slopes.

They started out on the bunny hill while Jonquil and Harrison showed Cleo and Rosemary the basics, but as the day wore on, they grew more adventurous and moved to one of the easy runs that wasn't built for toddlers.

Despite the fact that Harrison became her personal instructor, Rosemary was still relieved when they all took a break for hot chocolate and lunch about one o'clock.

As they sat around the table in the lodge, Cleo looked at the ski resort tags on Jonquil's coat. "How come you have two tags?" she asked.

"One is for Deer Valley, and the other is for Breckenridge."

"But why do you have two. Don't you ski here?" She played with her own Deer Valley tag.

"Most of the time." Jonquil smirked over her cup of coffee. "I just keep the other one on to tweak Gage's ego. He's such a hothead about locals going elsewhere to ski."

"You're so bad." Rosemary nodded.

"It's a gift." Jonquil didn't look the least repentant.

Rosemary considered the way Gage acted toward Jonquil. It wasn't like she had done anything to earn his disdain. That reminded her of the way she had jumped to conclusions about Harrison and she wondered what was behind the attitude in this case.

"Don't look now, but your gift is about to lose its strength." Harrison raised a hand in greeting and Rosemary glanced over to see Gage approaching them.

"How are you all doing? I trust you're enjoying yourselves on the slopes." He greeted them all, then turned to Cleo. "You must be the newest DiCarlo lady. I'm Gage, one of Vince's best friends." He extended his hand for a shake, making her smile. "Have you ever skied before today?"

Cleo brightened. "No, but it's so much fun! I'm going to get Rosemary to bring me lots!"

"Yeah, don't get ahead of yourself there, bug." Rosemary wasn't feeling nearly so in love with the sport. Maybe because she was incredibly bad at it and fell three times for each one of Cleo's falls.

The little girl laughed, covering her mouth. "She's not very good."

"Dad loved to ski," Jonquil said. "Maybe the ability skips a generation now and then."

Gage looked at her, his voice dropping into icy civility. "I trust you're enjoying the powder?"

"Of course. A fresh snowfall is always nice, no matter where I'm at."

His lips thinned, and he turned to Harrison. "And you?"

"I'm having a blast. I'll have to bring Cleo back, since her m . . . I mean, since Rosemary doesn't seem inclined." He glanced surreptitiously at Cleo, who didn't appear to have noticed the blunder—or the one Jonquil made a moment earlier.

Gage could be trusted with the truth, but there were a lot of people around, and Rosemary was *trying* to respect her daughter's wishes to just be her guardian as far as the public was concerned. But it made her feel just like when her father was alive and she wasn't good enough for him to acknowledge in public. She was still a second-class citizen when it came to her closest relatives.

"Well, I hope you have fun this afternoon. I'll see you around." He shot a quick glare at Jonquil, and took off.

She smiled slightly to herself and returned to her meal.

Rosemary didn't feel much like eating, but Harrison kept glancing at her plate and frowning, so she dutifully forked up more of it. She was working it off with all that falling on the slopes, after all. She could handle eating a little more of what she ordered.

The afternoon went well and she fell less often. Harrison didn't seem to mind following behind her to pick up her skis or poles so he could return them to her if she fell, but she felt guilty for forcing him to take it easy.

"You should go on alone. You could do three trips to my two," she told him after he brought over one of her skis for the dozenth time since lunch. "Really, I'll be fine." Jonquil was glued to Cleo's side, and they always made sure to keep her in sight. One of them might as well have real fun today.

He took off his glove and brushed some snow from her hair. "You're cute like that, like a snow angel." Their eyes met and time seemed to slow down. "I think snow angels need to be kissed."

When he leaned forward, she shied away, breaking their eye contact. "Not with my daughter watching." Her lips tingled though, already anticipating the touch of his.

He glanced down the slope. "She's not watching. They're out of sight. Probably waiting for us at the lift." Then he cupped her cheek with his cold fingers, leaned forward and kissed her. She melted into it, indulging them both for a moment, reveling in the gentleness of his touch, the fresh mountain air and the wisp of his cologne that stole into her senses. Something moved inside her, shifting in her heart.

"Mmmm, we should do that again. Soon," she said with a grin when he pulled away. She made herself focus back on the discussion they'd been having before the kiss. "Go ahead and finish up the run. I'll be right behind you. I promise."

"You're sure?" He brushed snow from her hair.

"You deserve to do at least one run at a speed that doesn't compete with a snail's," she said.

His lips twitched. "Okay. See you at the bottom." He kissed her nose, made sure she had all of her equipment, then took off for the bottom of the run.

Rosemary smiled, still amazed that she was getting along so well with the guy she had been fighting with—fighting her own attraction to, really—for months. How had that happened? She didn't know, and she didn't know how long it would last, but she decided to ride the tide for now and put all of the questions out of her mind.

She pointed herself down the slope again and got moving to a nice, smooth pace. Enough speed to enjoy the thrill, not so much that she thought she would fall over at any second.

She was starting to get back up to speed—with people zooming past her, when she approached the section of the run that had one side blocked off with red police-style tape. A posted sign said there was a drop-off, and though there had been a fence in place, it looked like one of the snow grooming machines had gotten too close and taken out a section.

She edged a bit closer to that side as people flashed past her. She was enjoying the thrill of speed and the air rushing across her cool skin when she heard someone behind her yell something. A moment later two hands planted in her back, pushing her over, right into the area where the fence was missing.

Rosemary tried to remember how to stop, all of her training going out of her head as she saw the edge of the slope rushing at her. Having a glimmer of sense, she forced herself to fall over, trying to land away from the edge, but the momentum carried her too far and she put her arms out as she started to tumble over the edge. She felt the tug and pull of her limbs, the groan of tendons, heard the snap of her skis releasing and more shouting in the moment before she rolled into a tree with a loud *ooph*. She could swear she was going to end up with bruises on top of her old bruises—the last of which still hadn't entirely faded from her accident in the garage.

She lay perfectly still for a long moment, trying to decide if all of her limbs were still connected to her body, and that she hadn't broken anything.

"Are you all right?" a male voice asked. She didn't open her eyes to see him, but she could tell he wasn't too near her yet, probably up on the run where she belonged. Strike that, she didn't belong anywhere near this place.

"I think I'm still alive," she called back up to him. "I can still wiggle my toes and fingers, so I guess I didn't lose my leg out there in the trees."

She shifted her head and arms a little, testing the muscles.

"Don't move. I'm a doctor." The man's voice was closer now and she heard him moving through the snow. "I can't believe he did that. I saw him moving toward you, too close, too fast. I called out, but he just looked like he'd lost control." Calls for others to get help from ski patrol ricocheted down the mountainside. "Just lay there and tell me where it hurts."

"Um, everywhere." She looked up at him. He was near fifty and only his face peered out between the layers of his clothing. The snow was deep and he had to wade through to her.

"Where the most?" he asked, pulling off his gloves.

She thought for a moment. "Where I hit the tree. I hit it pretty good with my hip. And my shoulder is sore," Actually, it hurt really bad, but she didn't think it was serious. She'd worry about that more later.

"Good. Just stay there, hold on. Are you too cold? Any trouble breathing or chest pressure?"

"No, it's fine. I'll be fine." She thought of her daughter and worry assailed her. "Cleo. My daughter Cleo should be waiting for me at the bottom of the run with my sister and friend. They're going to worry about me. She's been through too much already. I don't want her to worry."

"You must be a good mom, worried more about her than yourself when you're hurt." He pulled off her goggles and looked into her eyes. "Ski patrol will have a radio and can let them know what's going on. Tell me about Cleo." He checked her over for wounds, touching her feet and making her squeeze his hands while he kept her talking about her family.

Rosemary tried to keep most of it vague—if her rescuer didn't know who she was, she didn't want to draw attention to it. They'd had more than enough problems with the press the previous summer and she didn't need any more.

Ten minutes passed before the first ski patrol member showed up, and it was another fifteen minutes before search and rescue arrived with more equipment.

"Load her in the stokes. Careful," a tall dark-haired man said. She vaguely remembered that his name was Hank, and he'd gone out with Jonquil a few times in the fall. "Take it easy. Sorry, Miss DiCarlo. We'll get you to the hospital just fine."

She didn't bother to correct him regarding her name. "Did you hear back from the guys at the bottom of the hill? I need to know my daughter is okay. She's with Jonquil." She had made the request when the ski patrol guy stopped, but he hadn't had any luck finding out where everyone was.

"Let me try." Hank pulled out his radio and she described what Jonquil and Cleo were wearing. A few minutes later as they loaded her onto the back of some kind of ATV with tracks instead of tires, he came back over. "They're waiting for you at the lodge. Someone mentioned it to the resort manager and he found them."

"Gage. We know him." She sighed with relief. "So they're okay? My daughter?"

"Is fine," he reassured. "They said she's with Jonquil and the guy. They're worried about you and will be waiting when we get you down there."

She let herself feel relief and refocused her attention on holding her arms tight across her stomach to keep her shoulder from jostling too much.

The trip to the lodge took much longer than she would have taken on the skis. She had a moment where she wondered what happened to the ski equipment she'd rented, then decided to forget it. If someone else didn't collect and return the equipment, she would pay for it and be happy she never had to use it again.

Still, through the whole ordeal, she couldn't forget the feeling of those hands on her back, the hard push that didn't seem accidental at all.

When she reached the ambulance in the parking lot, Harrison, Cleo and Jonquil waited for her.

"Are you okay?" Cleo asked, reaching for her, wet trails on her cheeks. "Don't die, Mom."

"I'm not going to die," Rosemary said, grabbing her daughter's hand and squeezing it. She wondered if Cleo even realized she'd called her Mom. "I'm fine, really. Only a few bumps and bruises. They just wrapped me up to be extra careful. Watch, I'll be up and chasing you around in a couple of hours."

Harrison touched her cheek—almost the only part of her face that wasn't covered with some kind of gear. "We'll meet you at the hospital. See you in a few minutes."

"Thanks." She wanted to tell him how much she appreciated that he was holding her girl, supporting her. But she couldn't do it here. They removed her from the back of the four-wheel drive machine and into the ambulance.

The EMTs took her blood pressure again, asked her all of the same questions that they'd already asked once and started an IV in the arm that didn't hurt as much. Harrison, Jonquil and Cleo arrived at the ER and checked in on Rosemary almost before she was fully settled in the new bed.

Harrison carried Cleo, who was still crying. Cleo grabbed Rosemary's hand as soon as she was close enough. "Why didn't they take that stuff off of you yet?" she asked, sniffling. Her eyes and nose were red and her face crumpled as tears slid down her cheeks.

Rosemary felt terrible for scaring Cleo. "The doctor hasn't even had time to see me yet, bug. Wait a few minutes, okay? I'm fine, really."

Harrison and Jonquil held a spirited discussion about the joys of their active childhoods, resulting in a multitude of bumps, bruises and sprains. They didn't mention any broken bones, which was fine by Rosemary. The last thing she wanted was to tempt fate into giving her a broken bone right now when she had so much on her plate. Jonquil was barely out of a cast as it was.

It was pushing two hours when the doctor finally released her from the backboard, gave her directions to settle the swelling in her sprained shoulder and a prescription for pain medication.

Back at home Harrison helped Rosemary inside. She was able to walk, but she was sore all over, especially around her hip, which left her with a bit of a limp. The stairs up to her bedroom looked about a mile long.

"I need to call to get someone to cover for me tomorrow," she said as he helped her sit on the sofa in the great room.

"I think you're going to want more than one day off," Harrison said. "How about if I call in help for three days. We can re-evaluate Tuesday morning." He squeezed her hand.

Three days when she had only been back from DC for a couple of weeks? "I can't be gone that long, there's so much to do."

"They'll survive without you. You keep saying Tate is capable; give him a chance to prove himself. Let it go. Be here. Take care of yourself and your girl." He studied her, touching her chin. "She needs you here. Needs to know you're okay—she was hysterical thinking you might die and leave her alone." He brushed the backs of his fingers across her cheek. "You need to restructure your life anyway. Consider this a chance to re-prioritize your time."

She felt a little angry that he didn't think she managed her time well—she was keeping it all together, wasn't she? Running a kitchen took a lot of work; she couldn't just walk away. Especially since her father's will required her to work there until the first of September. She pressed her lips together rather than responding. She was angry and in pain, which she knew would automatically make her testy, and things were going so well with him, she didn't want to ruin it. "Hmmm."

"You must be using amazing restraint not to be arguing with me." Harrison brushed fingers over her forehead, down her cheek and along her bottom lip. "Or you're a lot worse off than I thought. The doc didn't give you any narcotics, did he?"

She smiled. "Morphine. It's wearing off, though. I'll need some Tylenol or something soon. There's a prescription for something stronger, but I don't want to fill it unless I have to."

He brushed his lips over the trail his fingers had just taken, a soft brush across her skin, soothing and comforting. "I'll take care of it." He ended with a light movement of his lips across hers.

Jonquil and Cleo entered and Cleo rushed over to snuggle, wrapping her arms around Rosemary's waist. "I thought you were going to die, like Mom and Dad. It scared me so much."

Rosemary hugged her daughter, holding her close. "I know, sweetie. I'm sorry I scared you. I scared me too." There hadn't been a deputy at the scene or the hospital, but they had said they'd send someone by when they finished dealing with something big that was going on downtown. It must have been huge to have all of the local law enforcement busy.

"Don't do that again," Cleo lectured.

"I won't. No more skis for me. I'm such a klutz! I don't know if you should be skiing either," she teased, though she really didn't intend to keep Cleo from going out with Jonquil or Harrison if they wanted to take her. She'd worry every minute, but she was determined not to overprotect Cleo if she could stand it. Maybe she'd keep her home for a little while, though—until she didn't have pain to remind her of what could happen.

"I liked skiing. You're just no good at it," Cleo pointed out. "I'm better than you." She looked a little proud about this fact.

"True enough. I guess if you go with someone I trust, you can still go." She leaned her cheek against Cleo's head. "But not right away. I want to hold you close for a few days, at least."

Jonquil came over with a selection of food from the fridge, offering them to mother and daughter. "Juice, milk, water, soda?" Jonquil asked while Harrison walked back over with a bottle of painkillers.

"Water would be good," Rosemary said.

"Orange juice," Cleo requested.

Over the next couple of hours, almost everyone in the family stopped in to see Rosemary and check on her condition—even Gage stopped by, claiming it was a courtesy, though he only spoke with Rosemary for a few minutes, then spent nearly half an hour verbally sparing with Jonquil about the best places to rock climb in the area.

Finally Deputy Oliver, a thirty-something man with a Southern accent, showed up, asking to see Rosemary. The house was full of people milling and talking and doing their own thing, but keeping an eye on her. It was a little suffocating.

"Is there somewhere we can get some privacy?" he asked, looking around at the room full of people.

Rosemary considered whether she could handle the stairs. "Let's go downstairs. We have a room there where we'll be able to hear ourselves think," she told Deputy Oliver.

The trip wasn't fun, but she decided it was mostly stiffness causing her discomfort, which she could live with. When she had settled on the sofa, he looked at her. "Seems you've been having a pretty rough time of it lately."

"You have no idea." She felt like everything was piling on her.

He took the chair a few feet away. "You want to run through what happened?"

Rosemary described the encounter the best she could remember.

"And you think the guy pushed you, that it wasn't an accident?" He jotted down notes.

Rosemary nodded. "I've thought about it a lot today. The guy who first came over to me said it looked like the man who pushed me lost control, but I don't think it was an accident. I felt both of his palms on my back, and there wasn't a hint of warning. He wanted me to go over the edge."

Deputy Oliver's eyes sharpened. "Why? Is someone mad at you? Any employees you fired since you moved here?"

She sighed, thinking about all of the people she had let go. "I'll have Harrison send you a list of disgruntled former employees." She didn't think there were issues with the people who were left on her staff, but she could be wrong.

"There are more than one or two in the, what three or four months you've been open?" His brows lifted.

She crossed her arms defiantly. "I have very high standards."

He grinned. "I'll just bet. I'll get that list and let you know what we find out. If you think of anyone else, you let me know."

"Thanks." Rosemary followed him back up the stairs and was happy to go to bed early that night. Cleo shared her bed again, too upset to sleep alone. Rosemary wondered if this was going to become a regular occurrence.

CHAPTER 17

Officially, Rosemary wasn't coming in to work Monday morning, but there hadn't been time to meet with everyone after the accident when Cleo wasn't around, and she needed to talk to everyone, to ensure they knew what was going on.

So, despite her desire to follow the doctor's recommendation and stay in bed, she made herself get up and went in for the morning executive meeting. Before the meeting, she asked Lana if she would have the family stay afterward.

"And what about catering and events," Lana asked Delphi when they reached the end of the executive meeting.

"We're on target for the Drummond wedding. Clare is up to date on all of the details and ready to take point on this and all of the subcontractors have been confirmed. Jeremy's scheduled elsewhere but Kyle Jenkins is taking the pictures. I'll be printing BEOs this morning for their review."

"Why is Clare taking point?" Rosemary asked. This was the first time she'd heard about it.

"I'm going to be in Denver over the weekend. Clare's good and the Drummond wedding is a lot less hands-on than many we've done. It'll be fine."

"What are you doing in Denver?" Rosemary pushed. Delphi's reticence only made her more curious, though that rarely did any good, as Delphi didn't share anything she didn't want to, no matter how much the rest of them nagged.

Delphi shot her an icy glare. "You went to DC several times and didn't share why. This is my weekend. Unless the world is about to end, I better not hear from any of you. Capiche?"

"Gotcha." But Rosemary intended to find out, if she could.

"Anything else?" Lana asked everyone. When no one answered, she ended the meeting, but the family stayed.

"So what's going on?" Joel asked Rosemary when the non-related staff cleared out. "Harrison said Trent wanted a list of everyone you fired or ticked off since you moved here." He and Deputy Oliver had been on a first name basis for several months now.

"It wasn't hard to put together," Harrison said.

"Who knows if someone else didn't like the way I looked at them or something," Rosemary pointed out, not enjoying her new role as the center of attention. "He's digging because the accident wasn't an accident." She ran them through events and what her rescuer had said. "Someone wanted to hurt me."

"Maybe to kill you," Joel took it a little further, causing a cold chill to rush down her spine.

"Anyone in particular who's mad, not just the general list of people you ticked off?" Delphi asked.

"Rulon," Harrison said. "He threatened her in the middle of the grocery store, drew some attention."

"So if someone else is mad, they might know that Rulon threatened you and try to throw it on him?" Joel suggested.

"Yeah, I guess, but I don't know if they have any evidence linking him to the incident. I left a message for Deputy Oliver this morning, but he hasn't returned it yet."

"All right, we batten down the hatches then." Joel's mouth was grim. "We've done it before and you know protocol."

"That was before we had a young girl living with us who likes to open the window to listen to the birds sing in the trees," Rosemary pointed out. "I keep catching her doing it even though it's freezing outside. She also forgets to lock the doors behind her."

"Then you're going to have to figure out how much to tell her, and check the door and window locks constantly," Joel said. "You probably need to vet all of her friends' families too, just to make sure you know where she is and who she's with."

Rosemary grimaced. "I know. I've been trying, but it's been hard to track everything. My work hours have been a little inconvenient. Thank goodness she's mostly been hanging out with Vince's niece at Etta's, so that's one less thing to worry about."

"Sounds like you need to restructure things," Harrison said, his voice light as he reminded her of his earlier comment. "And maybe do some of your paperwork from home instead of at the office. And there are all of us; we can fill in and keep an eye on her if you need to be at work when she's not in school. You probably need to let her school know something's going on, too, so they can watch out for her."

All of this talk made Rosemary's stomach feel a little unsettled. "I think I'm going to be sick. How am I supposed to keep her safe if we don't know who's trying to hurt me or how far they're willing to go?"

Harrison reached over and took her hand, giving it a squeeze. "We'll find them and take care of it."

She appreciated the sentiment, but it didn't make her feel any safer.

Rosemary sat at her bedroom desk that night after putting Cleo to sleep. The pile of paperwork from the lawyers had been growing, but she'd been putting it off, overwhelmed with adjusting to motherhood and problems at work. She was just as overwhelmed with the thought of handling the Markham estate. So she'd ignored it.

Now she flipped through the papers, her eyes crossing as she looked at lists of assets and liabilities. She really just wanted to turn the whole pile over to Alex and forget it—he could work out the details with the Markhams' attorney. She'd have to do that. Later.

She sighed and pushed the papers away, unable to keep her mind on anything except for the fact that someone wanted her or Cleo dead—if the snake was part of this—or maybe both of them.

There was a light knock at her door. "Rosemary?" It was Sage.

Rosemary glanced at Cleo to see if she was asleep, then stood and moved into the hall. "What's going on?" she asked softly after shutting the door behind her.

"Joel has some news. We thought we'd bring it over now."

That sounded ominous. Rosemary followed her to the great room where Joel waited with Jonquil and Delphi. She took a nearby chair while Sage commandeered the spot next to her husband and he took her hand. She seemed so dainty sitting beside him, her dark hair and eyes a crazy contrast next to his Vin Diesel exterior.

"I've been working with Deputy Oliver. It turns out Rulon has an alibi for the day you were skiing. He was temping in a kitchen in Denver. The chef there verified that he came in early to help set up for a banquet and worked until well after lunch. He doesn't have a good alibi for the car windows, but we can't prove anything about that. Not yet, anyway."

Rosemary deflated a little, more confused than ever. "So then who pushed me? It could have been almost anyone."

Amusement leaped into Joel's gaze. "I don't think the list of people who are out to get you is that long."

"Ha, ha." But she wasn't amused. "Where do we search next?"

"We keep working on the list and stay more vigilant. We'll catch him." Joel's voice was soft, but his face was determined.

She nodded, a sick feeling rising in her throat. "Yes, but will you catch him before he hurts my little girl?"

That was the thought that ricocheted through her head at odd hours of the day and night. She believed in Joel, he'd kept Sage safe when a stalker was bent on killing her, but Rosemary couldn't move Cleo in with him and have him watch her 24/7. So what could she do to keep her daughter safe?

Cleo huddled on the balcony overlooking the great room, listening to the news. No one would tell her anything, so the only thing she could do was to listen in. Right now, she kinda wished she hadn't. She'd been nearly asleep when Sage knocked and Cleo pretended not to notice.

She swallowed, terror and worry forming a greasy ball in her stomach. Rosemary was getting hurt; someone was after her. Was it Cleo's fault? Her parents had been hurt, then blown up in the bombing. Just thinking about that made her feel bad; she missed her mom and dad more every day. Now someone was coming after Rosemary. Maybe Cleo *was* to blame. Was she bad luck, like a curse on everyone who loved her?

She was scared to stay, but scared to go too. It was the middle of the winter and she didn't really know anyone here except Rosemary and her sisters—and Cleo didn't want any of *them* hurt, either.

She saw Joel and Sage stand to leave and she ducked even tighter into the corner. Maybe Rosemary would stay down there to talk to Delphi and Jonquil and she could hear more.

Cleo wasn't sure what she thought about Delphi—her name was short for Delphinium, which was really long. No wonder she went with the nickname. Cleo thought if she had a name like that, she'd make up one for herself. Then she could be Princess Adelaide or Queen Abby. Delphi was really serious, always working and didn't smile very much. She had sad eyes but she didn't talk about it. Cleo didn't blame her. She wondered if Delphi was as sad about her dad dying as Cleo was about her parents. Rosemary didn't talk about her dad much, even when Cleo asked about him, and she didn't know why.

The door shut behind Joel and Sage. Jonquil locked the door and set the alarm. They were always setting the alarm and locking the door and windows. It was like a prison here, but to keep everyone out instead of in. They had to lock the doors back home too, but her parents didn't freak out about her opening the window like Rosemary did.

"Well, that's almost worse," Rosemary said, pushing her braid behind her shoulder. "At least when I thought it was Rulon, I knew who to watch for. Now I'm just stressed about everyone all of the time."

"We'll figure it out. We won't let anyone hurt Cleo. You know that," Jonquil said.

Rosemary closed her eyes, looking tired even though it was still early for her. "I hope you're right. I don't know how to fix this."

When they didn't say anything else for a long moment, Cleo decided she better get back to bed before someone noticed her. She sneaked back to the room, being careful to make sure she shut the door quietly behind her.

Guilt pressed on her as she climbed into bed and huddled under the covers. If she hadn't come, Rosemary wouldn't be so upset. Maybe if she was really good, Rosemary would feel better. She tucked the blankets over her head and let the tears flow.

CHAPTER 18

"The CISM group will be in Conifer and Oak for the day, and then just in Conifer tomorrow. I've already double-checked the menu with Rosemary," Delphi said, wrapping up her report at the executive meeting. "What about for the anniversary party? When does that arrive?"

Gina, Lana's office manager, interrupted the meeting. "I'm sorry, but someone is on the phone for Rosemary, and she says it's urgent. She says she's from the school."

Rosemary's heart rate tripled and she leaped to grab the phone in the middle of the conference table. "Hello, this is Rosemary."

"I thought that would get your attention." It was Wanda's voice on the line.

Anger streaked through Rosemary as she sat back in her chair, relieved that Cleo was obviously fine, and irritated by the ruse. "Mother, you freaked me out. What do you want? I'm in a meeting, and I'm pretty sure Gina told you that."

"Too busy to talk to your mother? Come on, Rosie, did that father of yours knock all good behavior out of you, coddling your bad attitude?"

Rosemary gritted her teeth. "If you have something to say, say it, because I'm hanging up in thirty seconds."

Harrison reached out and covered her hand with his. She didn't think he really believed how awful her mother was, but the whole group was about to get a taste of the way things worked between her and Wanda if she didn't bite back the hurt and anger that always filled her when she heard her mother's voice.

"I still need that treatment, Rosemary. I really need five grand so I can start feeling better. You owe it to me."

139

"I don't owe you anything. I need to go. Some of us work for a living." She hung up, closing her eyes for a few seconds to get the emotions under control. "Is there a way to block her calls so they don't make it into the building?"

She held up a hand and shook her head. "Never mind, she'll just change her number or something." She sucked in a breath, looking at the group again. "Sorry, Delphi, go on." Her heart still pounded like crazy from the adrenaline that poured into her when she thought something had happened to Cleo. How could her mother scare her like that? Of course, Wanda had never had that kind of reaction when Rosemary had been hurt or in trouble. She would've had to care for that to happen.

Harrison squeezed her hand, drawing her back into the room. She looked around her. "Sorry, I got distracted."

"We understand," Lana said. "Delphi asked about the food for this weekend." Concern showed on her face as she studied Rosemary.

"Right." She managed to refrain from apologizing again and plowed ahead about preparations. She still felt muddled, but the report came out reasonably well organized anyway. The meeting finished and the other department heads left, but the family members stayed seated by silent agreement while the others filed out.

"Your mom again?" Harrison asked.

"Yeah." Rosemary smoothed back her braid. "She has this thing—she refuses to work and Dad's not around to shovel money into her bottomless pit of a bank account anymore, so she thinks I should start paying up."

"Is she mad you won't support her?" Joel asked.

"Yeah, she gets uptight when her credit card at Bloomies isn't getting a lot of use." Resentment shot through her and she clenched her teeth to hold it in.

"Is she upset enough she might want you out of the way?" Joel asked carefully. "Your inheritance isn't exactly a big secret—or at least the fact that you inherited big isn't a secret."

"Yeah, but she doesn't know how much there is, or that if I die, all my money goes to some stupid program for under-privileged cheerleaders, among other stupid groups. I hated those girls in school," she mumbled the end of this under her breath.

"Hey, I was a cheerleader," Jonquil protested.

Rosemary tipped her head to the side, studying Jonquil. "Yeah, why doesn't that surprise me?"

"You hate all cheerleaders?" Jonquil asked, crossing her arms over her chest.

Rosemary sat back and eyed her sister—she was Rosemary's favorite by far. "Well, I liked you fine until I knew about your deep, dark past. How come *that* didn't come up in our family scandals last summer? Seriously, if someone wanted people to hate us, they totally should have gone after Jonquil's secret past. Me getting kicked out of two schools doesn't even compete."

Jonquil stuck out her tongue at Rosemary, who tossed back a squinty fake smile.

"All right, children," Cami said, sounding a little harassed. "Back to the issue at hand. Wanda—could she be our bad guy or do we just hate her on principle because she's selfish and cruel?"

"Oh, hey, hate her on principle. I doubt she's the person who's after me. She probably thinks she can get paid faster if I'm alive. She'd be wrong, but it's probably what she believes." There were days when she was tempted to pay up to get her mother to go away, but she knew it would never end.

Harrison lifted a finger and she turned to watch him—as did almost everyone else. He was still holding her hand, but didn't seem to notice anymore. "Cleo says your mom always upsets you when she calls. What does she say? The day in your office I walked in on a call; it sounded nasty."

Rosemary repeated what she could remember of the most recent call, and the call before. "She said she'd make me pay. But I really think that's literally, because that's what she understands. She doesn't have the follow-through to attempt murder."

"Regardless, I'll check her out," Joel said. "If she's getting desperate, we don't want to overlook her."

"She can't ski. She doesn't even like the snow," Rosemary said. "No way she did that. Besides, the guy who helped me out claimed it was a man who pushed me."

"She could have paid someone to hurt you," Cami suggested.

"Hey, I'd do it for free," Delphi quipped.

Rosemary ignored the last part and pushed on. "She's mean and narcissistic, but I don't think she'd have anyone killed. Not even me."

"And still, I'm going to check." Joel scribbled something on his tablet computer.

"Fine. I hope it is her, because then I can see her in jail, which would make my year." Rosemary had enough of the discussion and stood, being her mother's meal ticket was bad enough without believing she would actually try to have her killed. It was more than Rosemary could handle calmly at the moment. "I have food to deal with. And last I checked, you all have things to do too."

"Hey, I haven't excused you," Lana protested.

"The main meeting is over. Are you going to write up the head of housekeeping and engineering because they took off already?" Rosemary asked as she circled the table. When Lana didn't respond, she nodded. "That's what I thought." She stalked out of the room, needing a few minutes to calm down before facing her staff.

Harrison couldn't get Rosemary's earlier distress out of his head. She'd held it in, but he could see it in her eyes, in the way she held her shoulders and the pinched expression on her face. The phone call had bothered her more than she would admit. When lunchtime arrived, he went straight to the restaurant. He greeted Marla, the hostess, and continued on through without an explanation. The staff was starting to get used to him just barreling into the kitchen to lock horns with Rosemary, so no one even blinked.

The kitchen was chaos as usual—the kind of organized chaos that defied understanding to an outsider like himself. The restaurant was busy and the convention running down the hall meant the kitchen was putting out a steady supply of food and snacks throughout the day.

"Have you eaten yet?" he asked Rosemary.

"Yes." She mixed a pan of rice pilaf, not looking up at him.

"Is that true?" he asked the girl standing next to her.

She looked at Rosemary from the corner of her eye. "Uh, yes, of course."

Rosemary sighed but didn't seem irritated when she glanced at the girl beside her. "You really have to become a better liar if you want to convince anyone over the age of two."

"Great." Harrison took that as permission to meddle. He moved to the corner where they put together the salads. "Two oriental chicken salads. And a side of those beer-battered fries for me. I love those things. We'll take them to another room so she can get away for a few minutes to eat." He really didn't care about the distractions of the kitchen—she managed to ignore those reasonably well from her office most of the time, but he wanted to get her talking about more private things, and she wouldn't do that in her office.

"You're so bossy," Rosemary said mildly.

"I have to be when I'm dealing with you," he answered in the same tone. "Come on, we'll have a few minutes of quiet, you'll be able to regroup, and you'll be calmer when you come back in."

One of the fry cooks shot him a grateful look that indicated Harrison was right that she'd been testy that morning. Considering the call from her mom, he wasn't surprised.

"If you're going to keep coming in here to bother me, I'm going to make you get a food handler's permit so I can put you to work." Rosemary grabbed a garlic clove and started mincing it.

143

"That could be interesting. But I don't think I need a permit to wash dishes, and I have a funny feeling that's where I'd end up."

She smiled. "You might be right. In that case, we have a sink full."

"Thanks for the offer, but I'm on my break right now. I can't do dishes."

"If you're in the kitchen," one of the guys said, "you're not really on your break, so you better get out of the way or get to work."

Harrison chuckled. "Why do I get the feeling she's said that a few times."

"You better believe it." Rosemary zoomed through several more cloves of garlic in way less time than Harrison would have believed humanly possible—especially since she still bore a sling for her sprained shoulder. He watched her work, appreciating the graceful way she moved through the task, answering questions and giving orders to the people around her without skipping a beat.

"Order up."

Harrison looked over to see the salads and a side of fries on a counter—they must have been anxious to get rid of Rosemary if they rushed his order ahead of everyone else's. "Perfect. Put down the knife, Rosemary. Time to eat."

"There's just something about a pushy man that gets to me," she said with an edge of sarcasm and gave a few directions to her staff. She grabbed her plate from the counter, allowing Harrison to follow her out.

He appreciated that she grumbled but didn't balk and he directed her down the hall to an empty room.

"Why are we eating in here?" Rosemary asked when Harrison picked a table.

"Because you need to get away from the minions for a few minutes. And I plan to pry about your mother, and you won't do that if everyone's hovering around you in the restaurant."

She lifted her fork and sighed. "They put the dressing on the salad greens instead of on the side."

"Yup, that's how the salad's made. Eat up." He forked up some chicken for himself and savored the flavor. He waited until she took a couple of bites before jumping in. "What happened between you and your mom? Did you always hate her, or is it something a little more recent?"

"Do we have to go over this? Really, it's so last year."

"Quit avoiding the question—you need to tell someone and we have to assess whether she's a real threat."

She stabbed at some lettuce with her fork, but slowly, reluctantly began to talk. "I didn't always hate her. I have vague memories of desperately wanting her to love me like I loved her." She paused for a moment. "That was a long time ago, though. I stopped trying to make her happy a long time ago. How terrible is it to say that? How much worse that I barely feel bad about it?" She rubbed the back of her neck, then returned to eating.

"Did she abuse you?"

She closed her eyes for a moment. "I really can't talk about her now. Please just let it go. It's over."

His heart ached for her, but he was starting to understand her. "If it were over, you wouldn't be so wound up about it." He watched her carefully, trying to nudge her without making her go over the edge. If she still refused, he'd change the subject, or at least shift it laterally a little.

She said nothing for a moment, then seemed to give in. "She's just self-absorbed, okay? Everything is about her, and how it affects her. It was never about me, unless I was what made her life worse than it would be otherwise, which was most of the time. You want to know why I got into so much trouble in school? Because I wanted my parents to pay, or to pay attention, I'm not sure which anymore. Both of them. Dad wouldn't acknowledge that I was his in public, and Wanda just didn't care about anyone but herself. She drives me crazy and she never gives up. But I'm not playing this time." Her face was tight and pain lingered in her eyes.

Harrison watched her. The urge to fix what was wrong was almost overwhelming, but he knew he couldn't, that it wasn't possible. He had strong feelings for her, ones that were growing stronger all the time, and he wanted to be her sounding board. That was what she needed most. The question was how to get her to keep sounding. "What will you do when she keeps contacting you?" He already knew the question wasn't *if* but *when*.

Rosemary's jaw clenched and she stabbed at the salad as if it were her worst enemy. "I'll get a restraining order. And maybe I'll take Cleo to Italy after September first. She'd like it there. It's perfect, and we could use assumed names so she can't find us and we'll spend the rest of our lives relaxing on the beach of the Mediterranean and drinking those fruity drinks with the umbrellas." She shoveled the salad into her mouth while she spoke, moving automatically when she was so upset.

His heart sank a little as he realized she didn't see him there beside her on that beach, but he wasn't going to be that easy to dismiss him. "Sounds like a plan. You think your beach might have room for one more?"

Her lips twitched a little. "Yeah, sure. I'll be happy to have Jonquil visit anytime." She looked up at him through her eyelashes.

"That was just mean." Harrison grabbed a fry from the plate and held it out to her. She eyed it warily. "Go on," he said. "It won't bite you. It's only one fry."

She bit her lip, then took it, closing her eyes as an expression of bliss covered her face while she ate it. "I haven't had fried food for so long. I love these things."

"Have another." He nudged the plate closer to her.

"No. One's my limit. Really, I can't eat them or I'll blow up like a blimp."

He slid his eyes over what he could see of her too-thin figure. "Give me a break, you will not. You're gorgeous, and even more so when you don't look half-starved." But he didn't push her any further. She'd eaten most of her salad, including all of the chicken. And she'd talked, though he hadn't been sure he would be able to get her to spill. "You need the energy to deal with what's going on."

She leaned back in her seat and looked at him, searching his face. "Why do I do that?"

"Say mean things about yourself and have an unrealistic body image? I have no idea." But he really wanted to understand.

"No," her voice was void of amusement. "Why do I talk to you about stuff like that? Why can't I seem to help myself? Lately it's like you set some food under my nose and I start talking."

The thought pleased him. "I should feed you more often. In fact, you and Cleo should come over for dinner at my place. Say, tomorrow night." He'd spent time with them almost every night since their date, but it wasn't enough. And he wanted to see her in his space, see how she acted when it wasn't her territory. See how he felt about it.

Rosemary crossed her arms over her chest, but the gesture was oddly self-protective rather than defiant. "Why don't you give me honest answers?"

He shrugged. "Why do you ask stupid questions I can't answer? Or questions I can answer, but which you don't actually want the answer to?"

"If I didn't want the answer, I wouldn't ask," she insisted.

He wasn't sure if that was true, but decided to take the risk. "Okay, then. You talk to me because it's me. I'm the one for you and somewhere deep inside, you know it. You're safe with me because I won't judge you for being angry with your mom and dad or any of the crazy things you've done. You know I'll love you no matter what, so I'm safe and you can get it all off of your chest." There, he'd said it, and it didn't make his insides twist up the way he'd expected. It was actually a relief to say it aloud, even if it meant risking her denials.

She started to protest and he pressed a finger to her lips. "I told you that you didn't want the answers. If you don't like it, don't ask."

He hesitated for half a second, then pushed just one inch further. "I love you, Rosemary. I'm in love with you and nothing you do or say is going to change that. Freak out if you want, but it won't scare me away." He leaned back and finished off his fries while she sputtered—it was nice to see her off balance for once.

"You're just... nuts... crazy. No way you could love me this soon. Forget it." She stood from the table and stalked off.

He decided challenging her when she was trying to process his words would be asking for trouble, but he couldn't just let her walk away without saying anything. "Thanks for lunch. What do you think about dinner tomorrow? Want me to pick you up, say around six?"

She turned to him in disbelief when she reached the door. "You have a lot of nerve."

"You have to eat." Making sure Rosemary didn't starve herself would be a nice bonus. "Come on over. It'll be fun."

Her lips pressed together and he wished for a kiss goodbye, but figured that wasn't going to happen now. She nodded. "Six. Don't be late."

He grinned when the door slowly shushed closed behind her.

CHAPTER 19

Rosemary told herself that it was only fair for her to play host to Cleo and Hannah sometimes. Cleo had been to Etta's to play with Hannah four or five times already, so though she had a pile of work to do, Rosemary agreed when Cleo asked for her friend to hang out, and she didn't argue when Hannah pulled out a game she'd brought along with her.

"*Beat the Parents*, huh? What's that all about?" Rosemary asked.

"We play against you," Cleo said. "Since you're the only parent, you can call one of the sisters if you can't answer the question, I guess. But if we beat you at the game we get to make cookies."

"Oh yeah?" Rosemary was fine with making cookies regardless of who won, but decided to play along. "What do I get if I win?"

Cleo's face scrunched up a little and she whispered to Hannah, who nodded. "If you win, we'll actually do the dishes after we bake the cookies."

Rosemary laughed. "It's a deal. Loser does the dishes. Set it up and I'll put my stuff away." She hibernated her computer and stashed it and the pages back in the carrying case—not entirely easy when one arm was still in a sling, due to the sprained shoulder—then took them to her room. When she returned, the girls had everything set out and ready to go. "Tell me how this works."

The girls explained the rules to her, though Rosemary had the funny feeling they were tweaking them to favor themselves. They started the first round and the girls answered the question of who was the first man to walk on the moon—she was impressed.

Then Rosemary's came up.

"Where was Daniel Radcliffe when they found him to play Harry Potter?" Hannah read.

Who? Apparently it must be the kid in the movie—or one of the kids in the movie, but how was she supposed to know that? "Um, how many times can I call one of the sisters for answers?" Rosemary asked.

The girls whispered again, though neither was very good at using quiet voices so she could hear every word. "Five," Cleo announced a moment later.

If all of the questions were like that, Rosemary had the sneaking suspicion she was doomed. She considered which of her sisters was most likely to know the answer and dialed Jonquil's cell phone. "Hey, I'm playing a game with Cleo and Hannah. My question is what, what's his name again?" she asked.

"Daniel Radcliffe." Hannah answered and the girls giggled together.

"Right, Daniel Radcliffe. What was he doing when they found him to play in *Harry Potter*."

Jonquil laughed. "Not to play *in Harry Potter*, you dork. He's the lead. You really need to spend a little less time in the kitchen and more at the movies."

"Do you know the answer or not?" Rosemary asked, not amused by her sister's teasing.

"Nope. Let's see, how about if you guess that he was in grocery store, or playing video games. I could swear I heard of some child actor being discovered at an arcade, but I don't know who it was."

"Thanks."

"Welcome, and hey, good luck with that. I hope you didn't bet them anything valuable. It sounds like those girls are going to take you to the cleaners."

"Yeah, I kinda got that feeling already." Rosemary shot the girls a look of censure, which only made them giggle again.

Jonquil's laugh echoed through the phone before she hung up.

"So? What's the answer?" Cleo asked. She had a cocky little grin that reminded Rosemary of herself at that age and she no longer wondered why so many people wanted to beat her up when she wore it.

"He was playing in the arcade."

"Nope. He was at a theater. Our turn!" Cleo sang and pushed the card holder to Rosemary.

The girls didn't know the sixteenth president of the United States was Abe Lincoln, but they declared that if they didn't know it, it must be too hard.

Amused, Rosemary let it go. "How would I know what Elmo's favorite food is?" she asked when that question came up. "I never had a kid who watched Sesame Street."

"Don't you remember from when you were a kid?" Hannah asked, all innocence.

"No, Elmo didn't come around until I was grown up," Rosemary said. "Ask me what Cookie Monster or Oscar the Grouch love best and I can help you out, but Elmo is a mystery to me."

"Just guess," Cleo said.

"It's too hard," Rosemary put on her biggest whiner voice. "It must not be a fair question if I don't know it."

"You're supposed to know everything, 'cause you're an adult." Cleo wasn't giving an inch. "Come on, just guess."

"Fine." Rosemary racked her brain and decided to go with Cleo's favorite food. "Pizza?"

"Yes! How did you know?" Hannah asked, wide-eyed.

"Who doesn't love pizza?" Rosemary was relieved she was going to have at least one move in this game.

It ended up being almost the only move she got before the girls won. Patently unfair, but Rosemary decided it was fun anyway, and started setting out ingredients for cookie dough.

"We need a hut to sit in while we eat these," Hannah said as she cracked an egg.

"Yeah. You should see her grandma's barn, Rosemary, it's so cool," Cleo enthused. "They set up a corner just for the kids to play in and it has little furniture and everything. We play in it all of the time."

"In this weather? It's cold out there." Just the walk from work to the car made Rosemary cold—but Cleo didn't seem to mind cold the way she did, which made Rosemary wonder if she had become a wimp as she became an adult.

"It's not that cold. The horses don't mind it, right?" Cleo grinned as she added a teaspoon of salt.

"How about if we make a hut out of the furniture downstairs and some blankets instead?" Rosemary suggested. It would probably irritate Jonquil and Delphi if they had to crawl through the blankets to get to their rooms if it wasn't down when they got home, but the furniture was easier to move down there than the sofas in the great room were and she wasn't much use with her injured shoulder.

The girls were quick to agree and as soon as the first tray of cookies was in the oven, they ran downstairs to start setting up their hut.

Rosemary smiled despite the fact that they'd already tired her out. Who knew parenting could be so exhausting? Or so fun.

"How come you live so far away?" Cleo asked as they drove to Harrison's the next evening.

Rosemary glanced at Cleo, who sat in Harrison's back seat. "It's not that far."

"But Vince and Cami are only a few blocks, and Sage and Joel are building next door to the house," Cleo said. "So how come you're across town, Harrison?"

"There weren't that many options," he said. "I didn't buy it. George leased it for me for the year. He said if I decide to stay, I could buy something else."

Rosemary turned to Harrison, curious, though it hadn't occurred to her to ask. "Are you planning to stay longer than the rest of us?" She reconsidered. "Then again, I don't really see Cami going anywhere anytime soon. Or Lana. They're both pretty entrenched." Lana had already accepted the job before she heard the terms of the will and said from the first that she intended to ride the current for as long as it lasted. Cami married a local, and Vince owned businesses in town, so he wasn't likely to go anywhere.

"I have the feeling most of you will be pretty entrenched by the time the year is up." Harrison took a quick glance, but his expression was hard to read.

"What's that supposed to mean?" His knowing tone said there was more to it, but he shrugged instead of explaining.

"Have you been talking to Sage? Is she reading the stars about it or something?" Rosemary had to know now that the topic had come up.

He sighed. "You never give up. Yes, Sage thinks you're all going to stay, at least for a while longer."

"And you? Are you going to stay?" Rosemary suddenly wanted very much to know.

His lips twitched. "I guess that depends."

"On what?" Cleo asked.

"On whether or not Sage is right."

"I thought you said she was *always* right," Cleo said.

"Yes, she is." He pulled the car into a curved driveway. "Here we are."

Rosemary let go of the questions about what exactly Sage had said—there would be time to go over that again later. She had never seen Harrison's house before, so she took a long look. It was covered in a stone facade, which gave it a cottage-y look, despite the fact that it was really too big to be a cottage. The forest encroached almost to the front porch with just a small clearing in the front for grass or flowers.

"It's hard to imagine what it'll look like in the summer—the snow kinda gets in the way," Rosemary said, but she liked it. It felt homey and comfortable.

"Yeah. Sage said it looks like a cottage in the woods—which it is, so it makes sense. She was talking about planting a bunch of wildflowers this spring." He pushed out and came around to open their doors.

"It's charming." Rosemary couldn't help but approve. It didn't have the sweeping grace and bank of windows that their father had built for his daughters, or the middle-class boxiness of her neighborhood back home. It was a perfect mix of the two, tucked into the forest like it belonged there.

"Yes. And wait until you see the inside." He led them up the front walk, onto the log front porch, and pushed open the door. "The whole place has hardwood floors and a few of the rooms have log walls. I have two wood stoves; one in here and one in the master bedroom."

"I guess they didn't want to get cold if the power went out," Rosemary said. The space wasn't huge, but it was nice, with an open floor plan into the kitchen. She walked over and stared at the tiny space. "How does anyone cook in here? Seriously, it's smaller than my bathroom."

"The bathrooms in your house rival the Taj Mahal," Harrison said.

"Don't exaggerate."

"You started it," Cleo said. "The kitchen is *not* smaller than your bathroom."

"She's right." Harrison leaned against the cabinet and snaked an arm around Rosemary's waist, pulling her close.

"Hey, not in front of the kid." Rosemary put a hand on his chest to push off. His warm, very firm chest.

"I don't care. And I'm not a kid." Cleo wandered to the counter and lifted the lid on the crockpot.

Harrison pulled Rosemary a little closer. "She doesn't care."

"I do." Her voice wasn't steady though. When he didn't kiss her, Rosemary looked over at her daughter. She had already smelled the meat simmering when she walked in, but the lid coming off poured scent into the room, making her salivate. This was bad. She'd known it would be. Dinner would be like a normal daily calorie intake if she wasn't careful.

Cleo took two more steps and lifted a second lid. "What's this?"

"Dump cake. It's a fruit cobbler. Put that back on. It needs more time and when you open the lid it lets out all the heat." Harrison spoke lightly, not upsetting Cleo, despite the fact that she had become very jumpy lately.

"Oh. It smells yummy. Do you have ice cream to put on top?" she asked hopefully.

"Of course." Harrison buried his face in Rosemary's neck and whispered, "You smell really good too." His lips brushed her neck, making her shiver, then he released her. "You ladies ready to eat? We can set the table."

Cleo kept up a lively chatter about a kid who got sick at school and how gross it was, though her eyes were filled with excitement. They all worked together to set out the dishes. Rosemary wouldn't let herself think about the way they worked in sync, how Harrison anticipated them, pointing out the right cupboards, testing the food, filling the water pitcher. It felt good, right—the three of them working together, preparing for dinner, to sit for a meal in his home. And the place was surprisingly homey considering he was a bachelor.

"Who decorated for you?" Rosemary asked. "I'm not buying that you did all of this."

"Most of the furniture came with the house," Harrison admitted. "Sage came in and dressed the place up a little more when I moved in, rearranged a few things to comply with Feng Shui. She said I shouldn't be staying in a place that was less homey than a hotel."

"She would be right. It's nice."

"Thanks. I'm comfortable here. Especially settling on the sofa in front of the fire at night with a nice cup of chamomile tea. It's cozy." Their gazes met and the promises in his eyes made her smile.

She could imagine it—with both of them on the sofa, of course. "Sounds cozy."

"Ugh. You two are so stupid," Cleo said. "If you want to kiss her, just do it. Don't stand there and make googly eyes at each other." Cleo was arranging the silverware, sending them covert glances.

"Okay." Harrison crossed to Rosemary in two long strides, pulled her close and laid his lips on hers almost before she could process.

Just before Rosemary closed her eyes, she saw Cleo peek at them again and grin. If she was happy about it, Rosemary didn't see why they shouldn't enjoy the moment. His lips were firm but yielding, his touch teasing, tender. His hands raced up her spine once, then settled around her waist, pulling her even closer. She settled into the kiss, lingering over it for a long moment, drawing it out until she felt her heart beating in her throat and she wished they didn't have an audience. She snuggled closer to him and sighed when he ended the kiss.

"Hello," he said in a husky voice in her ear.

She smiled, almost giggled aloud despite the fact that she hadn't giggled in years. "Hello. It took you a while for you to greet me properly."

"I won't wait next time." He pulled back and picked up the hot pads. "Time for dinner." He turned off the heat in the main crockpot and carried the crock onto the table.

Rosemary took a large helping of carrots, a small one of meat and skipped the starchy potatoes. It tasted fantastic. Though she tried to turn away dessert, Harrison served her some anyway, and she found herself unable to resist the sweet aroma, finishing half of it.

After they ate, they sat down to a rousing game of canasta, which Cleo won handily, and then Harrison put on the latest family movie release, which Cleo had seen in the theater, but neither Harrison or Rosemary had paid attention to before. Not surprisingly. Cleo snuggled under a fluffy blanket on the easy chair, and quickly fell asleep.

"It must be all that excitement with the puking kid at school that wore her out," Harrison suggested.

"Right. It always makes me tired when I see people puking around me," Rosemary agreed.

He pulled her a little closer, and she set her hand on his shoulder. She should be seriously freaked out right now, crazily freaked. The day before he said that he loved her, that he thought they were going to be together, and in the car, he insinuated that he would stay in town if she did.

He was actually serious about them, and she wasn't freaking out. She pushed the thought away, just really glad to be there with him, to feel reasonably safe at the moment, despite the troubles they'd been having. She needed a night without any troubles, time to just relax with Harrison and Cleo. A night to ignore the echoes of the bad decisions she'd made in her past.

So when he tipped her chin up and kissed her, she let everything around them drop away.

CHAPTER 20

Rosemary stretched the muscles across her back and sighed. She'd been at the resort since five, getting things up and running for the breakfast service. It meant Jonquil had to get Cleo off for school that morning, but that Rosemary would be able to pick her up and spend the rest of the day with her. She walked through the kitchen and got reports for the afternoon snack service and dinner preparations for the meeting being held in one of the small conference rooms, then checked her watch. Two o'clock. Time to go if she was going to be at the school on time. Mornings did have the advantage of allowing her to spend the afternoon with Cleo, so she accepted the trade-off of the too-early hours.

She grabbed her winter coat, packed her laptop and paperwork to work on after Cleo went to bed and walked out through the restaurant.

Everything appeared to be running like clockwork. Good, she thought, at least something was going well. She smiled to herself as she passed the spa and waved to Sage, then stopped to ask the new head of housekeeping for some fresh towels for the kitchen.

She was searching for the keys in her pocket when she heard someone calling her name. Sort of.

"Rosie, I knew you were here. They said you weren't but I knew you were."

Rosemary stopped where she was as her mother's voice carried across the large foyer. Her stomach clenched at the sight of Wanda standing beside the check-in desk. Why hadn't she parked around back again?

Wanda rushed to Rosemary, arms flung wide as if in anticipation of a hug. Rosemary stepped back reflexively as she grabbed her cell phone and speed dialing Joel's number.

"Wanda's at the check-in desk," she said when he answered, then hung up before he could respond. "What are you doing here, Mother?" she asked in a low voice. "You're supposed to be in DC."

"I thought I'd come see where my daughter works." She pulled Rosemary into a hug—as she was wont to do when they were in public and people were watching. Ever the actress. "Aren't you happy to see me?" She barely touched her daughter's shoulders as she did the social hug, but her breath stank of alcohol.

Rosemary's mind flipped through the scenarios, trying to decide where to take Wanda, what to do to minimize the scene she could already see ahead of them, the potential for public embarrassment and disruption at the hotel. "I was just leaving for the day. Walk me out to my car."

Joel approached, coming to a stop beside them. His eyes slid over Wanda as he sized up the situation and chose a response. An affable smile spread over his face like he was getting a real treat. "Hello, I'm Joel Watts. You must be Rosemary's mother." He extended a hand to her. "I married her sister, Sage."

"Another one of George's throwaways," Wanda said with an expansive gesture. "He was lousy with them."

His face tightened a little. "He certainly has a big family," he agreed without breaking his smile. "You haven't been here before, have you? How about if we show you around?" He took her elbow and gestured toward the hall where his office was.

"It is rather nice, but I thought I'd check in first." She pointed back to the front desk. "Settle in before I have Rosie take me on the grand tour."

"It's too early to check in," Joel said, though most of the rooms would be clean by this hour. "Come take a walk with us." Joel was rather stoic and quiet by nature, and Rosemary had rarely seen him like this—only once before, on the evening of his wedding when she saw him talking with his SEAL buddies. If it hadn't been for that one evening, she would have sworn that this man, the charming, social guy, was a pod person or something.

Whatever his end game was, she would go along with it. Even if she was getting a little too close to when the last bell would ring at the elementary school. She checked her watch again and figured she had five minutes to get out the door.

A moment later they were maneuvering into the security office. "What are we doing here?" Wanda asked as she looked around uncertainly.

Joel pulled the door closed behind them. "I just wanted a quiet place to talk with you." He sat beside her and gestured for Rosemary to take the chair behind his desk—the one furthest from her mother. "So what brought you here today?" he asked Wanda.

"I just wanted to see my daughter."

His voice was smooth, but his eyes held a glint of hardness. "I was surprised you didn't come when the hotel opened in September. Most of the girls' mothers came in then. It was a big accomplishment getting this whole place set up. You should see Rosemary when she's in the kitchen. She's a master. Like a symphony conductor. You must be so proud."

Rosemary was a little stunned at the compliment. Was he serious or just laying it on thick for Wanda?

"Well, it helps when you have Daddy Warbucks backing you and making sure you get all the best opportunities." Wanda's comment was slightly slurred and full of spite. It made the knot in Rosemary's stomach grow from the size of a quarter to the size of an apple.

"It doesn't hurt to have the financial and emotional support her dad gave her, especially when she has natural talent and is willing to work her guts out to become the best." Joel flashed Rosemary another one of those easy grins. It was starting to freak her out, even if she did appreciate the fact that he was standing up for her.

Her cell phone rang and she noticed Harrison's number on the other end. When she hesitated, Joel nodded that she should answer it. "Hey, what's up?" She checked her watch again.

"I heard your mom's here. Would you like some company?"

"We're with Joel in his office. Do you think you could get away for a while? It's almost two-thirty."

He hesitated for a second. "Are you looking for company or someone to pick up Cleo, because I could do that if you want."

"I'd really appreciate it if you could run that errand for me. My mother caught me on my way out the door."

"Do you want me to bring her here, your place or would you rather I take her to my place?"

"Yours, if it's okay. Can you get away for a while? I know it's early." It's not like he would get in trouble, but she knew he had work to do too.

"Yeah. I'll take care of it. No worries."

"Thanks." That was a big relief. She said goodbye and hung up. She smiled at Joel when he lifted a questioning eyebrow at her. "Just rearranging my two-thirty appointment." Everyone in the family knew that's when school got out. Sage had picked up Cleo a couple of times too, so she was pretty sure he'd understand. She'd rather not bring up Cleo with her mother around, especially when they didn't know for sure who was behind everything that was happening.

"Good." He turned back to Wanda, still projecting affability. "You just hopped on a plane at the last minute? You must be exhausted after the trip."

"I've been in Denver for a few days. Traveling always wears me out," she said, waving her hand a little as if it was only to be expected. "Besides, there are some great shops there."

Rosemary tried not to grind her teeth when she heard her mom talking about all of the shopping she was doing when she'd been on the phone begging for money only a few days ago. "I didn't think you'd want to come up here in the middle of the winter, Mother. You never did like snow very much."

"It's ghastly. Thought I was going to go off the road a few times on my way up here." Wanda patted her pocket and brought out a hip flask. "Luckily I brought something to warm me up." She had to tip it almost upside down to get anything out of it.

Rosemary swallowed back the bile. She hated when her mother drank. It didn't happen as often as it could have, but she was unpredictable—sometimes friendly and almost caring, while other times she was mean and nasty. At least Joel was with Rosemary this time. The question was how they were going to get rid of her.

"How long are you planning to stay?" Joel asked.

"A day or two. Rosemary and I have issues to settle and I want to see my granddaughter."

Over my dead body, Rosemary thought. "It's too bad I'm so busy for the next few days," she said. "If you'd called ahead maybe we could have worked some time into my schedule." Or she might have arranged to be *out* of town.

"You're in charge; reschedule work." The slurring grew worse.

"I can't do that. It's the weekend, when it's the busiest here." Rosemary stood. "I need to get moving. There's so much to do."

"You can't go," Wanda protested. "You have to give me money. That's why I came. I knew if I came to you, you'd take care of me. I just needed to remind you. You owe me, Rosemary." She went from calmly drunk to angry and insulting in the blink of an eyes. Rosemary had expected it, had even pushed for it, needing whatever Joel was waiting for to happen so he could get rid of her.

"There's not going to be any money," Rosemary said even as guilt twisted her gut. Why should she feel bad about not enabling her mother?

"But you have to help me." Wanda's face grew red and she reached out to her daughter.

"No, I don't." Rosemary stood her ground. "If you could find the money to fly out here, spend a few days in a hotel, go shopping in Denver and rent a car, you have enough to take care of yourself until you find a job."

"But I haven't worked since before you were born," Wanda protested. "How am I supposed to get a job now? Do you know how hard it is for someone to get work at my age? I mean, I'm almost forty."

She was over fifty, but Rosemary wasn't about to dicker over her age. "I can't help you. It's time you help yourself." She felt like a mean, ungrateful child, but unless she wanted her mom to come to her with a hand out for the rest of her life, she had to cut her off now. No question about it. The fact that her mother was mean and nasty about everything made saying no much easier.

"You can't do that, you useless brat." She lifted her hand to strike Rosemary.

Joel grabbed her wrist before she let it fly. "I wouldn't be doing that if I were you." His affability was gone, his voice had become low and hard. "Let me tell you how this is going to go, Ms. Keogh. You're going to leave this hotel and leave this town. You aren't going to contact Rosemary again. Not by phone, not by letter, not online. You're not going to come back here. Ever. Or to any of the other DiCarlo properties. I'm going to have your name listed in the system so they won't make a reservation for you. Rosemary is going to talk to the cops today, give them your name and see about getting a protective order."

That last one, at least, was an exaggeration. Rosemary didn't think she had enough grounds for one, but it sounded nice.

"That's what you think. She's my daughter and I can talk to her if I want to." Wanda struggled, rounding on Joel and hitting him this time. Joel grabbed her other wrist, then twisted her arm up behind her. He whipped a long ziptie from one of the many pockets in his cargo pants and tied her wrists together while she screamed and cursed him. Rosemary stood back, watching, shocked by his actions and relieved that he was on her side.

"Rosemary, call the sheriff and get someone out here. I'm pressing charges for assault and battery," Joel said.

She sucked in a breath and nodded, then picked up the phone from his desk and dialed out.

It was almost an hour before Rosemary was able to get away from the hotel to check on Cleo. She found her daughter sitting with Harrison at his kitchen table, a chessboard between them.

"Harrison's teaching me. Want to play?" Cleo asked.

"It's kind of a two-person game, sweetie." Rosemary leaned over and pressed a kiss to her daughter's head. "How was school?" She smiled her thanks to Harrison, intending to give him a much better reward once she had talked to her daughter for a few minutes.

"Well maybe you can play it with me later at home." She scrunched up her face. "Do we have a chess game?"

"Nope, I don't think any of us has a chess set. But if you like it, maybe we can pick one up. It's good for you, teaches you strategy and critical thinking skills." Or so she'd been told. "But Harrison will have to teach it to me, because I've never played before, either."

"You haven't?" Harrison asked. "How could you consider yourself an educated person without knowing how to play?" He stood and reached for her, reeling her in. When his lips met hers, the kiss was soft and much too short. "Glad your unexpected meeting didn't keep you all afternoon."

She set her forehead against his shoulder for a few seconds, relieved to be there in his arms. "Thanks for picking her up and playing with her."

"Anytime." He brushed his chin along her forehead, then released her.

"You had a *meeting*?" Cleo asked, her tone saying it wasn't a good excuse. "You promised to pick me up today so we could go shopping for Cami."

"I know. Sorry, hon." Rosemary put a hand on Cleo's shoulder. "It wasn't a meeting. My mom showed up as I was leaving to get you from school."

Cleo's nose wrinkled. "Your mom? What's she doing here? She doesn't even like us."

And how sad that the little girl could tell so easily. "Yeah, she came to the hotel and we talked and then we told her to leave and not to come back. So, we're all done with her. No more Wanda." She hoped. "Do you want to go shopping still?"

Cleo looked at Harrison and then back at Rosemary. "Harrison said he'd let me make him crepes. I really want to try by myself, Mom."

Rosemary felt the lump rise in her throat again, as it did on the rare times when Cleo called her 'mom.' She wondered if Cleo said it intentionally, or if it was a slip. "Well, we can always shop tomorrow. There are still a few days until the party."

"All right!" Cleo rushed to the fridge and started pulling out ingredients.

Harrison took Rosemary's hand. "How did it go, really?" he asked in a low voice.

"Pretty crappy. She showed up drunk and friendly, as she often does when she's trying to get something she wants. Joel met me in the foyer within a couple of minutes and got her into his office. It was freaky weird. He was like, friendly and charming and stuff. I didn't know he could do that."

Harrison chuckled. "It's a little out of character."

"Exactly. Anyway, it didn't take long before she showed her true colors. She tried to slap me but he stopped her, then she hit him instead and he restrained her and called the cops. She's in jail at the moment, though I don't know how long she'll be there."

"Not long, probably." He touched her face. "Sorry you had to deal with that. It couldn't have been fun."

"It's my curse. We all have them." She looked over at her daughter who was cracking eggs into a bowl. "Life gives us compensations. Thanks again. Really, it was a big relief knowing she was safe and would be happy with you, even if I couldn't keep my promise to her."

"No problem. I have a flexible boss." He squeezed her hand.

"Isn't that lucky?" Rosemary crossed to the kitchen and took a seat at the bar so she could supervise without being in the way.

"What did your mom want?" Cleo asked.

Rosemary considered, but wanted to be as honest as possible with her daughter, and she definitely wasn't going to lie. As crazy as things had been, Cleo needed to believe that Rosemary would tell her the truth, and she needed to know when something wasn't worth worrying about. Like this. "She wanted money. My dad was paying her bills for a long time, and now he's not."

"Did you give it to her?" Cleo asked.

"Nope. And I won't, either. She's not going to bother me anymore. Or you." She tapped Cleo on the nose.

"Good. She's mean." She added milk and some melted butter to the bowl and then dug through the drawers until she pulled out a wire whisk. "We should stay for dinner again. We should eat with Harrison a lot. He cooks good like you."

"I think that can be arranged," Harrison said, joining them at the counter. "If Rosemary's okay with it."

Rosemary looked up at him and felt a flutter in her chest. "Yeah, I think I'd like that."

CHAPTER 21

"I think we should get her that statue of a unicorn," Cleo said as Rosemary urged her from the store window.

"Are you sure she's the one who wants it? I could swear one cute little girl is really the person who has a thing for unicorns," Rosemary said as she guided Cleo into a boutique next door.

"Clothes." Cleo frowned, looking at the merchandise around them. "She has a lot of clothes. She doesn't have any unicorns."

Rosemary just grinned and led the way back to the accessories. "She does have a lot of clothes. Cami likes clothes. You know what she doesn't have, though?"

"What?" Cleo was a little sullen now that it was clear she wasn't going to get her way.

"A really fabulous scarf."

Cleo stared her down. "She has lots of scarves."

"Not like this." Rosemary reached for a hand-felted alpaca wool scarf in swirls of peach and green that would go beautifully with Cami's new pea coat. "It's even pretty soft. Feel." She brushed the wool against her daughter's cheek.

"It tickles a little." Cleo said, starting to thaw. "I think Cami would like it better than a unicorn."

"How about you?" Rosemary picked up a raspberry one and wound it around her daughter's neck. "Are you sure you don't like this? Because I think you might need one."

It was too fancy for a girl her age, but Rosemary decided Cleo could use something nicer to go with her dress coat, and the bright smile that flooded Cleo's face when she caught a peek of herself in the mirror took away any second thoughts.

Cleo stroked the soft wool and twisted it a little to catch the sparse synthetic fibers that winked in the light. "It's pretty. Can I really have it?"

"It's not for rough housing in the snow," Rosemary said.

"I won't. I promise." Cleo bit her lip and gave Rosemary a hopeful look.

"Okay. Is that the color you want, or do you like one of the others better?"

"I like this one! And that one is perfect for Cami too. Can it be from me?"

"Yes. I'll find another gift to put my name on." Rosemary picked through the store and ended up with a funky but understated necklace in gold and semi-precious stones that would go perfectly with a new blouse Cami had worn to work a few days earlier.

"Can we get ice cream now?" Cleo asked as they waited for the clerk to run the transaction.

Rosemary had hoped Cleo would forget about that. "You want ice cream? It's fifteen degrees out there."

"You promised!"

"I didn't promise," Rosemary said. "I said 'we'll see.' That's not the same thing." Still, it was nice to have a day out with her girl instead of being cooped up in the hotel or at home and she'd like to extend the time a little, so Rosemary nodded. "Frozen yogurt then. There's a nice place around the corner." Cleo wouldn't really know the difference between the two, and Rosemary didn't need the extra fat from ice cream.

The roads were busy. It had snowed the previous day and five inches of fresh powder brought the skiers out in droves. The sidewalks had been cleared and salted, but Rosemary was still careful about her footing. "Why couldn't Dad have opened his new resort in Florida instead?" she asked no one in particular.

"Then we'd have alligators come onto the grass and scare people away." Cleo frowned a little. "I don't like alligators, 'cept in the zoo, because they can't hurt anyone there."

"That's right." It had been a long time since Rosemary had been to a zoo—she had gone with the Markhams when they took Cleo for her third birthday, but that seemed like a lifetime ago. "I've heard rumors that there's a zoo in Denver. You want to go when it warms up a little?"

Cleo's eyes widened. "Yeah! Do you think they have unicorns there?"

Rosemary laughed. "Honey, you know unicorns aren't real."

"Mom said there are unicorns in the Bible so they *must* be real."

There was no arguing with that. "Well, then. There you go—they were real. But they must be extinct because I've never heard of any sightings these days. I bet they have a lot of other really cool animals at the zoo though." She slid her free hand into Cleo's and felt contentment wash over her.

"Can we call Harrison to have ice cream with us?" Cleo asked.

"Not this time." But Rosemary thought the idea was a good one—if it weren't middle of the afternoon on a Wednesday. He'd been able to get away to pick up Cleo from school for an emergency, but she was pretty sure this didn't count as an emergency.

She reached for the door handle to the frozen yogurt shop when she heard a light crack and the window in the door shattered. She yanked Cleo to the side as two more shots fired off and people inside the store started screaming. No stranger to drive-by shootings—despite her middle-class address—Rosemary pulled Cleo close and hunkered behind a nearby car, putting the engine block between them and the street. Her heart pounded and the taste of fear was strong in her mouth while Cleo screamed into her coat.

"Are you okay, honey?" Rosemary kept her voice low, trying to give comfort, but heard the quavering in it.

Cleo didn't remove her face, just kept crying. She didn't seem to be bleeding, so Rosemary turned her thoughts to protecting her daughter. She fumbled with her cell phone even as she tried to figure out which direction the shots had come from, but all she knew for sure was that they had originated outside the store, and not from the sidewalk, or she would have been hit instead of the window. While she dialed 911, her mind zoomed through the possibilities of who would want to kill her or Cleo.

"911, what's the address of the emergency?" A woman's nasally voice asked.

"I'm outside Pauline's Fine Frozen Yogurt in Juniper Ridge. Someone shot at me and my daughter." Rosemary held Cleo tighter to her.

"Is the shooter still there? Did you see them?"

"No. I don't know. We were just about to go inside. I didn't see anyone. Maybe someone else did." It happened so fast, Rosemary was having trouble putting it all together.

"Was anyone hurt?"

"Not that I know of." She looked into the yogurt shop and saw a couple of people wiping at little streaks of blood off of their faces or hands, but there wasn't a crowd around a body on the ground, so the shooter must not have hit anyone. "It looks like there might be a few cuts from the glass, but I don't know about more." She tried to make her mind work, but it refused to click into gear.

"Okay, I'm sending officers and an ambulance. Can I get your name and phone number?" The dispatcher took the information and Rosemary heard her talking in the background as she paged officers.

The wail of sirens seemed to appear immediately and Rosemary put up a silent prayer of thanks and relief. No way was she moving an inch until she knew for sure they were safe, or that their current location was less safe than moving.

In ten or fifteen seconds, the sheriff's office cars double-parked in front of the store, their lights flashing.

Rosemary stayed where she was as a couple of cops—some with the county sheriff, and some state troopers—spilled out of their vehicles and walked around the area, checking it out, their guns ready.

Rosemary squeezed Cleo between herself and the car, covering as much as possible while Cleo sobbed, the sounds still muffled against her.

A moment later a state trooper approached her, his gun back in the holster. "A couple of the other guys are still checking out the alleys, but it looks like the shooter is gone." He hunched beside them. "Are you Rosemary?"

"Yes." She looked up and around them, still not feeling safe.

"You told the dispatcher that you thought the shooter was aiming for you?"

"Yes. I've had several odd things happen lately, accidents that didn't seem to be real accidents. I don't know why, though."

"Tell me everything."

Rosemary ran back through the details from the time they left the boutique until the black and whites arrived. By the time she finished, the ambulance had pulled in and the EMTs had come out to check on the people who had straggled out of the shop, trying to keep them separate from the people spilling out of the nearby stores. The other cops returned to take statements and scribble notes. Cleo still had her arms wrapped around Rosemary, but she was sniffling and listening, adding a detail here and there instead of crying. It was a big improvement.

"Why does someone want to hurt you?" Cleo asked Rosemary when the officer stood and moved away.

"I don't know, hon. I wish I did."

"Rosemary?" Joel's voice rang over the din of the milling crowd and Rosemary stood, her legs cramping, and looked for him. She'd sent him a quick text while they spoke with the officer, saying that there had been an incident and to come get them. If she had someone shooting at her, she wanted him and his Glock by her side.

He caught sight of her almost immediately and headed in their direction. Rosemary grabbed Cleo's hand, and just barely remembered to collect the bag with their purchases in it. Looking nervously around her, she met Joel halfway.

"What happened?" he asked.

"Details later. We need to get somewhere safe now." She felt an itch between her shoulder blades and couldn't help wondering if the shooter had joined the roaming crowd.

He took her back to his Range Rover—they'd send someone else for her car later. When they were headed for home, Rosemary filled him in on what happened, though she tried to downplay things a little. She couldn't believe she'd put her daughter in danger by taking her out in public when someone obviously wanted her dead. Eventually Cleo would get caught in the crossfire. How could she be so stupid?

"Okay," Joel said as he pulled into Sage's spot in the garage and closed the door behind him before letting them out of his vehicle. "Here's what we're going to do. You stay here while I check out the house. I'll double-check all of the door and window locks and close all of the blinds. Then you're staying home, out of sight. I'll have everyone come home for a meeting tonight and we'll see if we can figure out what's going on. An officer might end up on your doorstep again, but other than that, don't let anyone in except for family."

Rosemary nodded, feeling both a tiny bit more nervous about his hyper vigilance and better about the situation knowing he was on the job, though she couldn't figure out how the two feelings could be inside her at the same time.

"Why does someone want to hurt you?" Cleo asked from the back seat again.

"I don't know, bug." Except it was looking more and more like nothing that had happened since they returned to Juniper Ridge could be considered an accident.

"I'm not stupid, you know. I heard you tell the cop someone's been trying to hurt you." Cleo's face crumpled a little. "Why?"

"I have no idea. I wish I did so I could fix it." Rosemary squeezed between the bucket seats and released Cleo's seatbelt so they could snuggle together in the back.

Joel was probably only gone for a few minutes, but it seemed like longer. He came back into the garage, looked at his vehicle—the only one parked there at the moment—and his eyes widened in surprise for a second before he caught sight of them in the back seat. When he pulled the door open he huffed. "You about gave me a heart attack when I didn't see you in the front seat. Everything's clear in there, but *somebody's* still opening her window and forgot to lock it." He shot Cleo a knowing look.

She glanced away, hunching into her seat a little. "Sorry. I won't do it again. I just like the bird sounds outside."

"I know you do, but until Joel says it's safe, we need to keep the windows locked, okay, and always while we're not at home. Always, always." Rosemary didn't think she quite managed to keep the exasperation out of her voice.

"Okay." Cleo sounded thoroughly chastened.

Rosemary pushed the hair back from Cleo's face and pressed a kiss to her forehead. "No harm done. Let's go inside."

"You better cook up a storm," Joel advised. "Our crowd always demands food."

"Great. Decisions by committee are always so much fun."

"Don't smile too wide, it might stick there," Joel teased, straight-faced.

"That's highly likely." Rosemary turned back to her daughter. "All right, kiddo. Let's go inside and warm up. You have homework, too, don't you?" She fought the shivers inside her, the way she wondered what would happen next and if they'd really be safe at home alone even as she tried to act unconcerned for her daughter's sake. If they went back to normal routines, would that help Cleo feel safer?

"I don't feel like doing homework."

"All right, you twisted my arm. You can do the dishes first."

"Rosemary!" she whined.

Rosemary laughed. "All right, if you insist, you can do homework and I'll do the dishes."

Cleo stomped inside, but at least she was irritated now instead of scared, so Rosemary considered it a win. "Thanks," she said to Joel before going inside.

"You're welcome. Call if anything looks hinky or I'll see you in a couple of hours. I'll queue up the surveillance system from work while I finish reports."

"Okay." That made Rosemary feel better too. If Joel kept an eye on the house via camera, she could breathe a little easier.

Harrison had been feeling twitchy all afternoon. The hair on the back of his neck kept prickling and he couldn't focus on work. He stood to take a walk around the halls; a few minutes away from his desk might help him focus for what was left of his day.

He had taken only a few steps away from his office door before Joel stopped him.

"We need to chat." He set a hand on Harrison's shoulder and guided him back into the office, then closed the door behind them.

"What's wrong?" Harrison's twitchiness increased.

"Rosemary ran into a little trouble downtown. She and Cleo are completely fine, but I have the feeling she might not call and I didn't want you to hear about it from one of the staff."

Alarm ripped through him. "What happened?" Rosemary *hadn't* called him; was she really okay?

"They were downtown shopping and someone shot at them." Joel shrugged as if it weren't a big deal, but the dark blankness in his eyes said differently. "The police haven't ruled out anyone else as the target, but it's pretty clear to me that it's about Rosemary. She texted me after the police arrived and I got them out of there and back home. They're perfectly fine, not even a scratch on them, just shaken up. I double-checked the house before I let them inside and everything's locked down."

Harrison felt both relieved that they were okay and more worried than ever that someone was so determined to kill her—and the shooter had put Cleo at risk as well. His stomach churned at the thought of either of them being hurt.

And then there was the nagging thought that she hadn't called him herself. She hadn't thought to let him know what was going on or apparently considered that he would worry about her or that he could help. How could he get her to think about him as part of her world, as someone she could lean on if she needed something?

"Hey, you okay, man?" Joel asked.

Harrison nodded, making himself push back the worry. "If she's okay, I'm okay. Is there anything I can do?"

"Get someone to take you out to get her car?" Joel passed over Rosemary's keys. "It's just down the street from the frozen yogurt place. I told her to cook for a crowd tonight."

"I'll do that." He clenched the keys in his fist and told himself that their relationship was still new, even if his feelings weren't. It might take a while to get her to think of herself as part of a couple.

Joel excused himself, mentioning something about dinner on his way out the door. As if anything would keep Harrison away that night. He turned his fist over and noticed his knuckles had gone white, felt the key digging into his palm and decided he needed that walk more than ever.

As much as he wanted to run straight to her place and check on her, in his current mood it would start an argument, and that was the last thing he needed to do. So he'd walk it off, then close things out for the day and pick up her car. There would be time to discuss their relationship that night—when he got her alone.

CHAPTER 22

Dinner was nearly ready when everyone started to trickle in through the garage doors a couple of hours later. Rosemary stood over the stove checking the vegetables when Harrison walked in from the garage. He set her keys on the edge of the counter and crossed the tiles, wrapping his arms around her. "Joel told me what happened. You should have called me. How are you doing?" He pulled her tight and she returned the hug, needing the warmth and reassurance when everything had gone so haywire.

"I'll live, apparently, but I'm scared to death. I spent the past two hours thinking of all the ways it could have gone wrong." She tucked her face against his shoulder, grateful for his strength and comfort. "I should have called, but I didn't want to bother you when we were safe."

He touched her chin and tipped her chin up until their eyes met. "Next time, bother me, okay?"

"Okay." It was all she could say before he touched his lips to hers, the contact brief but reassuring.

A wolf whistle split the air and Rosemary pulled away to see Cami grinning at her.

"I couldn't help myself, not after the way you teased me when I got together with Vince."

"You're funny." Still, Rosemary extricated herself and returned to the food on the stove. "We'll be ready to eat in ten minutes if you lazy butts will get out the dishes."

Cami and Jonquil set into motion while Cleo called Harrison over. He sat beside her, holding her hand while she talked to him earnestly about what had happened that afternoon. Rosemary could only hear occasional words through the chatter going on around them, but Harrison's soothing tone seemed to calm the little girl. A moment later Cleo crawled into Harrison's lap, though she was getting a little too big for lap sitting. He interlocked his fingers as his arms surrounded her and Cleo fidgeted with his shirt collar as she had her dad's when she was younger.

Rosemary felt a sharp pain as she remembered how close Cleo had been to her father, how she had always hung on him, kept him company by playing on the floor of his office while he worked. She loved going out on the job with him.

Tears rose to Rosemary's eyes and she brushed them away, trying not to let the others see—it would damage her reputation as the tough one in the house. Thankfully Lana entered through the garage door with her six-month baby belly preceding her and attention shifted toward her. Blake came up behind, but didn't garner nearly as much attention. By the time everyone was finished patting the belly—something they didn't do at work—Rosemary was in control of herself again.

"I smell something awesome," Lana declared as she approached the stove.

"And it'll stay awesome if you don't touch," Rosemary said, shifting so she stood between Lana and the food. "Go take a seat and rest." While Lana may not be bad luck in the kitchen, she wasn't exactly skilled in the culinary arts, either.

"I've been sitting all day. Seriously, I'm pregnant, not disabled." Lana grumbled some more under her breath as she moved away.

Rosemary would have agreed with her, knowing how it felt to be over-protected while pregnant, but Lana looked like death warmed over. They were gearing up for the prince of Denmark and his entourage to visit in a couple of weeks and everyone was on overtime making sure things would go perfectly.

She opened the oven and smiled as the cheese bubbled nicely on the enchiladas. "Dinner is served. Where are the others?"

"Just in time," Delphi swept in with Sage and Joel right behind her. "Smells good. I'm starving. Do you think the snow is going to go away anytime soon? I need to get out for a ride."

"Wishful thinking," Rosemary said, imagining buttoned-down Delphi on her motorcycle—an incongruous image, if she'd ever seen one.

"I'll have to settle for a big helping of whatever you made, I guess." She smiled—something she didn't often do—or at least Rosemary rarely saw it.

"It's a nice consolation prize if you need one." Rosemary set the first pan of enchiladas on the trivet and went back for a second.

"Where's Vince?" Sage asked as Cami joined her at the kitchen island.

"Coming. He's still pushing snow in a couple of parking lots and he has one more driveway to clear before the owners arrive this weekend." She snagged one of the chips Rosemary had baked up from the extra tortillas.

"Did he come home last night?"

"For about five hours. The new plow's arrival was pushed back again. At this rate it'll be June before he has it." Cami frowned a little.

There was a knock at the front door and Joel opened it to let Vince in.

"Great, the whole family's home. Guess it's time for solution by committee," Joel said, shooting Rosemary a look.

She rolled her eyes—because it was expected—and plated up some dinner for Cleo and Harrison, who were still snuggled on the sofa. Cleo's head rested on his shoulder, her eyes at half mast. Rosemary watched them for a moment while she waited for Jonquil to finish with the veggies. Then she took a moment to survey the room. Six months ago she'd thought there was no way the six half-sisters would come together the way their father wanted them to. Now she wasn't so sure. Imaginary boundaries were being erased or redrawn, friendships had formed and she was starting to think maybe they wouldn't return to being total strangers when this all ended.

Maybe.

She'd been mostly without a family of her own for so long, she hadn't thought she could get used to so many other people surrounding her, in every pocket of her life, but she'd been wrong. She wondered what other surprises were still in store for her.

Cleo stayed awake long enough to eat, but then started to drift off again—still in Harrison's lap.

"Hey, bug, let's get you to bed." Rosemary was surprised Cleo was sleeping so early; it was barely seven pm and she usually had to be dragged to bed at eight-thirty. She touched Cleo's forehead, but didn't feel a temperature. Maybe the days' excitement had worn her out.

"Don't wanna go. Stay here. All night." The corners of her mouth tipped up like she was trying to hold back a smile.

Rosemary shook her head, but had to keep her own smile in check. "Let's get you ready for bed anyway, then we'll see."

Harrison shifted Cleo in his arms and stood—a significant feat considering the almost-ten-year-old was tall for her age. "I'll take her up."

Rosemary didn't protest, enjoying the play of muscles under his shirt as he shifted Cleo in his hold. She followed him up the stairs to Lana's old room. He removed Cleo's shoes while Rosemary grabbed pajamas and then he returned to the living room while Rosemary helped her daughter change.

"I want to stay downstairs and listen," Cleo said.

"You're too tired. Besides, it's grownup talk." She didn't want to risk scaring Cleo worse than she already was.

"I'm not a baby."

"No, you're not." Rosemary kissed her forehead. "I'll tell you all about it in the morning, okay? Get some sleep."

"Rosemary?" Cleo called her back when she was nearly to the door. "Will I have to go live with Mike if something happens to you?"

Rosemary returned to sit on the edge of the bed, disturbed by the question. "Nothing is going to happen to me, bug. Do you really think all of those people are going to let me get hurt, or send you to live with Mike?" Rosemary feathered the hair back from Cleo's face, loving the sweet, tired expression, noticing her own features there, and those of the biological father. She felt a fleeting moment of regret that he didn't get to see what a great kid Cleo was, then she let it go. "Sleep tight. I'll see you in the morning."

Cleo shifted onto her side and curled up before Rosemary even stood.

When she reached the great room a moment later, Rosemary wished this could just be a powwow about their 'ghost' like the ones they'd had a few months ago instead of about her situation.

"So, tell us what happened." Cami got down to business as soon as Rosemary took her seat beside Harrison again. "And don't leave anything out."

"I don't know what to say—we were out shopping and someone shot as us. I didn't see who it was, or notice anyone strange or unusual watching us, and we got away fine. Joel's probably been in touch with the detective and can tell you more than I can." Rosemary shrugged as if it wasn't a big deal, but she could still hear the echoes of the gunshots and shattering glass. She shivered a little and Harrison wrapped an arm around her shoulders. She shifted closer.

Joel continued the report. "Someone from another store thought they saw a man in his mid-to-late forties, brown hair, medium build lingering in the alley across the street a few minutes before the shots, but she didn't get a good look at him and wasn't able to give a better description."

"And it might not have been him anyway," Rosemary said, discouraged.

"Right. The police department is trying to get more details or find a store security system that might have caught him to see if the woman can identify him, but that might take a few more hours to confirm. He said all of the store owners on that street are cooperating, though. It scared everyone that something like this could happen in this sleepy little town." He said these last words with a twist of wryness. Considering the troubles they'd been having at the hotel, there had to be a lot more going on in town than most people knew.

"So we're stuck with nothing," Delphi said.

"Nothing useful, anyway. At least not right now. Except the general description the woman gave the officers." Joel turned to Rosemary again. "Does it bring anyone to mind?"

"Only about two dozen guys who fit it," she said. "Could it be any more generic?"

"Well, if that was the guy, it wasn't Rulon, because he's too young," Harrison pointed out.

"True enough, but who does that leave us? The only people I know in town are the ones I work with and I don't think I've ticked anyone else off enough to shoot at me."

"What about your mom? If she's looking for a payout, she could be after you," Delphi suggested.

Rosemary was shocked by the feeling of betrayal that rushed through her system that her mother could try to have her killed. She'd thought that Wanda couldn't hurt her anymore and that nothing she did would shock her, but that thought did. When she shook her head, it was mostly because she couldn't face the possibility. "No, she couldn't do this."

"She is in town, Rosemary. And it's possible she paid someone," Joel suggested.

"As if my mom knew any thugs who do wet works." She took a cleansing breath, then considered it a little more. "No, she's grasping and underhanded, and I wouldn't be surprised if she calls again, begging—despite Joel's threats—but she wouldn't have me killed. I'm sure about that."

But why would someone want her dead? She knew she was a little abrasive at times, but she didn't think she'd been that bad. "My first concern is keeping Cleo safe. Can I do that if someone is after me? What do I do?"

"I've been thinking about that." Harrison rubbed his thumb across the back of her hand, which he was holding. "Maybe the two of you should take a trip somewhere. My mom loves to have visitors."

Sage's eyes brightened. "Yes, and she thinks you're great. She said you have a sweet old soul."

"I guess you pulled the wool over Darla's eyes. How did you manage that?" Delphi asked Rosemary.

Rosemary ignored the cut and shook her head. "I can't take off right now, not with everything going on. But maybe we could send Cleo for a visit." She touched her stomach, feeling a little sick at the thought of being separated from her daughter so soon.

Cleo waited until she heard raised voices from the adults downstairs, then crept out of her bed to listen in. She hadn't been that tired, but knew they wouldn't let her stay for the conversation, and hoped if they thought she was asleep, they would talk about things they wouldn't tell her.

She sneaked onto the balcony just as Harrison suggested they visit his mom. At first Cleo thought that sounded great—she loved Harrison and Sage was really cool too, so their mom was probably nice, even though they said she didn't ever eat meat or eggs—weird. Then Rosemary said she wanted to send Cleo there by herself. Cleo crumpled a little at the thought. Rosemary didn't want her? She wanted to get rid of her?

"Just a question," Jonquil said, raising her hand a little to draw attention to herself. "How do we know that this is about Rosemary? Is there a chance it's actually about Cleo?"

Cleo felt the air whoosh from her lungs. She had wondered when someone would realize it was her fault. It had to be her fault because her parents were dead and now someone was after her and Rosemary again—even Jonquil could see it and Cleo thought they were friends. Maybe Jonquil didn't really like her, either.

Rosemary looked at Jonquil, wearing her scary face. "What? Why would anyone want to go after Cleo? She's just a kid."

"I know, don't shoot me, but all of this did start after she arrived," Jonquil said. "And the snake was in her room. It's possible this isn't really about you at all."

"Then how do you explain my little ski accident? And the car windows?" Rosemary's words floated up to Cleo as she returned to her room, feeling a little sick. It was true, it was all her fault and she had to do something to keep Rosemary from getting hurt. Even if Rosemary didn't really want her anymore. Cleo couldn't blame her; she caused a lot of trouble for everyone. She was surprised they didn't try to get rid of her before now—send her to live with Mike. But he didn't really want her either.

The tears started before she even reached the bed. She climbed inside and pulled the covers over her head, turning her face into the pillow so no one would hear her. She had to do something to make this better for everyone else.

"Do you really want to send Cleo to my mom's alone?" Harrison asked.

Rosemary shook her head. "No. I couldn't stand sending her away to stay with a stranger and not knowing how she is. But what do I do? I can't have her here, at risk, either."

"I think you need to stop driving to work," Jonquil said, holding up her leg, which had been in a cast until a couple of weeks ago. She'd broken it in a car accident with Sage. "You never know if the guy will go after that—someone already took out some frustrations on it. With these winding roads, it's not exactly the safety zone." She shot a glance at Sage, who flushed a little.

"I'm so sorry about that," Sage apologized.

"It wasn't your fault. We didn't have any reason to think your car wouldn't be safe," Joel soothed.

"In either case," Harrison said, looking at Rosemary, "maybe you should take turns in different people's cars until we figure out what's going on."

She realized how rough this must be for him too; he'd come close to losing his sister and now the woman he was dating was in danger. Their relationship might be new in a lot of ways, but he was serious about her, even if she didn't understand why. "And maybe Cleo shouldn't be out in public with me for a while." She slid a hand over her roiling stomach.

"Let's not get ahead of ourselves yet," Joel said. "Tomorrow morning I'll see what's going on with the investigation, if the detective doesn't contact me first."

"I'll hang out here for now, then return to get them to work and school," Harrison offered.

"Yeah, I bet that'll be a real chore," Delphi said dryly.

"He'll hate it, but he'll throw himself on the proverbial sword for our Rosemary," Cami agreed, her lips twitching.

"I'm just a nice guy, what can I say?" Harrison wore a smirk.

"That's our cue to leave," Vince said, standing and taking Cami's hand to pull her up. "Call if you need anything at all. We're just down the street."

"Ditto. And double-check your daughter's window," Joel suggested as he stood.

Rosemary nodded and watched the others leave. Delphi and Jonquil both went down to their rooms, leaving Rosemary sitting on the sofa with Harrison.

CHAPTER 23

"We really should check Cleo's window," Harrison suggested when the silence between them grew uncomfortable. It was a feeling he hadn't experienced with Rosemary lately, but he had things he wanted to say, things he wasn't sure she was ready to hear. He decided to wait a few more minutes, at least.

He followed her up the stairs and stopped in Cleo's bedroom doorway, watching as Rosemary walked over and tested the lock, then stopped to pull back the covers that almost completely covered her daughter's face.

"Rosemary, has everyone gone home?" Cleo asked, her voice sleepy.

"Most everyone. Harrison's going to hang out for a while longer," Rosemary said as she tucked the blanket under Cleo's chin.

"He should stay. I don't want him to go home." Cleo's voice was more alert now, but her face was obscured by darkness.

"He has to go eventually," Rosemary said.

"No, he doesn't. Sage's room is empty. He's her brother, he can stay there again. I don't want him to go home." There was a trickle of fear in her voice.

"Honey," Rosemary started to protest, but Harrison walked over and touched her shoulder.

"It's okay. I'll stay if it'll make you feel better," he told Cleo.

"Good. You should. I like you. Don't leave us. Rosemary needs you." Her voice turned sleepy again and she turned away, curling into herself again.

"I like you too, bug. I'll stay and I'll see you in the morning." His heart nearly broke when he heard the longing in her voice. She'd

185

lost so much already—what would she do if something happened to Rosemary? What would *he* do now that he'd finally gotten her to let him in—even if it was only a toe-hold? Was she really opening herself to him, or had the fact that she hadn't called him today proved that she was keeping her distance?

"Thank you." Cleo's words were barely more than a whisper.

He led Rosemary out to the great room.

"Thank you for staying so she'll feel better," Rosemary said when he pulled her down to sit beside him.

Harrison wrapped his arms around her waist, drawing her back against his chest. "I didn't do it just for her. I did it for me too."

"You're worried about us?" Rosemary asked with a bit of laughter.

"Yes." He kept his irritation out of his voice, which left it flat and matter of fact.

"Come on, we're at home," she blew off the threat with her usual bravado.

"I know, but being at home hasn't always meant you were safe, has it? Not here, and not before you came here." He referenced her childhood, knowing it was a dirty tactic, but wanting her to take this seriously. "I feel better being with you, having you in my arms so I know you're safe."

Rosemary's brow furrowed. "Are you upset about something—something besides the shooting, anyway?"

"Depends on how you look at it, I guess."

"Then how I'm looking at it is that you're upset about something and I want to know what the deal is. I've had a really crappy day and don't need you to go all passive aggressive on me."

That irritated him even more. "Okay, here it is straight out, then. I'm mad that you didn't call me after you were shot at."

Her brow furrowed. "Do you carry a gun? Because I thought Joel was the obvious choice." She pulled away a little, but he wouldn't let her get far.

"Yeah, he is the obvious choice. At first. But once you were safe you should have called to tell me what happened. Didn't you think I'd want to know?"

She rolled her eyes and turned a little condescending. "So this is about you? You need to know every detail?" She glared at him.

He huffed a little, managing not to grit his teeth. "No, this is about me wanting to be there for *you*. Me wanting to be someone you know you can turn to when you're upset or need someone's shoulder to cry on."

"I'm a big girl, Harrison. I don't need your shoulder."

"Right, because today wasn't rough for you at all?" He stared her down, knowing she was bluffing.

She shunted her gaze away. "It wasn't a picnic."

He took a moment to breathe off his frustration, being mad at her wasn't helping. Maybe lightening the conversation would. "Why do people say that about picnics anyway? They have ants and the grass ends up being wet half the time. There's nowhere really flat to put your soda can and the wind blows away your paper plates."

She smiled.

"Talk to me, honey."

She swallowed hard and he watched the movement in her graceful neck. He reached out, running his finger down the pale column, loving the softness of her skin and the way she shivered in response to his touch. He hated the thought of her being scared or injured.

"It terrifies me to think that I could lose her." Rosemary had one arm crossed protectively over her stomach and wadded a handful of her shirt in her fist. "I can't stand the idea that she could get hurt because of me. It's even worse knowing I can't stop it because I don't know why someone is doing this." Tears leaked onto her cheeks and he wiped them away, gently rubbing his fingers over her skin.

"It's not your fault," he said, "and we'll figure out who's behind it." If she would let him help.

She huffed a little and looked away.

"We will," Harrison reiterated. "Has Joel failed us yet?"

She gave him a half smile. "Nope. But no one is that strong all of the time. He's got to miss sometimes."

"He won't be working alone."

She rested her head against his shoulder and he just held her while she silently cried. He felt useless, like he should be doing something to fix the problem, like she needed help and he wanted to be the one to give it, but he didn't know what to do.

"I'm such a baby," she said after a long while.

"No you're not. You've probably had that coming for a long time." He kissed her temple. "Feel any better?"

"I don't know. They say crying helps, but now I just have a stuffy head and puffy, red eyes." She chuckled a little and grabbed a tissue out of the box Sage kept stocked on the end table. "Why do you put up with me?" she asked.

He tipped her face up so he could look her in the eye, wishing he could make her really understand. "Because I love you."

She sucked in a breath. "You keep saying that, but how can you know? You must be mistaken. It can't be real. Not this fast."

"It's real," he said, frustrated at her refusal to accept his feelings, even if she didn't return them. "This, between us, it isn't my imagination, and my love for you has grown for so long—it's definitely real. Tell me it isn't."

Then he kissed her, sliding his hands up her neck and into her hair, gliding his mouth over hers, taking it slow and easy, even as part of him urged for hot and fast. He brushed his fingers down the column of her neck again, down her shoulders and arms, then threaded their fingers together, using only his mouth and soft, sweet kisses to show her what he really felt.

She had become his world in the first moment he saw her on that ship. She'd become part of him that day, though he'd fought against it. He'd dated and tried to find that moment of connection again, but he'd never felt it with anyone else. It had always been about her, even while they argued about stupid things at work.

Now he wanted to show her the other side of the man she'd been sparring with for more than six months so when she tried to intensify the kiss, he refused to give in, keeping it soft and loving, showing her what love was, with every slide of his fingers, every brush of lips. He needed her to understand that she made him feel complete, whole.

She lifted her head and looked at him, her eyes a little out of focus. "What was that? I've never..."

"Been so loved?" he asked and brushed his mouth against hers again. "Let me show you."

She turned and looked over her shoulder to Cleo's room with the door opened a few inches, then back and nodded. "You have to sleep in Sage's room, though. If she comes to my door during the night..."

It hadn't been his intention, but he could work with that. "Deal." He kissed her again, then stood and followed her to her room.

Cleo had pulled back into herself by morning and Rosemary watched her get ready for school, wondering if the previous day's shooting had finally become real for her little girl. "Are you okay?" she asked.

"Fine." But Cleo didn't look up from her bowl of cereal where even the marshmallows were starting to get mushy.

Rosemary touched her forehead, looking for a temperature, but it felt fine.

Cleo pushed the hand away, scowling. "I'm not sick. Why do you always think I'm sick?"

"You're just not acting like yourself." Rosemary moved to the sink, trying not to feel hurt by Cleo's grouchiness. "I wanted to make sure you were feeling all right."

"I'm fine." Cleo looked over at her. "What did you guys talk about last night?"

"Not much," Rosemary felt like all they did was go around in circles. "Harrison stayed in Sage's room last night and Joel's going to get back with the police today to see what they found out. Then we'll figure out what to do from there."

"Okay." Cleo took another listless bite of her food.

Rosemary sat beside her daughter. "Are you worried because of what happened yesterday? Because we're going to make sure you don't get hurt, you know?" It was a bald-faced lie, she shouldn't promise anything of the sort, but Rosemary didn't know what else to do, and she'd give up anything to protect Cleo.

"How can you promise that? You don't know! Something could happen as soon as we walk out of the house." Her facade of listlessness lifted just long enough for her to yell at Rosemary, then she looked worried and returned to the quiet little girl Rosemary didn't know at all.

Harrison came down the stairs just then, looking all freshly showered and shaved and way too well rested considering how late they'd been up the night before. "Hey, ladies, are you having an old fashioned family argument over breakfast?"

"We're not arguing," Cleo grumbled.

"Apparently we're not arguing." Rosemary shot him an exasperated look. "Cleo's worried that we won't be able to keep her safe. I can't blame her, it was pretty scary yesterday."

Harrison slid a hand onto Cleo's shoulder and gave it a squeeze. "We're going to find a solution and do everything we can to figure out who's been trying to hurt your mom."

"She's not my mom," Cleo said fiercely. "My mom is dead. She only brought me here because she had to." She pushed away from the kitchen bar and rushed up the stairs.

Rosemary was horrified to hear her daughter say that. Had she said or done anything to make Cleo think she didn't want her there? "Cleo, that's not true."

190

"Yes it is. Don't worry. I won't get in your way." She went into her room.

"Cleo," Rosemary called, disbelief filling her.

"I'm getting my backpack!" she called down the stairs, her voice filled with anger and tears.

Harrison slid an arm around Rosemary's shoulder. "Try not to over-react. She's upset and she has every right to be. All you can do is show her that you love her and we'll find out who this is and put an end to it."

Rosemary turned her face into his shoulder for just a moment, taking in his scent and enjoying the feel of his arms, remembering how it had been for them the previous night. Just the memory made her tremble. She'd never known a man's arms could make her feel like that—special, cherished. Had she ever felt that way before? If so, she didn't remember it. All of that layered on her distress about Cleo's behavior. "I don't know what to do."

"I know. I'm sorry."

Cleo came back down the stairs, wearing her coat and with her bulging backpack flung over one shoulder. "Let's go. I want to go to school."

Rosemary had her own things to deal with, so she didn't fight— she'd have Cleo as a captive audience in the car, after all.

They went out to the garage to Harrison's car and Rosemary held open the back door for Cleo to climb in.

"Why are we taking Harrison's car?" Cleo asked when they were all seated.

"He offered to drive."

"Is he going to pick me up after school?"

"No, I might have Jonquil bring me to pick you up."

"Why not just take your own car?" Cleo crossed her arms over her chest, staring sullenly at Rosemary.

Rosemary looked at Harrison, feeling helpless to explain without scaring her daughter worse. He gave her an encouraging look. She sucked in a breath. She had promised not to lie, but how much did she want to say? "Last fall Sage's car was tampered with at work. She was in an accident."

"That's when Jonquil got hurt, isn't it?" Cleo asked.

"Yes. We decided it would be better if I didn't drive for a few days. Just to be safe."

"Mom and Dad and I were in an accident," Cleo said, staring out the window.

"You were?" Rosemary hadn't heard about that. "When?"

"About a week before... the bombing." Her voice choked a little.

"What happened? Did someone hit you at an intersection?" Rosemary wished she'd known. Had this been bothering Cleo for a long time?

"No. We went to see Uncle Mike and when we came back something happened to the engine and Dad lost control. The car rolled. That's why they have that new one."

Rosemary remembered the shiny new Honda in the garage, still sporting the temporary plate printout in the back window. "That must have been really scary. Were you hurt?"

"No. But Mom had scratches on her face and got kinda bloody and we hurt the next day."

"I bet you did. I'm so glad you were okay." But wheels were starting to turn in her head. Jonquil's suggestion that maybe this wasn't about Rosemary, but somehow about Cleo was starting to gain traction—but it still didn't explain why both of them seemed to be targets. She thought of the Honda again and remembered the accident in the garage. If that had been Cleo who set the avalanche of equipment off, she could have been killed by the flying Dutch oven or camping paraphernalia. Had she been the intended target all along?

The elementary school was ridiculously close to their house, apparently, because Harrison pulled up in front of the school before Rosemary could respond.

"Yeah, sure you're glad I was fine," Cleo said. "Because we all know I've made things so much easier for you." She slammed the door behind her and ran toward the school.

Pain ricocheted through Rosemary. "What did I screw up?"

Harrison covered her hand and threaded their fingers together. "You don't have to do anything for her to be upset. She's been through a lot. Let's see what the cops have to say and go from there. There's always this afternoon to work things out with her."

Rosemary decided not to argue—he was right, and that would give her time to mull over what Cleo had just told her about the accident. Could she know something about someone that would make her a target?

CHAPTER 24

Rosemary wanted to rush straight to Joel's office and demand answers, but she knew he would let her know when he had any information. That left her antsy and irritable as she worked the morning rush. She kept her mouth closed as much as possible to avoid snapping at people and focused on what had to be done. When Sage showed up at the kitchen door mid-morning, Rosemary didn't pause to ask what she wanted, she just turned the work over to someone else and headed out the door. Joel seemed to like having her there as a buffer when he dealt with difficult issues for the sisters. "Joel heard back?" Rosemary asked.

"Yes. He asked me to bring you to his office. Harrison will join us there." Sage didn't say anything more.

Rosemary wasn't sure how she felt about Harrison being automatically added to the discussion, as if he belonged. His declaration of love at lunch the other day had nearly knocked her off her feet. Hearing it again the previous night hadn't been much better. She liked having him around, and was learning to trust him, but she wasn't ready to completely ignore everything she'd learned through the years about men and relationships. Watching her sisters with their husbands proved not all relationships were like her mother's, but she still didn't trust she could maintain a healthy relationship for the long haul—even if Harrison *did* think he loved her.

Still, she'd never had someone show her tenderness the way he had the previous night. He told her he loved her and then he'd shown her with every action. Would he suddenly open his eyes one day and realize he'd made a mistake? That she wasn't the person he thought he saw?

194

Sage filled the few minutes it took to reach Joel's office with chatter about something that had happened in the spa that morning and Rosemary made sounds of interest as she tried to anticipate what Joel had to say.

Harrison was already there when they arrived. He looked up when they came in and smiled at Rosemary, though it was a tighter smile than the one he'd said goodbye with that morning. Did he already know?

"Tell me they learned something," Rosemary said in lieu of a greeting.

"I have a picture," Joel said and pulled a page off the printer. He passed it to Rosemary.

It didn't matter that the picture was grainy and out of focus, Rosemary recognized the man in it immediately—she sat in a nearby chair, her legs feeling weak. "It's Mike. Don's brother. He thought he should have had custody of Cleo. He told her about me being her birth mother and tried to stir up trouble at the reading of the will." She tried to figure out why Mike would come after her. "Cleo said he told her he wanted to take care of her, but he talked down to her like she was a stupid kid. She didn't want to live with him and wondered why he wanted her to live with him when he didn't like her very much." She was stumped. "Why would he come after *me?*"

"That's a good question. Why would he want to raise Cleo if he didn't like kids much and you were taking care of her?" Joel asked, but the words sounded like he was trying to make her think, as if he already had an idea or two.

Harrison walked over and took the seat next to Rosemary. "Did the Markhams leave anything major to Cleo?"

Rosemary thought about it. "There are some papers the lawyer sent me dealing with the estate, but they still owed money on the house, and the car was brand new, so it was probably a bigger liability than asset. Don made a decent living, but he didn't get paid that much and she was a stay-at-home mom."

"Wait," Harrison said, holding out a hand. "Didn't Cleo say they were all in an accident the week before the bombing? Some kind of engine malfunction when they were coming home from visiting Mike?"

"Yeah, but—"

He cut her off. "And didn't you say the lawyer keeps sending papers and talking about the estate? And that Mike said you were looking for a payoff?"

Rosemary stopped breathing for a second. "Yeah. But there can't be that much. I haven't really looked at the amounts but there just can't be."

"What if there is?" Joel asked.

She stared at him. Why had she just pushed the papers to the side and figured she'd get around to them later? "I guess there could be."

"How would Mike get his hands on it?" Joel asked.

"By taking over as Cleo's guardian—"

"Which you won't allow as long as you're alive," Harrison interjected.

"And there's very little money for the guardian anyway—or to kill her so he and Cecelia's brother become the only people left to inherit." That made a little sense, anyway. Rosemary yanked her phone out of her pocket and scrolled through the contacts list to the estate attorney, then hit send.

It took several minutes to navigate through the receptionist and get into the attorney—Rosemary considered herself lucky that she didn't get stuck waiting for a call back. It only took a few minutes for the attorney to give her the bottom line for the estate's value. She was still in shock when she ended the call. "They have investments of nearly a million, and each had half a million in life insurance. Then there's the equity in the house. We're talking serious money here."

"So he does have a reason to want Cleo dead. That much cash is nothing to sneeze at," Joel said, picking up the phone. "I'm calling

Detective Carlson and I'll have him check into the car accident as well. We'll see if they thought it could be sabotage."

Rosemary's heart clenched with worry. "I have to call the school, let them know someone might try to hurt Cleo and they have to keep a closer eye on her. Maybe we should bring her home for a few days, until they can catch Mike." Her hands shook as she searched for the school's number in her phone's contact list and Harrison had to take the phone from her and find the number himself. "He wouldn't have come if he didn't want to get rid of me or Cleo, would he? He would have asked to see her if he actually cared, wouldn't he?" Could she be jumping to conclusions? But it didn't feel like it. It finally felt like everything was clicking into place, and that scared her even worse.

"I'm sure she's fine," Harrison said. "We'll just ask for them to check with her teacher to make sure she's doing okay, and then we'll tell them to keep her inside until you pick her up." When he passed the phone back to Rosemary, she could hear the school's phone starting to ring.

"Juniper Ridge Elementary. How can I help you?" a woman's voice greeted her.

"Hello, this is Rosemary Keogh. My," she had to stop herself when she nearly said daughter, "I'm the guardian for Cleo Markham, who's in Mrs. Shepherd's class."

"Yes, I remember when you registered her."

That made Rosemary feel a little better. "Well, apparently someone might be trying to hurt her. It's her uncle, Mike Markham. Can you check with the teacher and make sure she's okay? Then keep her inside until I get there to pick her up?"

"I'd be happy to, Ms. Keogh, but, um, she didn't come in to school today. I thought you were calling to excuse her."

"What?" Rosemary felt all of the blood drain from her head and thought she might pass out. "I dropped her in front of the school this morning. She should be there."

"I'll double-check with her teacher, but I looked at the absentee list about fifteen minutes ago, and she was on it. Just a moment."

Rosemary leaned on Harrison's shoulder, unable to blink or think of anything but her little girl and wondering if she was going to turn up dead somewhere. She forced that thought away as quickly as she could—they were going to find Cleo, and she was going to be perfectly fine. Thinking otherwise would just be borrowing trouble—and drive her crazy.

The receptionist came back on the line. "Ms. Keogh, I spoke with Mrs. Shepherd. She said she hasn't seen Cleo at all today. I'm sorry. We'll check the school grounds and see if she's hiding out somewhere. I'll let you know if we find her."

"Thank you." Rosemary hung up and thought for a moment that she would pass out. "Cleo didn't make it to class today. She's gone. What if Mike has her?" She looked into Harrison's eyes and saw her worry echoed back to her.

Harrison was glad Joel picked up the phone and called the cops the second Rosemary mentioned Cleo was missing because Harrison had his hands full making sure she didn't pass out on the floor. "Hey, honey, stay with me. Cleo was mad when she got out of the car. Maybe she decided to go for a walk and then went back home instead of into school." He was trying to think of what he would have done at that age; sneaking back home would have been high on his agenda—if his mom hadn't lived on the land where she worked. She would have caught him for sure.

"Or maybe she went to a friend's house," Sage suggested. "I'll drive home and check for her there." She grabbed a pad of paper and a pen from Joel's desk and placed them in Harrison's hands. "You two think of everyone she knows, all of the places she's liked best or asked to visit since she got here and we'll have the police search them, talk to her friends, that kind of thing."

"Right, of course." Rosemary seemed to snap out of her shock a little, taking the paper from Harrison, then started scribbling furiously.

"Do we have a recent photo of Cleo?" Sage asked.

"I think Jeremy took some pictures when he did that wedding the other day—we were in the hall." Harrison thought for a moment. "The girls probably have some too. I think Jonquil snapped a few on her phone while we were out making snowmen." He had to swallow back the surge of panic rising inside him at the thought of that sweet little girl in the hands of a killer. He pulled out his phone and called Jonquil first. When she said she thought she had a good one, he asked her to send it to his phone. He started a list of what Cleo had been wearing that morning, as close as he could remember. Rosemary added to the list and Harrison smiled when he pulled up Jonquil's picture of Cleo, hair sticking out of her cap, her bright eyes shining as she held a snowball like she was getting ready to launch it at the camera.

Harrison wondered if they would really need all of this for the deputy, but decided if not, Joel and Sage were being smart to keep them busy. He was slightly less freaked when he was doing something reasonably productive.

Deputy Oliver came in and had Harrison send the picture of Cleo to an email address to be disbursed to the rest of the department. He sent the description of the clothes she'd been wearing that morning and then grilled them for anything more they could add to the list of friends and locations that Rosemary could come up with. He also said they'd run an Amber Alert with Cleo's and Mike's descriptions.

"What else can I do?" Rosemary asked when the deputy folded away the paper.

"Keep your cell phones turned on and handy and we'll call if we come up with anything else. It's possible she'll try to contact you, too," he said. "You should probably go home and wait for her."

Rosemary's phone rang then and she fumbled a little with it before hitting send. "Hello? Oh, you're sure? Okay. Can you wait for her? Thanks." She looked disappointed when she hung up. "That was Sage, she said she's been all through the house and Cleo's not hiding out there. She said she'd stay in case Cleo goes back."

"Okay, we'll work on this list and see what we come up with." Deputy Oliver stood and moved to the door. "Don't worry, we'll do our best to find your daughter."

It was only then that Harrison realized they had been referring to her as Rosemary's daughter, even though they hadn't announced that to the world—Cleo hadn't made that decision yet. He stood and followed the deputy out the door. "I'm sorry, just a second, if you don't mind?"

"What?" He looked impatient.

"Sorry, I know we need you out there but I just realized—Cleo found out a few weeks ago that Rosemary is her birth mother. She hasn't told anyone yet, as far as we know. Can you refer to her to the others as the guardian for now? If it turns out she is hiding in someone's basement or something, I don't want her to be upset that we told the secret when we told her it was her decision."

The deputy nodded. "I'll take care of it."

"Thanks." Harrison watched him walk away, then stood and let the worry and fear rush over him for a moment. He loved that little girl as much as he loved Rosemary and while he'd been trying to keep it together since the attack the previous night, he only managed it by pure determination. He took another deep breath and returned to Joel's office. Rosemary was in there and she was going to need his support—so he needed to be able to give it.

CHAPTER 25

Rosemary was only able to sit in Joel's office for ten minutes before she was going out of her mind. She turned to Harrison. "I can't go back to work and I can't sit here. Take me out to see if I can find her somewhere."

He nodded, looking relieved.

"Trent said to hang around," Joel objected. He had already sent word through the network of employees to keep an eye out for Cleo in case she showed up and he had several employees going out to check out the grounds for her.

"We'll stay where we have a cell signal," Harrison said, joining Rosemary. "It's not like Cleo would have wandered outside of that area anyway. Not on her own. Maybe Rosemary will see something that will help us know where to look." He took Rosemary's hand and gave it a squeeze. "I'll go get my jacket. You do the same. I'll meet you back in the parking lot."

Relieved she was going to actually do *something*, Rosemary exited and hurried to her office in the kitchen.

"We have a problem," the assistant pastry chef said as Rosemary walked back into the kitchen.

"Then you'll have to handle it. I have to go."

"It's a big deal," he insisted.

"My little girl is missing and we think someone may be trying to hurt her—I think my problem is bigger than yours. Have Tate handle it or take care of it yourself. As long as you're not stupid, I don't care what you do today." She snatched up her coat and strode out. The assistant stared as she walked away.

Rosemary thought she handled that pretty well considering she didn't call him any names or scream at the top of her lungs—both of which were serious temptations.

She met Harrison at his car and slid inside.

"Where to first?" he asked.

She considered for a moment while they drove through the parking lot. "Your place. She doesn't have a key or anything, but she likes it there, and you have that covered porch that's out of the wind."

"Gotcha." He turned his car left at the intersection.

They checked every nook and cranny of his place and came up empty. They went to the park down the street from the school—Cleo had mentioned wanting to play there, but Rosemary hadn't taken her due to the heavy snow pack. They checked the woods behind the sisters' house and swung by a few of the stores Cleo had liked the most during their few shopping trips.

The sheriff's office has sent out a CodeRed message to the locals' telephones with Cleo's description, so when they were downtown, Rosemary got stopped every few minutes by someone who recognized her and wanted to know if they'd found Cleo yet. After fifteen minutes, she was ready to head out to less popular areas.

"They're canvassing her friend's houses," Harrison said when they were stumped about where to go next.

"Yeah." Rosemary's brain wasn't working at top speed, but she had another idea. "Did we mention Etta Talmadge's place?"

Harrison turned the car toward Vince's mother's home. "I don't remember seeing it on the list. You think she went there?"

"It's the only other place I can think of in walking distance that we didn't tell the deputy about. She spent a few afternoons there with Hannah, playing in the barn. Maybe she'd hiding out there." Hope welled in her chest, but she tried not to let herself believe it too strongly.

"We're stretching now," he cautioned.

"I have to keep hoping. The alternative is that Mike got to her and I can't," she stopped as a sob rose in her throat. "I just can't think about that."

"I know. Me either." He touched her knee, then pulled into Etta's driveway. The large Alpine cabin loomed out of the forest with a bank of south-facing windows so big the reflection could blind passing jets.

A new thought struck Rosemary. "What if we find her but Child Protection Services learns she ran away and they decide I'm not fit and take her away?"

"That won't happen." He took her hand and squeezed it. "They have to understand that she'd be upset—it's been rough for her, but it's not your fault."

She faced him, desperate for reassurance. "How do you know that?"

Harrison took her face between his hands and turned her to look at him. "It's going to be okay—hold on to that for now." He kissed her forehead. "Let's go inside."

Rosemary felt a little better as she waited for Harrison to come around and open her door. "I hope Etta's here."

"All we can do is hope," he answered when her hand was in his.

Etta greeted them at the door, a bright smile on her face. "What are you doing here today? I didn't expect a visit."

Harrison took the lead this time. "Cleo ditched school today. We're trying to figure out where she went. We remembered her talking about that play area you had built into the old barn for your grandchildren and hoped you'd let us check it out."

Her brow furrowed with worry. "Of course, just go on back. I haven't seen her. Is everything okay?"

"I'm sure it'll be fine." Rosemary made herself act certain because the alternative was unbearable. "We're just looking around. It's a scary world out there."

"Don't I know it? If you find her, bring her in for some cookies. I just pulled some out of the oven."

"Thank you, I might do that." Rosemary thought that Etta's cookies could have won international cookie contests and had been trying to get the recipes from her.

She was glad Vince was so diligent about ensuring his parents' walkways were cleared as they circled the house to the barn. The structure was ancient and rarely used except to keep vehicles for repairs, store kids' toys and house their play area.

Harrison opened the well-oiled door into the play area and Rosemary held her breath. They had already determined that calling out her name was unlikely to get them an answer, and more likely would make her run, so they didn't yell into the semi-darkness now.

Rosemary's stomach dropped when they walked in and she didn't see Cleo. She felt ready to melt into a puddle when she noticed a pile of blankets shift from the corner of her eye. She found Cleo huddled against the wall, covered in the old horse blankets and with her arms wrapped round her. She had a frown on her face, even as she breathed deeply and evenly—a sure sign she was asleep.

Relief flowed through Rosemary as she reached out to touch her daughter's cool face, and Cleo shifted slightly in sleep. "Hey, honey. Wake up. You've got to be freezing."

Cleo moved again. "Mom? Why's it so cold?" She shivered a little, then opened her eyes. Confusion filled them for a moment before she placed where she was. "Rosemary, Harrison." She glanced around her and then looked a little cowed. "Am I in trouble?"

"Not until I get you warmed up. We can discuss everything else later." Rosemary reached for her hand while Harrison shouldered Cleo's backpack. "Why didn't you go to class today?" Rosemary asked.

It took a long moment before Cleo answered. "I didn't want to. I was mad and I didn't want to talk to anyone, but I thought about this place and decided to skip school." She turned her face down, but looked up at Rosemary, as if she expected to be in big trouble.

"Did you skip school in DC?" Rosemary wondered if she was in for eight years of fighting Cleo's truancy.

"No." She frowned and kicked at the pile of blankets she'd been huddled under a moment ago. "But things were easier there."

204

Rosemary glanced at Harrison, who was on the phone with someone, telling them to call off the search. She considered their new theory about who was behind everything and decided she needed to take the rest of the day off and spend it with her daughter. "I think we need to go home so you can tell me all about it."

"Home? You're not making me go back to school?" Cleo asked, confused.

"No. We're going to spend the afternoon together—just you and me, but you're going to bring home all of the work you missed today and you'll have to catch back up before you can go skiing with Jonquil again." Since they had talked about going out that weekend, Rosemary had the feeling Cleo would get to her work pretty quickly.

"Okay." Cleo grumbled a little under her breath as they reached Etta's front porch.

"I'm just going to let Etta know we found you, so she doesn't worry," Rosemary explained.

Etta was sorry they wouldn't stay for cookies, but plated up almost a dozen and sent them home with the trio. Harrison delivered Cleo and Rosemary to the house, walking them inside. He hesitated for a moment, watching the mother and daughter absorbed in each other. Rosemary glanced up and saw his pursed lips and furrowed brow. He scooped Cleo into a big hug, picking her up. "I was worried about you, sweetie. Don't scare me like that again, okay?"

Cleo looked a little shame faced. "I'm sorry. I didn't want you to worry about me."

"We always worry about you because we love you." He pressed a kiss to her forehead and set her down again before turning to Rosemary.

"Thanks for helping me search." She felt oddly awkward.

"I wouldn't have wanted to be anywhere else." He slid his hands onto her waist and pulled her to him, laying his lips on hers. "You two are so important to me; I always want to be here for you."

"I'm starting to get that." Warmth filled her chest as she realized he was straight-up serious.

"Good." He looked torn, but finally released her. "I ought to get back to the office and leave you two to work things out. Don't have too much fun without me. And make something yummy for dinner—I'll need a consolation prize if I have to work while you two play hooky."

"Play hooky?" Cleo got a confused expression on her face.

"Skip school and work," he explained and added to Rosemary, "Double-check the locks and call me if you need anything."

"We will." Rosemary leaned in and gave him a kiss goodbye before watching him return to his car. There was a pensiveness about him she didn't understand. Something she needed to figure out. Later. Apparently some quiet time with her daughter was on the menu. Now to get her to open up and talk.

The first order of business was a change of clothes to something warm and snuggly and a cup of hot cocoa for Cleo, who was shivering from her morning in the barn. Rosemary made herself a cup of Sage's calming tea mix and then whipped together some tomato soup and grilled cheese sandwiches for lunch.

Rosemary kept up a steady stream of chatter about going to the Markhams' sometimes after school when she was a kid and the cozy afternoons she shared with Cecelia when things were bad at home or she was frustrated with people at school. She didn't ask about that day, though. That would wait until Cleo was warm and full.

She nearly skipped the sandwich for herself, but Cleo piped up, "Did you already eat lunch? Where's your sandwich?"

She debated for a few seconds—cheese was pretty fattening, and she was for sure eating one of Etta's cookies. Still, she had a weakness for grilled cheese and she could always stick to veggies at dinnertime. She had the feeling this afternoon was going to be difficult, so she probably better do it on a full stomach. "Nope, I'll have a sandwich with you." When she saw the relieved expression on Cleo's face, she was confused. "Were you worried?"

"You're too skinny, it makes you look sick and I don't want you to be sick."

Rosemary was floored—Cleo thought she looked too skinny too? "Did Harrison put you up to saying that?"

Her brow wrinkled. "No. But you don't eat very much. You tell *me* to eat healthy, but you don't."

Rosemary hadn't realized she was so obvious that Cleo noticed it. Had she taken the diet too far? Harrison had commented that she was too thin. She'd thought he was just being difficult—he was the one who had said she was too fat during the cruise where they first met. But a couple of her sisters had made comments about her thinness too. She would think about it. "Maybe I worry about my weight too much. Have you seen pictures of me when I was in high school?" She sliced some more cheese for her sandwich, trying to get some perspective on the situation.

"No. You never showed them to me."

That was probably true. Rosemary wasn't sure she had any with her, either. "When we finish talking this afternoon, we can dig through some of my things and see if I've got one hiding out somewhere. I was... not skinny back then. Not at all." She'd been on the chunky side even before she became pregnant. When she'd met Harrison it had only been a month or so since the birth and she was heavier than ever.

"No you weren't."

"No, really. I was a *chunky monkey*." Rosemary tried to lighten the mood by laughing off her body size, which had been so painful for her.

This made Cleo giggle a little. "You're making that up."

Rosemary pulled out her cell phone and dialed the spa. When someone answered, Rosemary asked if Sage was available. A moment later, she put it on speaker phone. She buttered two more slices of bread while she asked, "Hey, Sage. You remember when you met me on the cruise?" She was pretty sure Sage would.

"Of course. You and Harrison sparked off of each other immediately."

"That's a nice way of saying I offended you both within seconds of meeting," Rosemary said, still feeling a little guilty about it, even after all of these years.

"Oh, there were the other kind of sparks too."

Rosemary decided to redirect the topic. "Don't try to be nice, but Cleo here doesn't believe it when I told her that I was a chunky monkey back then."

That elicited more giggles from Cleo. "No way!"

"I wouldn't say that," Sage said carefully.

"Oh yeah? How would you put it?" Rosemary knew Sage would be honest but kind at the same time.

"Hmmmm. I guess I would say that your curves weren't packed on in quite the same way they are now. Or like they were in May, when you had curves."

Rosemary ignored the last comment and laughed. "In other words, I was round all over." She pointed the spatula at Cleo. "I told you so."

"You were beautiful even if you weren't so thin then—and Harrison could barely take his eyes off of you, regardless of your shape."

The thought made Rosemary's stomach quiver a little. He'd said as much, but she hadn't believed him. "Really?" she asked it in a dry tone.

"Oh, yeah. He pointed you out to me before we met—you drew him to you even then."

Could it be true?

"Rosemary and Harrison sitting in a tree," Cleo started to chant, loudly.

Sage joined in for "K-I-S-S-I-N-G."

"All right you two, that's enough. Sage, don't you have a treatment or something?" Rosemary wasn't really annoyed—she was embarrassed, and that was a hundred times worse.

"I do. See you tonight. Cook plenty; I'm sure there will be another powwow." She said goodbye and hung up.

"So see," Rosemary changed the subject away from her and Harrison kissing in the tree and then marrying—she was so not ready for that kind of commitment. "I really was overweight back then."

"You were not. Sage didn't say that."

"That's because she's really sweet and doesn't ever want to hurt people's feelings. You should really try to emulate her when it comes to that. It's part of why everyone loves her so much." She flipped the sandwiches and wondered why she'd followed the impulse to call Sage—better yet, why she'd *had* the impulse to call Sage.

"You aren't mean to people," Cleo said. "Not unless they deserve it."

Rosemary beamed at her. "That's right, so when I ground you for a week, you'll know you deserve it, right?"

Cleo's eyes widened. "A week?"

She considered that. "Well, not this time, maybe. But sometime before you go off to college I'm sure it'll be a week—you're my daughter after all."

"So you were naughty?" Cleo asked, intrigued.

Rosemary hedged, not wanting to encourage bad behavior. "Not without a good reason." Of course, her *good* reasons sometimes ran along the line of 'because I want to' or 'because Wanda doesn't want me to.' No need to tell Cleo that though.

Cleo grew quiet. "I had a good reason today."

"I'm glad to hear it. And after we've talked about it, you and I can decide what kind of punishment we think you deserve for scaring us all half to death."

Cleo stirred the dregs of her cocoa. "Were you really worried about me?"

"Of course, bug. Always." Rosemary poured the soup into their bowls. "I worried about you when you were still with your parents too, you know? Cecelia used to send me weekly updates with what you were up to and funny things you said and did." Especially when she was in Europe studying under culinary masters and couldn't make it home much.

"Really?" Cleo tipped her head and narrowed her eyes. "Then why did you want to send me away?"

Goggling, Rosemary nearly dropped one of the sandwiches on the floor. "I didn't want to send you away. What makes you think that?" She managed to transfer both sandwiches to plates.

"I heard you guys talking after you put me in bed last night. I wasn't sleeping." She looked a little sheepish. "I knew you wouldn't let me stay and listen."

Rosemary tried to remember the conversation. "You heard Harrison suggest we go to his mom's for a while where it's safe."

"And you said you were going to send me alone. Because I'm so much trouble that you don't want me around." Hurt filled Cleo's eyes.

Rosemary completely forgot the food as she circled the island and pulled her daughter into a hug. "I want you to be where it's safe—that's the most important thing to me, but I couldn't send you to a stranger's all by yourself—even if you would probably love Darla even more than you love me. Everyone does. She's special. And she loves everyone; she never seems to get mad and, well, she's just really terrific. Except she doesn't eat any kind of meat—not even eggs or cheese. Weird, right?"

Cleo wrinkled her nose. "Who doesn't eat cheese? That's just wrong."

"Agreed." Rosemary pushed the food in front of Cleo and started her own meal. She had scraped most of the cheese off her enchiladas when she made them the previous day, but she loved the stuff and savored the buttery sandwich and soothing soup. She'd work out longer tonight. Then she remembered what Cleo had said about her weight. She'd have to think about it.

"Why did you think I would send you away?" Rosemary asked when they were both seated.

"You did before."

Her heart broke all over again. "I've never done anything so hard as the day I signed the papers for you to live with Cecelia. It was the right thing for all of us then, but it wouldn't be the right thing now." She touched Cleo's arm when she didn't look over and waited until their gazes met. "There's nothing on this planet that would make me give you up again. I love you, Cleo, and whether you decide to tell anyone else or not, you're my daughter. Your Uncle Mike can't have you and no one else is going to take you from me, either."

"What if you change your mind?" Tears started to leak down Cleo's face.

"I won't. No matter what happens, no matter what crazy things you do, I will never, ever stop loving you or ever not want you to be around, okay?"

Cleo studied her, uncertainty on her face for a long moment. "Promise?"

"Promise." It seemed like a reasonable segue, so Rosemary took it. "Why did you run off today?"

"I didn't want to go to Harrison's mom's house," Cleo muttered. "I thought you didn't want me anymore."

"Why would you think that?"

"Because this is all my fault."

"What's your fault?" Rosemary was totally lost.

"Everything was fine before I came here. Then you started to get hurt and stuff, and that didn't happen before I came here, so it must be my fault. Mom and Dad probably died because of me too. Mike said I was a brat—that day before the car accident. He said they never should have adopted me."

Fury roared through Rosemary. No one had a right to speak to a child like that—not any child, never mind hers. "No way. Your parents died because someone wanted to kill a senator..." she trailed off, suddenly realizing maybe she was wrong about that. As far as she knew, they hadn't heard back on the car, whether it was an accident or sabotage, but if it was sabotage, could the bombing have been about the Markhams, and the senator had been collateral damage? She mentally shook her head. No way was Mike psycho enough to kill a restaurant full of people just to get two out of the way. Was he?

"See, you know it's my fault." Cleo set down her barely touched sandwich, as if not hungry anymore.

"No, it's not." Rosemary pulled herself together though her mind still raced. "Look. We don't know for sure why this is happening, but we think it might be about money. Your mom and dad had a bunch of investments that had paid off and we think someone wanted the money and maybe that's why they died. That's not because of you."

Cleo's eyebrows lowered, making her forehead furrow. "But how would they get the money if Mom and Dad were dead?"

Rosemary considered how to tell Cleo that Mike might be behind everything, but how did you say something like that? "There are ways, but only if your parents weren't around anymore." She wanted to warn Cleo that Mike might try to hurt her, but she didn't want to admit her suspicions if there was even a tiny chance she was wrong. "I don't want you to freak out, but I don't want you to trust anyone but my family—not even your Uncle Mike. Not until we clear this up."

"Not even Harrison?"

Rosemary realized she had been counting him in as part of the family. When did that happen? "Harrison is fine. And Vince and Joel and Blake, but don't trust anyone else right now unless I specifically tell you it's okay, all right?"

Cleo's face was pinched and her eyes wider than usual. "I'm scared."

"I know." Rosemary pulled her close. "This is really hard, but we're going to catch whoever did this so it won't last forever."

"Okay." She didn't seem convinced.

"I'm not sending you away and you're not responsible for what's happening. Is there anything else that's bothering you?" Rosemary asked when a moment had passed.

"I hate math."

Laughter and relief bubbled inside Rosemary and she couldn't help but let it out. "I can't fix that, sorry."

"Am I in big trouble?" Cleo's voice was worried.

"Nope. But next time you decide to skip school—even if you have a great excuse—you will be, okay? And you're going to have a whole lot of homework to catch up on after skipping today." Catching up would give Rosemary a reason to keep Cleo close until they caught Mike.

"Deal." They shook on it.

"Now, eat your lunch before it goes totally cold."

Cleo sipped at her soup and pulled a face. "Too late."

Rosemary stood and grabbed their bowls. "Microwave, here we come."

Cleo's smile was tentative, but showed her relief.

Rosemary decided to consider it a successful chat. Now if they could put all of her daughter's and her own fears to rest.

Cleo's words that she was so skinny she looked sick popped into her head again. She tried to remember how hard she'd worked to lose the baby fat, but in that moment, she just thought of the way so many of her clothes hung too loose on her now. Had she been starving herself and didn't realize it? Had she let Harrison's words—words that were nearly a decade in the past—influence her when she ran into him again last summer? She had the feeling that they were right. Maybe it was time to take stock of things again.

"How are you holding up?" Sage asked from Harrison's office doorway shortly after he returned to work.

He smiled and gestured for her to come in. "I'm doing okay. I think worrying about her shaved a few years off my lifespan, though."

Sage closed the door behind her and took a seat across his desk. "It was pretty scary. I wondered if you'd stay there for the rest of the day."

He noticed the careful way she phrased it, as if not wanting to make it sound like he was slacking on the job because he hadn't stayed at the house. "I thought about it—seriously almost turned around and went back half a dozen times before I reached the hotel—but it wouldn't have been the right move."

"Why not?" Sage studied him. "You can't seriously think you don't belong there, not after everything that's happened."

He played with the pen he'd been writing with, turning it end over end. "I don't know what to think. Last night..." How could he put the way he'd felt holding Rosemary in his arms into words? Or the disconnected way she'd made him feel when she didn't call him for help? "It's two steps forward and one step back with her. And all of them baby steps. Besides, I was able to see that they were fine, settled at home and safe. I think Rosemary needs to have some quiet time with Cleo without anyone else there as a distraction. If Cleo's running away or skipping school, she needs someone to focus wholly on her. I told them that I was just a phone call away."

"Good." She tipped her head, studying him. "Have you told Rosemary you're in love with her?"

He remembered how she'd acted the first time and an ache entered his chest. "Yeah. It kind of wigged her out," he said, appreciating that Sage smiled in response. He put on a good front. "I think I like keeping her a little off balance. She's such a control freak sometimes."

"That she is. And a little off-balancing can be good, but don't overdo it, especially with the rest of her world being such a mess."

She paused for a moment, studying him. "You two are good together, you know? I see good things for you. Don't forget your own gift. You had that impression for a reason. You don't need to feel disconnected anymore."

"Duly noted." He tried to make light of it, but felt chills slide down his back that she could read him so well. Holding on wasn't proving simple, but he couldn't let go yet. He just hoped the baby steps they were taking led to the place he wanted end up.

CHAPTER 26

"I don't know if I can take this much family togetherness," Delphi said as she dished up a bowl of Rosemary's fragrant stew that night. "Cami's birthday in a few nights makes three this week with everyone gathering 'round the table. My parents weren't really into family togetherness unless we were putting on a nice face for society. And there are way too many of us now."

"We're going to have to start charging admission to cover the cost of dinner so they don't bankrupt me," Rosemary agreed.

"Bankruptcy is so likely, considering your great number of designer clothes and shoes and your itty-bitty income," Delphi said with a voice so devoid of sarcasm a stranger never would have realized it was implied.

"Shut it." Most of her sisters had nagged Rosemary to buy a few new outfits—some fancy party dresses and new designer boots. But she spent most of her life in a chef's jacket and didn't see the point to updating her wardrobe with expensive items just for the sake of owning them—though her tennis shoes were the highest quality she could find when it came to comfort. It's not like she ever wore a dress other than weddings anyway. Well, there was that date she had with Harrison, but that was an aberration. "My top-of-the-line cooking and baking equipment is more expensive than some of those four-inch heels you all think are necessary anyway. Footwear should be comfortable first. Fashion is a distant second." Of course, the melding of the two was important, but her idea of fashion and theirs didn't often coincide.

"Rosemary, we still have so much to teach you." Cami patted her shoulder. "Don't worry, when this mess is over, I'll drag you to Denver for the day to show you what Nordstrom is really all about."

"Yippee. I can't wait."

Cami just smiled.

"Any word from Deputy Oliver?" Rosemary asked Joel when he walked past with two large chunks of fresh bread on his plate.

"A few things. I'll fill everyone in when we're all sitting. Did you mention our suspicions to Cleo about the perpetrator?"

She shook her head. "I talked to her about the money issue and not to trust anyone outside this room, but that was it. She thought it was her fault that everything was happening." Though Cleo was across the room, they were both careful not to mention Mike aloud.

His lips pressed together in a tight line. "I'll take that into account when I give the report."

"Thanks."

As soon as everyone had their food and were seated in the great room, Joel started the topic that had drawn them all there. "I heard back from Detective Carlson today. He said the police department back east confirmed that there was tampering with the Markham's car."

"Someone wanted to hurt my parents?" Cleo's voice quavered and she huddled closer to Rosemary.

"It looks like it. And no, that's not your fault," he said as her face started to crumple.

"Have any groups taken responsibility for bombing the cafe?" Rosemary asked carefully.

His face tightened. "No. Which supports your theory about the senator being a casualty. I called a buddy who works Homeland Security now and he thinks we might be right."

That made Rosemary's stomach twist with fear and anger. Mike had killed all of those people to get to his own brother. She nodded and a glance around the room confirmed that most of the others were aware of her suspicions. "So now what?"

"I put them onto other options. They're going to try for a warrant for the home. We'll see what they come up with. The sheriff's deputies have been chasing their lead here, but the place he had been staying said he checked out yesterday and no one seems to know where he is now."

"Do they think he went home?" Rosemary doubted it, but staying here was the height of stupidity, so it depended on how big his ego was.

"The detective thinks not. There's no plane ticket in that name, in any case. Carlson's spreading the search into towns a little farther away but still in driving distance of here. Hopefully they'll get something soon."

"In the meantime, what are you going to do about staying safe?" Lana asked.

This had been on Rosemary's mind, even while she talked about everything and nothing with Cleo as they cooked dinner. Sending Cleo to school without protection seemed foolish at best. She didn't want to make her stay inside while the other kids went out for recess, but she couldn't let her be exposed—and if Mike was willing to kill a café full of people, what would stop him from hurting a classroom of kids? Sticking her in the kitchen office to work on school stuff while Rosemary cooked seemed extreme too, though. "I've been mulling over options, but nothing feels right."

"I was thinking about it," Joel said. "The presidential suite is open for the next four or five days. It would be easier to control who comes and goes there, and to keep your location a secret. There are too many ways to get into this house. We could send you away, but if he thinks you're still in town, he's more likely to hang around and it'll be easier to catch him."

"You could hire a couple of the off-duty cops again to monitor the hall so they could be armed and make an arrest if he shows up, too," Lana said.

"That's what I was thinking," Joel agreed. "And there aren't many rooms down that hall. It would be easy to block them out— find an excuse to work on them so they can't be rented. Then we won't have any guests with a legitimate excuse to be in the area, minimizing risks and possible issues."

"Because corporate is totally going to believe that we need to do work on them five months after the hotel opened?" Jonquil lifted her brows in punctuation.

"So she rents them all for a few days, it's not going to break her," Cami said.

"I say do it," Delphi added. "Then I won't have to listen to Rosemary snoring through the air vents."

"I do not snore," Rosemary protested, though she had no idea if she did or not.

"Yes you do," Cleo said. "Not loud though. I can't hear it from my room."

"Great, not loud. That's so much better." Rosemary crossed her arms over her chest and feigned irritation.

Harrison grinned at her from across the room. She met his gaze and felt warmed by the affection in his eyes.

"So, everyone's agreed?" Cami asked.

"Yes. And I pre-emptively blacked out the rooms to keep them empty, so you can go there tonight," Joel said. "I also contracted for the guard—apparently Lana and I are on the same wavelength. He'll be relieved to know he'll be in the hotel and not doing surveillance from his car out here."

"What about Cleo's school?" Rosemary wondered.

"Call them and explain that you're going to home school for a few days. I'm sure the principal or school counselor can be trusted with the truth and to smooth the way for you," Sage suggested. "Have the teacher get the homework together. One of us can pick it up, along with her extra school books. And you can do kitchen paperwork from your room, or pop down to berate and harass your employees once or twice a day if you need to."

"Hey," Rosemary threw a pillow at her. "I do not berate or harass. Often." But she felt unbelievably relieved to have the decision made. She really hoped Mike made a mistake soon so they could end this unending worry.

"I don't get it." Cleo threw the pencil across the room. She liked the presidential suite, but she hated not being able to go to school—and still having to do homework. What was the point of being in a hotel if she still had to do the stupid math?

"Go get your pencil." Rosemary's voice was perfectly even and her face didn't look even a little annoyed, no matter how hard Cleo had tried to rile her that day.

Cleo crossed her arms over her chest and slouched in her chair. "I'd rather be at home."

"I'd rather be in Aruba, but I'm not. Finish your math and English and we can cut out for a couple of hours to watch a movie." Rosemary pulled a newly released DVD from the bag of goodies Jonquil had brought up earlier.

Cleo squealed and jumped up, running over to grab the DVD case.

Rosemary held it out of reach. "When your math and English are done."

"I hate math. When am I ever going to use it?" Cleo crossed her arms over her chest.

"Every day." Rosemary's eyes never left her spreadsheet. "Ask any of us; we use it all of the time."

"That's what calculators are for." Giving up, Cleo snatched up the pencil she had thrown.

"Sometimes I can't find a calculator, and sometimes it's just better to be able to figure something out for yourself."

"Well I can't figure this out. It doesn't make sense. I can't make it come out right and I don't know why." Cleo slumped back into her chair and started tapping the pencil eraser on the table.

Rosemary sighed and clicked a few keys, then came around to her side. "Let me see what's going on."

Cleo pointed to the problem and held back a smile. It was nice having Rosemary here helping her. It reminded her of her mom—her real mom. She wasn't sure what to think yet about Rosemary being her birth mom. Why had they kept it a secret? It wasn't like she couldn't handle it—she was almost a teenager, wasn't she? Well, okay, she was almost ten, but that was practically a teenager.

She wondered if Hannah's grandma was mad that she sneaked into the barn without permission—would she decide Cleo couldn't come over anymore to play there? She missed Hannah.

"You forgot to carry the three."

"What?" Cleo came back to reality with a mental thud. She hadn't been paying attention to Rosemary at all.

"Here." Rosemary tapped the spot with her fingertip. "You forgot to carry the three. That's why it didn't work out right."

"This is so dumb."

"Good thing, otherwise it might talk back to you," Rosemary stood and returned to her side of the table. "You'll be fine, just keep working hard and it'll come. I promise. Math wasn't my best subject either."

Cleo erased the part she messed up. "What was your best subject?"

"PE. And when I got to junior high, they let us take home ec. I suck at sewing, but the kitchen arts part was pretty cool."

"You sewed something?" Cleo found that hilarious. She could see Rosemary trying to pick out a seam she sewed wrong and swearing under her breath like she did when she worked on reports.

Rosemary picked up a Lifesaver mint from a nearby bowl and threw it at her. "Yes, and it was terrible. I ripped it into rags after it was graded. No I don't have any pictures, get back to your math."

"This is terrible," Cleo said of the assignment. "Can I rip it into rags too?"

"After it's been graded." Rosemary clicked the mouse a couple of times and scribbled a note on the paper beside her.

221

Cleo leaned back to see the corner of the DVD sticking out of the bag. She really wanted to watch that, so she ought to get her homework done. She guessed. "Are you and Harrison going to get married?" The thought had been on her mind a lot lately—Rosemary and Harrison were always kissing, and didn't people get married when they kissed a lot? She didn't think she was ready to call anyone dad, but she liked having him around. He was really nice, and he made her feel safe.

Rosemary had been reaching for her water bottle and her head whipped over to look at Cleo. "Where did you get that idea?"

"'Cause you kiss him all the time and I heard him say that he loves you before he left last night. You didn't say it back. Why not?" She watched Rosemary's jaw twitch and congratulated herself for making Rosemary act funny. Usually she was so focused she could hardly be pulled away from her paperwork. It was so boring!

"I, um. Well. Hmmmm." Rosemary turned red and looked as if she didn't know what to say. "We haven't been dating that long. I think we need to date for a long, long time so we don't make a mistake if we decide to get married." She took another swig of her water. "I'm not thinking about marriage yet. I'm too young."

"You're almost thirty. That's not too young to get married. Hannah's mom got married when she was only nineteen. You were pregnant with me when you were only nineteen, too."

"See how handy math came for figuring that out?" Rosemary said brightly. "I was only nineteen. But I wasn't ready to get married that young. Some people are—apparently—like Hannah's mom. Some of us need more time first. Like me. And I'm not almost thirty—I'm going to stay twenty-five forever. No matter how wrinkled I get."

Cleo giggled, though she knew Rosemary was trying to avoid the questions. "Do you love Harrison?"

Rosemary stopped at the window and looked out, not saying anything for a long moment. Just when Cleo was going to nag her again, she finally spoke. "I don't know. I feel something for him. He's pretty great, isn't he? But do I love him?" She turned to Cleo. "I love you. I loved your parents, but that's really different. Loving Harrison comes with complications." She put a hand to her heart. "It's a little scary to think of loving Harrison like that."

The movies never made love look scary. "Why? In the movies it's just all kiss, kiss, I love you, let's get married."

That coaxed a chuckle from Rosemary. "Relationships aren't easy. Just ask Lana and Blake. That was one big mess of not-easy almost from the start. Screwing things up *is* easy, and I don't like to screw things up."

"But Blake and Lana are still married. They're happy." Cleo didn't get why adults made it so hard.

"They are. Insanely, disgustingly happy. And the baby just makes it all that much better. They can't wait to hold their little boy." She smiled at Cleo. "Just like your parents and I couldn't wait to hold you." She walked over and crouched beside Cleo. "You're my best thing, you know that? It might have been hard, but I've never, ever regretted having you, and your parents loved you more than anything—as much as I did."

Cleo slipped her arms around Rosemary's shoulder. "I love you too." She missed her mom and dad so much. Everything was so much easier when they were around. Tears squeezed out of her eyes, but she didn't want to turn into a baby, so she wiped them away before Rosemary could see and changed the subject back to Harrison. "So are you going to marry Harrison? I think it would be cool to live at his house."

Rosemary stood again. "I don't know. You'll have to wait and see like me. Now get back to work."

Somehow the math didn't seem so bad after that, but Cleo decided she was going to make sure Rosemary married Harrison—it would make everything somehow a little bit better.

CHAPTER 27

Cleo woke from her nightmare with a surprised scream, sitting upright in bed as if the pillow were hot. It took her a moment to realize it was just a dream. She wasn't on the sidewalk being shot at. Rosemary hadn't really been hurt like she had in the dream. She still heard Rosemary's last words echoing in her ears, blaming Cleo for her death.

"Hey, honey, are you okay?"

She blinked in surprise when she realized the form in the doorway was Harrison. She rubbed away the tears from her cheeks. "Where's Rosemary?"

"She went downstairs to finish decorating Cami's birthday cake. How are you? Did you have a bad dream?" He entered the room and sat in the chair next to the bed.

"Yeah. It scared me, but it wasn't real." She tried to be strong like Rosemary, to pretend she wasn't scared, even though her hands felt shaky.

"No, it wasn't real. You want to talk about it?" He took her hand, rubbing the back of it, soothing her.

"No. I'm fine." She didn't want to admit that she was still scared, that the thought of having Rosemary blame her for everything that was going wrong made her tummy feel funny.

Harrison waited for a few more seconds. "I had something I wanted to talk to you about."

"What?" She eyed him curiously.

"I know you've been through a lot the past couple of months. It's been pretty crazy."

"Yeah." Sometimes she felt like she couldn't catch her breath, it changed so fast.

"You know I love Rosemary. How would you feel if I married her someday? I don't know if it'll happen anytime soon, but... someday." He looked kind of nervous.

She smiled. Rosemary said she wasn't going to marry Harrison for a long time, but Cleo knew better. "I'd like that. I like you, and I think Rosemary does too. She doesn't talk about it, but I can tell."

"I hope so. What do you think about my place—do you think you'd be okay living there? I know Rosemary said she'd consider moving back to Washington DC when she finished her contract here, but we both have jobs here. Would you be okay with staying?"

Cleo didn't say anything at first—he was asking her what she wanted? Most adults didn't care, they just did what they wanted and dragged the kids with them. "Would you move to DC if I wanted to?" Would he tell her the truth?

He pursed his lips for a moment. "I don't know. I know we'd definitely consider it if you really feel like you need to move back there, but I don't know if Rosemary can live in your old house. It's close to her mom's place, isn't it?"

Cleo nodded. "Yeah. She's not nice. I don't like her."

"It probably wouldn't be easy for Rosemary if she lived that close to her mom."

Cleo hadn't thought about that, about anyone except for herself. She missed her friends back home and the comfort of her own furniture, her stuff, and the quilt her mother made for her. She meant to ask Rosemary to pack the quilt, but forgot. But she was friends with Hannah now and some of the other girls were nice too. Did she want Rosemary to want to keep her this time? "Would I be able to bring some of my stuff here, like my furniture?"

He smiled. "Yeah, I think we could manage that. In fact, I bet Rosemary would be happy to have your stuff shipped here anyway. Have you talked to her about it?"

She frowned. "No. She's so worried all of the time. I'm in the way. I try not to cause too many problems." She still worried

Rosemary would send her away again, like she had when she was a baby.

He brushed the hair away from her eyes. "Not so much like Rosemary, are you?"

"What?"

"Nothing." He shook his head and the skin by his eyes crinkled when he smiled. "We'll talk to her when things calm down, see if you two can take a few days off to go back and pack the things you want most."

"What if she doesn't want to?" Cleo asked.

"She will. She wants you to be happy and comfortable. So do I."

Cleo considered that. The funny feeling in her tummy had changed so she felt happy again. "I think I love you, Harrison."

He smiled. "I definitely love you, bug."

She had a sudden thought. "I don't know if I'd ever be able to call you Dad. I still miss my dad."

"That's okay, I know you loved Don. Rosemary said he was a really good dad, and I don't think I could ever replace him, even if I wanted to. You can just call me Harrison if you want and if you change your mind later, that's good too. Do you think you can go back to sleep now?" His voice was a little husky, like he might cry, but she wasn't sure.

She felt better, not scared anymore. "Yeah."

"Goodnight. I'll see you in the morning." He pressed a kiss to her forehead, then got up and walked out, leaving the door partly open so she could see the hall light.

A moment later she heard the main door open and she got out of bed to see if he was leaving her in the hotel, alone. She didn't want to be alone. She saw Harrison pull Rosemary close and kiss her, so she must have just arrived.

"How's Cleo? Did she sleep through?" Rosemary whispered so quietly Cleo could barely hear it from her crack in the door.

"She woke for a few minutes, but she's going back to sleep now. She had a nightmare, but she didn't want to talk about it."

Rosemary shifted out of his arms and Cleo could see her face—there was worry in her eyes. "I wish she would, but she never does."

"I think she's missing some of her things from home."

"Then we'll have to make a trip back to get them." She brushed her mouth against his. "Thanks."

They moved to the sofas and Cleo returned to her bed. Just like that and Rosemary would make a trip to get her things? Starting to feel secure in her new place, her new life in this big family for the first time, she snuggled under the covers. Maybe everything would be okay after all.

Rosemary stood in her bra and panties staring at herself in the mirror. Cleo's words kept echoing in her head, accompanied by all of the remarks she'd heard from Harrison, Sage and the others. Was she too thin? She considered how loosely her clothes fit her now and how she had liked her body shape before moving to Colorado. She'd been content, so when had that changed?

Now that she studied her reflection, she realized part of her mind had automatically reverted to that wounded nineteen-year-old when she met Harrison again. He'd never so much as hinted that she was overweight in the past six months, but somehow she'd convinced herself that she wasn't good enough, thin enough, nice enough. She couldn't change her character much, but she could change her weight. So she had.

But Cleo was right—she was too thin now. And she grew tired faster than she used to. She'd excused it as stress about Mike and being a full-time mom, but it wasn't about that. She knew it now.

And Cleo needed her to have the energy to keep up, so Rosemary was going to have to make a change. She stared at her own eyes in the mirror. "This stops now." Then she nodded and dressed for bed. Once again, this was something she could control. So she would.

It had been three days since Cleo skipped school and took ten years off Rosemary's life. They were both bored out of their skulls despite the fact that Rosemary's sisters had all stopped in more than once and Harrison spent all of his break time and into the wee hours of the night in their suite.

There was no sign of Mike, but the detective confirmed that he hadn't flown anywhere—unless he was using an alias—and the police in his hometown had raided his home and found evidence that he was behind the bombing. Meanwhile, she really needed to get back to her kitchens and Cleo needed to talk to someone under the age of twenty-seven.

Feeling thoroughly ready to walk out on strike, Rosemary picked up the phone and called Vince.

"What's up, Rosemary?" he greeted her.

"Can you make sure your sister brings Hannah to the party tonight? Cleo needs another little girl to chatter with before we both go stir crazy."

"I'll call Monica and make sure, but I can't see Hannah passing up the chance to see Cleo—she's been asking about her. How are you two holding up?"

"I'd be doing better if there was any change in sight, and if this room didn't have a guest coming to sleep in it in a couple of days. I'm pretty sure they won't want to share. They've got to find Mike so we can get back to real life."

"They're working on it. Don't worry, the police are finding leads all of the time."

"I hope so." She looked out the window and wished she could go for a walk. "I've been thinking Joel needs to come up and review some self defense moves, but there's no real defense against a gun."

"I thought when he reviewed them with you girls last fall you said you didn't need any help," Vince teased her.

"I didn't have to protect myself and a nine-year-old then."

"True enough." There was sound of paper being shuffled in the background. "I'll see what I can do about Hannah. See you in the private dining room tonight."

"Thanks."

"Is she coming?" Cleo asked as soon as Rosemary ended the call.

"We'll see. How's the social studies coming?"

"It's so boring!"

"Everything with you is boring! When it's done, we can move on to art." It was a constant struggle to keep them both on task and Rosemary was absolutely certain—supporting what she'd already known—that she didn't want to be a teacher or home school her kids.

"Okay." Cleo didn't seem all that excited.

"I thought you loved art."

"I did at my old school. We got to paint and work with clay and other cool things. Here we just draw stuff, which is all right, but I'm not really that good at drawing."

"Me either. You saw the drawing I did for Cami's cake."

Rosemary had been sneaking down to work on the cake after Cleo went to bed the past few nights, leaving the officer at the door to keep an eye on things outside and Harrison inside. Her time alone in the pastry end of the kitchen with basically no one around to bother her had been her saving grace. Otherwise she was afraid she would have thrown something at someone by now. She glanced over at the countertop in the hotel room's wet bar and wondered how badly it would stain if they mixed fondant on it.

Deciding to deviate a little from the plan, she called down to the kitchen requesting a list of tools and supplies that would overwhelm most home bakers. They were delivered fifteen minutes later.

Rosemary thought this was the kind of thing her father would have done with her—not the cake decorating, of course, but finding something they could enjoy together. His face was too well known for them to go out much in DC, so he found ways for them to hang out together and talk. She'd forgotten about that and wondered why.

Cleo looked over at Rosemary curiously as she set things out. "What are you doing?"

"We're going to have a different kind of art lesson when you finish social studies. Your pencil drawing can wait."

"We're going to decorate cakes?" Cleo sounded unimpressed.

"Just wait and see."

She set out the rolling mat and pin, looked at the gum paste they'd sent and the modeling chocolate, inspected her gum paste tools to make sure they were clean, and nodded in satisfaction. When it was all laid out, she looked over at Cleo again. "Done yet?"

"Almost. Stupid Magna Carta." She scribbled a couple more lines and stuffed her paper into her book. "Done. What are we doing?"

"I think you need to learn to make some flowers and butterflies. They're adding a few cupcakes to the cake for dinner tonight, since more people are coming than I planned on, so we'll add these to the frosted cupcakes to dress them up. The cake is garden themed, so it'll be perfect."

"I get to help?" Cleo looked intrigued.

"Yes, but first, pull back your hair in a ponytail and wash your hands, then we'll get to work."

They were still working on it when Harrison walked in holding a bowl from the kitchen an hour later. "Hey, what are you ladies doing?"

Cleo looked up, happiness sparkling in her eyes. "I'm making butterflies for some cupcakes."

"Cool." He walked over and slid an arm around Rosemary's waist, easing her back against him and pressing his lips to the bare nape of her neck. "I think this is one of my favorite spots, right here," he muttered as his slid his mouth up along her skin and around to the hollow under her ear.

Rosemary shivered delightedly, turning her head to accommodate his explorations. "You sure about that?"

"I said 'one of,' didn't I?" he murmured low enough she doubted Cleo could understand.

"I see." Her mouth felt suddenly dry and she had to take a drink from her ever-present water bottle. "Take a closer look at the butterflies. Aren't they awesome?"

He pointed to one that was flawless. "You really need to watch that piping bag, you messed this one up, Cleo."

She giggled. "That one is Rosemary's."

"Really? I thought they were all yours." He set the bowl on the table, revealing that it was a mix of fresh fruits. "Thought you might need a break from your hard paperwork, but I see I'm mistaken."

"Hey, fruit is a nice break anyway. Cleo's been learning all about color and how to mix them to make other colors, when outlining is helpful and when it's not. She's going to draw some of tonight's cupcakes for her school project."

"That's brilliant." He set an approving hand on Cleo's shoulder for a couple of seconds, then moved on to the coffee table, pulling it closer to the sofa.

Rosemary and Cleo bookended him when they sat down and they talked and laughed for fifteen minutes while they demolished the selection of melon, apple, orange slices, pineapple chunks, and strawberries.

"I can't believe we ate all of that when dinner is in," Rosemary checked her watch. "Two hours. I won't want any dinner."

"I will. You said I could order pizza if I want!" Cleo bounced off of the sofa. "I'm going to finish my butterflies."

"Good plan." Rosemary watched her put on fresh food-safe gloves and return to work with great concentration.

"She's enjoying herself," Harrison said.

"Yeah. It's been good to have this time together, I think. Good for her to know I don't think she's in the way." She leaned a little against his shoulder.

"Has she called you mom again since the ski accident?"

"Once." It made Rosemary sad that it hadn't stuck, but she promised to let Cleo make her own decisions about this—she wouldn't push. "How are things going down there?"

"Been better. It's getting a little frenetic planning for our big visitors next week—I keep hearing whispers from the employees, speculating on who it might be."

She imagined it would get worse when the prince and princess of Denmark actually arrived. "Anyone guess right yet?"

"Not that I know of." He slid his hand into hers. "How are you doing?"

"I just want them to catch Mike, or tell me that he's home again so we can get back to real life. I can't stand having this hang over my head. And I want to be doing something about it—not waiting for someone else to fix my problems for me." She'd never been good at letting someone else be in control.

"You don't do well with that, do you?"

"Not at all. Inaction gives me hives."

"Funny," he said, leaning in for a kiss, "I don't remember seeing any hives."

She smiled as their lips met. "Not very observant, are you?"

"Yes, I am."

"Hello, I'm standing right here," Cleo said when the kiss lingered for a long moment.

"I know. If you don't like it, turn your head." Rosemary pulled away though. "You probably ought to be getting back to work," she said to Harrison.

"Probably. It was nice to get away for a little bit, though. I needed a break from my desk."

"Yeah, it's like you're chained to it, you spend so much time there." They both knew she worked more hours than he did, but that was the nature of their jobs—and partly her choice since she insisted on cooking more than most kitchen managers did.

"Forty-hours per week is a lot to ask of a man," he returned.

She wished she only worked forty-hour weeks. "You're just mean."

He grinned and stood, pulling her up with him and leading her to the door. Before he opened it, he brushed his lips over hers once, twice, three times. "See you later tonight."

"You bet." She sighed a little as he left the room, then turned back to Cleo.

"And you're not in love with him?" Cleo's brows lifted the same way Cami's did when she was making a point.

Rosemary smiled. "Shut up, squirt."

Cleo laughed and did as she was told.

Rosemary was left wondering if she'd recognize love if she saw it—was that what this was? She felt so good when Harrison was around—cherished, as if there was nothing and no one more important to him. And she wanted to make things easier for him too, but he was a man who seemed perfectly content in his life. What did she have to offer him?

Chapter 28

"Careful, don't break them!" Cleo said as Rosemary set the new butterflies on top of the two-dozen cupcakes that had been baked and set aside to go with dinner that night.

"I'm not going to break them." If she did that at this point, she would be humiliated—she'd managed to get them all back downstairs safely enough, after all.

"You better not."

Rosemary finished with the last one and then pulled out her phone to snap some pictures. Then she carried the tray of cupcakes into the dining room. No one else was there yet, just servers, so she set up the cake on an elevated plate and arranged the cupcakes around it. They had opened a room on one end of the ballroom. Another group was on the other end, but the air wall was up between them, and the doors to the hall and other room were locked.

"That's what I want to draw for school," Cleo said.

Pleased with the way it turned out, Rosemary snapped a couple more pictures. "Remind me to print one of these for you tonight so you can draw it."

"Okay. Do you think my teacher will care that it isn't the same as everyone else's?"

"I bet she won't mind at all. Where did you put the presents?"

"Under the table. These tablecloths are really long. I bet she won't even know they're there until I pull them out." She grinned.

When Rosemary took the tray back to the kitchen, she waved to the off-duty deputy, Trent Oliver. He stood in plain clothes near the entrance to the private room where they'd be eating tonight. Everyone had to go past him to get in, which made Rosemary a little more comfortable about leaving her daughter alone—even for a minute. "Is this what parenting's supposed to be like?" she muttered to herself. Paranoia about her daughter's safety had begun the moment she'd found out she had been named as guardian, but it had grown exponentially since the attacks began.

She was returning to the dining room when she heard Cleo screaming, "Leave me alone! I don't want to go with you."

Rosemary pushed past the hostess who was leading a couple to their table, and was tight on the officer's heels as he preceded her into the room.

The air backed up in her lungs when she saw Mike holding Cleo around the waist, a gun to her head. "Out of the way or she dies." His eyes were a little wild as he stared at the deputy, who had a gun trained on him.

Had he been in there the whole time? Cleo had said something about how long the tablecloths were. Rosemary felt frozen in place, trying to figure out what to do. Mike wanted Cleo dead, so letting him go with her wasn't the answer.

"I'm with the sheriff's office." Deputy Oliver's hand was rock steady. "Come on, Mike, you know you're not getting out of here alive if you hurt her. Put the gun down and let Cleo go."

"If she had just died in the car accident, I wouldn't have had to do this. Or if her parents had left her to me to take care of, to manage her money. I knew Scott didn't want her." He glared at Rosemary. "Why did you have to get in the way? You left her once; you should have just stayed away."

"I've never stayed away," Rosemary said feeling cold all over. "Didn't you know I was always around, visiting and spending time with Cleo? She was my daughter and I needed to know that she was happy and healthy. That goes triple now."

He glared at Rosemary. "You are so much trouble. I swear you have more lives than a cat. First you aren't hurt in the garage accident, then the snake doesn't bite anyone, you're barely wounded in the ski accident and I missed when I shot at you. But I won't miss

235

this time." His hand was shaky as he nudged the gun against Cleo's head.

Rosemary's lungs seemed to seize as she kept her eyes on the gun. "Mike, is this really about a little bit of money? We know you caused the car accident, and you were behind the bombing. Even if you did get away today, which you won't, it will only be a matter of time before they catch you and take you in." She heard anxious voices behind her and glanced out of the side of her eye to see a couple of the servers whispering together and watching her.

"Wow, you're smarter than I thought. I didn't think you'd realize the bombing was me. Everyone blamed it on terrorists taking out the senator. It was so simple—and it was a total fluke that he was there. What were the chances I'd take out someone important enough to cover the truth?" His gaze never left her face.

"If you hadn't kept coming after me, you would have gotten away with it." Rosemary glanced to the side again, and motioned to the servers to move away.

"What are you looking at?" Mike demanded.

"There are a lot of people in the restaurant, Mike. Let me clear some of them out. We don't want more innocent people involved here, do we?" She watched Cleo, saw the terror in her eyes, heard the way she whimpered. She had to get Cleo free, and she had to get these people out of here.

"No. If you clear them out, you'll call for help. I don't think we need anything extra."

Rosemary saw Joel come into the restaurant at a full-out run, then slow as he approached. He stopped so she was close enough to hear him, but out of Mike's sight.

"Is it Mike?"

She nodded just a little.

"I've already called 911. Help is on the way." He touched the gun in his shoulder holster, then turned to the servers near him and whispered something to them. They started clearing out customers on that side of the restaurant.

Glad to have that issue under control, Rosemary turned her full attention back to Mike and Cleo, who was sobbing. He held her around the waist so her feet didn't touch the floor.

"Come on, Mike," Trent said, stepping further into the room. "You don't want to hurt a kid. It's not her fault. None of this is."

Mike's face tightened. "Not another step or I'll shoot her. I mean it!"

Rosemary froze. "What do you hope to gain, Mike? The deputy here has already told you he'll take you out if you hurt Cleo. What good is this doing?"

"I'm not stupid, I've managed to get this far, haven't I?"

Rosemary could have commented, but she held her tongue. "Are you in a financial bind? Do you need some money to straighten things out?"

"Like you would understand what it's like not to have the money you need," he said, his voice growing a little hysterical. "But you had to take mine away from me too, and it's nothing compared to what you're getting from your father."

"I didn't do anything to you. I just took in Cleo, my daughter, when *you* killed your only brother and his wife. How could you do that to them, after everything they did for you?" The outrage of his actions against Don was almost as strong as her terror for Cleo.

"Uncle Mike, you're hurting me," Cleo said, whimpering. He didn't seem to notice.

Rosemary made her voice a little lower, hoping it sounded calming. "You don't have to hurt anyone. You can still walk away." It was a bald-faced lie. The only way he was getting out of here was with a bullet in him or in handcuffs—and at the moment, Rosemary hoped it was the first option, as long as Cleo wasn't hurt first.

Rosemary glanced over when she saw movement and caught sight of Joel slipping through the door in the air wall and moving in behind Mike.

Her already racing heart seemed to double again as she worried his presence would make things worse. Having someone with Joel's training in this situation was a definite advantage, but she didn't know if it would be enough.

Deputy Oliver didn't take his gaze from Mike and showed no reaction to Joel's arrival. He did talk to her for the first time though. "You should get out of the room, Ms. Keogh. It's not safe for you here."

"Not while he has her." Rosemary decided she needed to keep Mike's attention on herself to give them a chance to do something about the situation. "Don't hurt my little girl, Mike. She's just a kid. She doesn't deserve that."

"She's a throwaway, just like her mother."

Rosemary went cold. She'd heard those words before, from *her* mother about her being like her father, and while the term throwaway never came up, it was implied on a regular basis. Now Rosemary wasn't so upset at the idea of being like her father—not the sleeping around part, but the good-parent part that made him take an interest in her, calling and visiting as often as he could get away with, being there to listen when she was upset.

Had he berated her when she told him about the pregnancy? No, he was sad, maybe disappointed in her, but he let her make the decision that was right for *her*, then supported it. He could have been better in many ways, but when she needed him most, he'd been there for her. She wanted to be that kind of parent for her daughter. And she would protect Cleo through anything.

If she just had the chance.

There was another rustle behind her and she glanced over without turning her head and recognized Harrison's silhouette.

"Is Cleo in there?" he asked.

Trent was talking to Mike, keeping him distracted, so she answered. "Yeah." She kept her words barely more than a whisper and didn't move her lips. "He has a gun on her."

There was a slight hesitation, then Harrison stepped into view, moving in front of Rosemary. "Mike. We haven't met yet, but I've heard a lot about you."

"Harrison, what are you doing?" Rosemary hissed, appalled. Now the two people she cared about most were in the line of fire and she didn't think she could take it.

"Don't move any closer," Mike warned him. "I know who you are. You're with her." He gestured to Rosemary with his chin.

"How did you know we would be in here tonight?" Harrison asked, his voice calm, though his hands shook a little.

"Silly waitress. I flirted a little and she said you were going to be down for some party tonight. I figured this would be my chance. They've been too well protected until now."

"True. We love our girls." He stepped closer to Mike.

"Sir, get out of the way and leave the room," Trent said.

"Stop it. Stop moving," Mike said, his voice turning a little hysterical. "Cut it out."

"That's my girl you've got there," Harrison said, though he did stop where he was. "I can't let you hurt her."

Joel had crept closer, almost close enough to touch Mike, who seemed wholly unaware.

Trent muttered something about idiot civilians. "Mr. Forrest, if you don't get out of this room, I'm going to arrest you."

"Fine, arrest me afterward. But I'm not going anywhere until my girls are safe." He took another step toward Mike, his movement casual.

"Harrison," she protested.

"Stop it!" Mike screamed. He moved his gun to point it at Harrison, Joel slammed the butt of his pistol into the man's head and Harrison managed to grab at Cleo as Mike fell forward. They all landed together in a heap.

Trent jumped toward them and grabbed the gun. Joel already had Mike's hands behind him and a ziptie ready but Mike was unconscious.

"Mom!" Cleo cried, looking at Rosemary, reaching for her with tears rolling down her cheeks.

Rosemary helped extricate her from the jumble, holding her tightly while Cleo clung back. Harrison stood to join them and wrapped his arms around them.

"Thank you," Rosemary said, kissing him firmly. She couldn't believe he had stood for her, stood for Cleo when she needed him most.

"I heard there was something going down here. I couldn't leave you to handle it alone." He ran one hand along her hair. "I can't believe I could have lost you two."

"We're not that easy to get rid of," Rosemary said, but her own cheeks were wet and she shook hard from the adrenaline that still pounded through her system.

"Good."

Cleo was sobbing hysterically and Rosemary cradled her closer. "Hey, sweetie. It's okay. You're okay. He can't hurt either of us ever again." She knew it would be a while before they all believed it.

Another deputy came through the door and took custody of Mike, who was starting to come around. "Looks like he got himself a goose egg."

"I guess we should have that checked out," Trent said, though he didn't sound sorry. "He could have a concussion."

"Sure hope you don't expect me to apologize," Joel said, stony faced.

"No, sir."

Joel came over and checked on Rosemary, Cleo and Harrison. "That was a gutsy thing to do, Harrison. Stupidly gutsy."

"And what you did wasn't?" There was no apology in his voice.

"I'm a trained professional," Joel protested.

"You're trained for action, I'm trained to talk. Looks like we both put our skills to use."

"You're trained to deal with people like that?" Trent asked, his brows lifting.

"I work in human resources—I deal with angry employees on a regular basis. Thankfully none of them have ever come at me with a gun before."

"Let's hope none of them ever do," Rosemary said, starting to feel like her feet were under her again. "And Harrison, as much as I love what you were willing to do for us, if you ever do anything that stupid again, I'll kill you myself."

He simply leaned forward and kissed her again. "I love you too, honey."

Not having a suitable response, she kept her mouth shut.

"Are you going to arrest me?" Harrison asked Trent.

There was a moment of silence, as if the deputy was trying to decide. "You get a pass this time, but don't get in my way again."

Relief filled his features. "I won't."

Rosemary hoped he'd never have a reason to change his mind.

CHAPTER 29

It took nearly an hour to handle reports and get the employees back into the kitchen, though everyone was shaken up. The family party switched to a new room—Rosemary didn't want to stay in that one, even if Detective Carlson had cleared it for use.

The family started to flood in as soon as they were allowed. Concern filled every voice and way too many hugs were dispensed for Rosemary's peace of mind—she didn't think she'd ever hugged so many people in a week, never mind an hour or less.

The eleven members of their family, if you counted Harrison, plus fourteen extra people from Vince's family, counting all of the children, made for quite a crowd.

Children's voices clamored for attention, Hannah and Cleo huddled in one corner sharing secrets, and Rosemary enjoyed the presence of so many people after the several days of near solitude in their suite and the nerve-racking events earlier.

Harrison's arm slipped behind her on the chair and she leaned into him, appreciating his strength and presence. For a moment there, she had been sure she was going to lose him, lose him when it hadn't been that long since they'd found each other.

"Now this is what a family is supposed to be like," he said as everyone talked over everyone else, her sisters bickered good-naturedly over little details and Etta dispensed wisdom of the ages, couched carefully in clichés—not her normal MO, but it fit the evening.

Rosemary watched Cleo interacting with everyone else, the stars in her eyes made of happiness, and possibly even tears. Rosemary had asked her if she wanted to skip dinner, go home instead, but

Cleo had insisted she wanted to join the party. Maybe she needed the feel of friends and family surrounding her—it seemed to make Rosemary feel better too, even though Mike was in jail now, and unlikely to get out anytime soon.

She remembered that good long look at herself in the mirror and focused on healthy portions and good nutrition, worrying less about calories. It hadn't been easy, but she was determined to make better decisions.

The past couple of months had been hard—for all of them, but Rosemary was starting to feel closer to her sisters—even to Delphi and her standoffish ways.

She rubbed her cheek against Harrison's shoulder and he kissed the top of her head. She'd never known such gentleness or steadiness. Was Cleo right about them? About Rosemary's feelings for him? And if she was, what would she do? What *could* she do? The thought of risking everything, of casting her luck to the wind and hoping it came back to her was terrifying.

They had finished presents and were savoring the cake when Cami elbowed Sage. "Go ahead."

"It's your day. I don't want to take the attention off you. It's already been split in so many directions."

Cami glanced at Rosemary, an apology in her expression—for allowing the subject to come up, even if it hadn't been mentioned directly. "You won't. It's just a birthday, and not even a major milestone."

"What's going on?" Rosemary asked.

"She's pregnant," Harrison whispered in her ear.

"What?" Rosemary stared at Sage, who nodded.

"We just confirmed that I'm pregnant. I've suspected it for a while. We're going to have a baby around the first of September," Sage glowed with excitement and Joel wasn't much different.

Hugs and kisses ensued as everyone—including Vince's family—congratulated her.

"How long have you known?" Rosemary asked Harrison. She felt a little shocked by the announcement, though she shouldn't have been. She'd just been so wrapped up in her own issues since the bombing that she hadn't thought much about what the others were going through.

"She didn't tell me," Harrison said. "I just guessed. She's been all glowy and happy for the past few weeks, and you've noticed that Joel barely lets her out of his sight."

"And that was different from before how? He's going to be the most overprotective dad on the planet. Can you imagine if they have a little girl?" Her eyes drifted to her own not-so-little one and she wondered how different things would have been if she hadn't met Harrison on the cruise. She had been recovering from the rejection of Cleo's father, the loss of her baby and the severe jealousy that stemmed from seeing Harrison watching out for Sage when Rosemary had spent the previous ten minutes trying to work up the nerve to go talk to him.

If they had connected then, would she have finished her degree, gone abroad to study? No, she knew she wouldn't have, and she didn't regret any of that, but more and more she did regret not having Harrison as part of her life for the past few months—why had she driven that wedge between them from the first? And how did she make up for it now?

Vince's sister offered to have Cleo over to sleep the next night, but Rosemary demurred, not wanting her little girl out of her sight after the day's events.

"Call me tomorrow?" Cleo asked Hannah when they were preparing to leave.

"Promise. Work on your mom. See if she'll let you come after all."

Rosemary stared at Hannah. She knew Cleo had other parents. Had Cleo told her about the adoption?

"Honey, Cleo's parents..." Etta's voice trailed off as if she didn't want to say it aloud.

"Yeah, but Rosemary is my birth mom," Cleo said, standing a little taller. "That's why my parents asked her to raise me when they died." She looked straight at Rosemary. "Because they knew she loved me already."

Rosemary smiled but couldn't say anything as a lump rose in her throat and tears formed in her eyes. "Yeah. I do," she finally managed to croak out.

"That makes Cleo extra lucky, I guess." Etta took Rosemary's hand and gave it a squeeze.

"Yep." Harrison picked up Cleo and swung her onto his back. She squealed a little and clung, laughing. "And I think it's nearly time for this little one to get to bed."

"But I want to stay up!" Cleo said.

"Not this time, bug. Let's go get our things from the room upstairs. I think it's time we went home," Rosemary said.

"Back to the DiCarlo mansion?" Harrison asked when they finished packing.

"DiCarlo mansion? When did you start calling it that?" Rosemary was exhausted and slumped back against the sofa.

"Just now. I was thinking that it seems awfully big, with all of those empty bedrooms."

"Are you angling to stay the night?" she asked.

"Maybe."

She really didn't know what to say about that. She wanted him close and in the next room was almost as perfect as in hers. "I guess we'll have to discuss terms, then, won't we?"

Cleo made it out to the car on her own steam, but just barely. Harrison carried most of their belongings, with Joel bringing up the rear, also well laden.

"Seriously, you were only there for a few days. What is all of this stuff?" Joel asked.

"We weren't there on vacation," Rosemary said. "We have her homework and my piles of work stuff—most of which is already down in the kitchen, just so you know, and then there are the clothes and other necessities." Perhaps they had brought more things to the hotel than absolutely necessary, but Rosemary had wanted to be prepared—especially since she was sharing a single suite with a wiggly nine-year-old.

They loaded everything into the back of Joel's Range Rover and he trundled them back up to the house.

"Let me know if you need anything," Joel said after he dropped his armload on the seldom-used dining room table.

"Thanks, I think we're going to take a nice, calm night and sleep like the dead." She definitely felt like she could sleep for a week.

"Good plan." He waved goodbye and Harrison locked the door behind him.

"Up to bed, sleepyhead," Rosemary told Cleo.

"Do I have to sleep in my own bed?" she asked. "Alone?"

"Mike has been arrested. It's safe now, sweetie," Rosemary said, hoping Cleo would settle for some reassurance.

She considered that for a moment. "Can you come up with me for a while?"

"Sure. I'll be right there."

"Both of you?" She looked over at Harrison.

Harrison stuffed his hands in his pockets. "You bet. I'll be up too. In just a minute."

"Okay." Cleo padded up to her room, yawning wide enough to drive a freight train through.

"Are you okay?" Harrison asked, sliding an arm around Rosemary's shoulder.

"I could have lost my baby." She buried her face in his shirt. "I can't believe he was that close to her."

"It's okay now." He tipped her head up and brushed his lips over hers in a light caress, but she wanted more, needed more this time and pulled him closer, deepening the kiss, losing herself in him and his arms, his love and strength after an experience that had left her feeling adrift.

"Thank you. You didn't have to risk your life for us," she muttered against his mouth.

"I really did."

He pulled her against him and for a moment she forgot that there was anyone or anything else in the world, but reality intruded and she pulled back, slowly, not wanting to, but needing to. "Can we put a bookmark in this and come back to it later?" she asked. "Cleo's waiting."

"Right. We should go to her." He swallowed hard, as if stopping wasn't what he wanted.

"Yeah." But all Rosemary could think of was how much she wanted to dive back in again—how much simpler life seemed when she was kissing him.

Cleo lay in the middle of Lana's queen-sized mattress and Harrison and Rosemary took opposite sides, squeezing on top beside her. "Sorry it took a minute longer than we planned on," Rosemary said.

"Yeah, because you were kissing. I know you were—he has a smear of your lipstick on his mouth." She closed her eyes and Harrison reached up to wipe at his mouth, embarrassment radiating from him.

"Fine. I was kissing him. I like kissing him, a lot." Rosemary decided brazening it out was the safest bet.

"Good. When people get married, they should like kissing each other. My mom and dad liked to kiss a lot too. I used to think it was yucky, but now I think maybe it's good."

Mildly embarrassed, Rosemary shifted the topic, asking about the plans Cleo and Hannah had started cooking up at dinner, and then Harrison spun out a story his mother used to tell him as a boy. Before he finished, Cleo was fast asleep.

They tiptoed out of the room and mostly closed the door behind them.

"She seems to be dealing pretty well," Harrison observed.

"For now. Tomorrow morning might be another issue. And she'll probably have nightmares tonight." She shivered a little and rubbed her arms. "Sage used to wake up screaming. Even before the stalker followed her here."

Harrison's brows furrowed. "She did? She never said that."

"She wouldn't. Though she can put on a nice face, it doesn't mean that there isn't plenty going on below the surface." She sent him a side-long glance. "You of all people ought to know that."

"I do." He leaned against the railing and urged her closer to him. "Are you going to have nightmares tonight? Would a little company make you sleep better?"

"Probably, but you can't spend the night in my bed, Harrison." She kept her voice to a whisper. "I have a daughter in the house."

"Are you going to let her go to Hannah's tomorrow night if she still feels up to it?" he asked, nuzzling against her ear. "Because I was thinking if she's not going to be here, maybe we could have a sleepover too. At *my* house."

She smiled and brushed her lips over his jaw line. "That sounds fabulous."

CHAPTER 30

Sending Cleo back to school on Monday wasn't as easy as Rosemary expected. She'd given Cleo an out, said she could stay home one more day if she wanted, give her time to think before she had to face curious kids and the rumors that had to be floating around already. Despite the two fiery nightmares that had woken Cleo screaming—along with everyone else in the house, she had insisted.

Rosemary dropped her off by the front office, then went in to talk to the school counselor to let her know what was going on and make sure they would call if anything happened.

Then she dragged herself back to work, exhausted.

Once she was fully alert, it was good to be in the kitchen again, barking orders and keeping her hands and mind busy with something that wasn't about the attack. Keeping Harrison off her mind was another issue entirely, though. He seemed to sneak in when she least expected it, reminding her that whatever was going on between them was still unresolved. She was even more confused about her decisions now than she was earlier.

He'd declared his feelings several times now, but the thought of going all-in terrified her.

She'd been putting off a decision, though, telling herself that when everything was settled with Mike, she would figure out what she thought about her situation with Harrison. Now she had to face her options and figure out what she wanted to do.

"Distracted today?" Tate asked around one o'clock.

"Huh? Oh, yeah, I guess." Then she realized the crepe she was cooking had been in the pan too long. She growled at herself and threw it away. "Yeah. Maybe I should take a quick breather."

"Go ahead. I'll keep an eye on things," he said.

Rosemary's eyes burned a little from staring at the food, so she grabbed her jacket and headed for the outdoors. The grounds were beautiful in the snow and the walks were cleared. Fresh air was just what she needed.

It was nice to be outside, alone, with no one watching. She sucked in a greedy breath of the frigid air and felt some of the clouds in her mind start to roll away.

"Taking a break?"

She turned to find Blake coming up behind her.

"Yeah. When I start making mistakes in the kitchen, it's time to clear my head. You too?"

"No, just coming in from a meeting downtown. There was a frozen water pipe in the childcare center we opened last summer and I had to handle some of the details. I saw you out here and thought I'd take a minute to see how you're holding up."

"Are you going to send your son there?" she asked as he fell into step with her. She wasn't looking to rehash the previous night's events.

"We'll see. It depends on what Lana wants to do. I mean, she might not want to come back to work after she finishes maternity leave. Or she might come back just to finish her contract."

Rosemary thought Lana would want to come back; she'd spent fifteen years working for her current position and giving it up didn't seem likely. On the other hand, Rosemary knew how strong the maternal instinct could be when you held that baby in your arms—much stronger than you thought before. "And if she doesn't return, how does that affect the inheritance?"

He smiled. "I checked with Alex about the will. He said there was a baby clause in it that would alter the contract. Seems George was very hopeful about us getting back together."

"Or for one of the others getting married and settling down with a family right off the bat," Rosemary said. "Seems a little too optimistic, even for him."

"He was nothing if not thorough. But really," he changed the subject back, "how are you?"

"Better than I expected, all things considered. I won't be sleeping well for a while, and Cleo might need counseling." She rubbed the back of her head. "I don't know what to do for her—she's been through so much. How do you deal with all of that at her age? I'm not sure how to deal with it myself."

"You haven't exactly had an easy life up until now."

"Have any of us? I think Jonquil's the most normal of the bunch and she isn't exactly scar-free, either."

He didn't say anything, which prompted her to ask, "What kind of mother am I going to make, I mean, really? I don't even know what I'm doing."

He laughed. "You think Lana and I have any idea what we're doing, or that Joel and Sage aren't freaked out about being parents—especially Joel. You think you had it rough; your life was easy compared to his."

Her feelings cooled at the comparison. "You don't know me very well if you can say that."

"I know your mom never appreciated you, had a string of boyfriends and thinks only about herself. But your father loved you and checked on you, made sure you had food and clothes and a decent education. He supported your decisions and you had a set of surrogate parents who gave you the love and attention you never got from your mom and couldn't count on regularly from your dad." He shot her a look. "How am I doing?"

She considered the way he put it. "Close enough."

Blake nodded. "Joel had a roof over his head and pretty much nothing else good from this list. You know something about healthy relationships, because you had the Markhams. You've seen from them what it means to be a mother, to love and care, and I can tell from watching you with Cleo that you're going to be just fine at the job. Not perfect because, well, you're human, and we all make mistakes as parents, but you give her what she needs most, so she'll turn out okay."

Rosemary's eyes burned. She hadn't seen her life in quite that way before. She did have the Markhams there to turn to. And while her feelings about her dad wouldn't be resolved anytime soon, he had cared about her, checked on her, supported her decisions—when she wasn't being an idiot. That was something, anyway. "Thanks. I think I needed to hear that."

"You're welcome. Next time you need a pep talk, you know where to come." He slung one arm around her shoulder.

She chuckled a little. "You're really good at this big brother stuff."

"I like having sisters. Most of the time. It's a nice change, and I don't really see eye-to-eye with my brother. He can't forgive me for what happened with Dad." His voice grew sad.

"Then he's the one missing out—what happened wasn't your fault and you're pretty terrific at what you do. It's not like you lack for family here."

He smiled. "No, I don't. Convenient that, just when I needed it." He gave her a squeeze. "So, you and Harrison, huh? I have to admit, I didn't see that coming."

She chuckled. "Me either, though it doesn't seem to have surprised him or Sage."

"You can't keep anything from Sage, though."

"Isn't that the truth?"

They reached the front doors of the hotel again and he gestured to them. "Ready to go in?"

"I guess so. I ought to check on my minions." Somehow it seemed less of a chore now than it had a few minutes earlier. "Thanks for the walk."

"My pleasure."

They parted ways in the foyer and she headed back to the kitchen, not just refreshed, but with a better outlook. Yeah, things had sucked for her growing up, but she hadn't been left totally to her own devices. And things now were better than they'd been in a long time.

It definitely bore thinking on—when she wasn't cooking.

"I like that dress. It's pretty," Cleo declared when she walked into Rosemary's room at a quarter after six.

"Thanks. I like it too." It was one of the few dresses Rosemary owned. She didn't think Harrison was planning on pizza and ice cream, and she felt like dressing up—it was Valentine's Day, after all. She picked up some lapis lazuli earrings her father had given her a few years earlier and put them on. She didn't have a matching necklace, but the chunky gold chain hanging in her armoire would do the trick just fine.

"When you marry Harrison, are we going to move to his house? And does that mean we won't move back to DC?"

Rosemary's fingers fumbled with the necklace clasp as she tried to open it. "What? Honey, why do you keep asking me about marriage?"

Cleo shrugged. "You love each other, right? What else do you need? I thought that was why people got married."

"Yeah, but there's more to it than that." Rosemary struggled for the words, then felt like she had been hit with a sledge hammer. She'd never admitted to anyone that she loved Harrison, wouldn't let herself even think that way, but she did. She sat in the chair and stared at herself in the mirror in shock, realizing she'd been in love with Harrison for a long time—maybe since before they officially started dating. How had that happened—and why had she been so pig-headed she hadn't realized it? She sucked in a breath, feeling suddenly light-headed.

"What else is there?" Cleo asked, oblivious to Rosemary's epiphany. "That's all that matters in the movies. Sometimes people get married without even loving each other—but what's the point of that? It's just stupid. You get married to someone because you want to be with them all of the time. You're always happy when Harrison is around, aren't you?"

"Mostly, yeah." Except for when he was driving her crazy, but that didn't happen very much anymore. She wondered who had changed so they had stopped arguing all of the time. Had that just been to cover up their feelings, and now they were dating, they didn't have to fight all of the time? Her head spun.

"Hey, are you okay?" Cleo asked. "You look kinda sick."

"I'm fine, bug. Just getting ready to put on my shoes. Did Jonquil get in yet?" She would be watching Cleo tonight since she didn't have a Valentine's date like Rosemary did—an oddity in itself as Jonquil was usually the one with the dates.

"Yes, and she bought a box of Ho-Hos for us to share while we watch movies." There was a note of mischief in Cleo's voice.

Rosemary shuddered theatrically, knowing it was expected. "You're not allowed to eat that stuff. Doesn't Jonquil know better? I could have brought something that was made with real ingredients from work if she wanted me to."

"You're so silly."

"You should put on your jams before I leave," Rosemary suggested.

"It's still early. Besides, Hannah's little brother got into my stuff and I think he pulled out my pajama top. It must still be at her house. He gets into everything."

"So pick a different pair from the drawer," Rosemary suggested, though she knew the Cinderella set was Cleo's favorite. "You were like that when you started to crawl, you know—into everything. Your parents had to bolt all of the shelves and stuff to the walls so you wouldn't pull it down on yourself."

"Are all babies like that?" Cleo wrapped her arms around her legs and set her chin on her knees.

"Pretty much. They like to explore."

"Maybe we'll have to bolt my shelves and stuff to the wall when Lana and Sage have their babies. Do you think Sage will let me touch her tummy to feel her baby moving like Lana does?"

"Probably. You'll have to ask her."

"And when you have a baby, will I get to feel that too?"

"Again with the getting ahead of yourself." Rosemary touched her stomach and felt it turn over a little. Not from sickness, but the thought of being pregnant again threw her for a loop. If she had another baby, she would plan ahead and would get to raise and care for it. It was scary, but somehow a lot more exciting than the same thought would have been a few months earlier.

"Don't you want more kids?" Cleo asked.

"Yeah. I do." Rosemary felt the certainty down to her toes, and for the first time in a long time, she knew what she needed to do.

CHAPTER 31

Harrison had rushed home from work to pick up his apartment and throw dinner together. Though he'd offered to pick her up, Rosemary had promised to come straight over when Jonquil got home.

He checked the time once more as he stirred the Alfredo sauce and checked the pasta he was cooking. Would she be on time, or would everything be mush when she arrived? He glanced at the roses he'd asked Jonquil to put together for him and told himself he shouldn't be so nervous, but he couldn't help it.

The doorbell rang and he sighed with relief, checked his shirt to make sure he hadn't splattered on it, then answered the door. "Hello, come on in."

She smiled up at him as she walked inside. When she unbuttoned her coat, he nearly lost his breath.

Rosemary stood in his entryway wearing an electric blue cocktail dress that clung in all the right places, hinting at the fact that she had gained back a few pounds, turning her sharp edges into perfect curves. The flowing skirt fell a few inches short of her knees, and her long legs stretched down to a pair of matching blue heels that did things for her calves that had his mouth watering. She seemed to glow—even her eyes sparkled as she look at him.

"Wow."

She grinned. "Right back at ya." She tugged on his jacket lapels and stepped into his arms, sliding her hands along the pale blue linen of his shirt and around his neck, planting her mouth on his.

He skimmed his hands up her side and back down again, leaving them to rest gently at her hips as he took his time with the kiss hello. Something about her felt different; she was more accepting and calm than he'd seen her in a while. Maybe ever. "Welcome home." He meant that more literally than she probably realized.

"Thanks." She shifted away with visible reluctance. "Whatever you're making smells wonderful. What is it?"

"Pasta." He took her coat and hung it in the closet. "I hope you're hungry."

"I ate light today, figuring you'd carb load me tonight." She didn't seem bothered by that possibility though. "Cleo kept talking about her new cousins being born and wondering if she would be able to feel Sage's baby move like she could with Lana's."

"Yeah, she seems fascinated by that. I can't blame her." The thought of holding Rosemary and feeling their baby's movements inside of her made his heart fill with longing, but he wasn't going to push her—he promised himself he wouldn't push, even though he wanted to.

"It's not as fascinating after the kid has been doing flips in your stomach all evening and plants their foot on your bladder so it has to be emptied every half an hour," she said a little dryly.

"I bet. It's still a miracle, though."

"Yeah. It is."

He checked the noodles and declared dinner ready. He dished it up and they sat to eat. "So, now you don't have to run off to Aruba or Bermuda, or some other island paradise that ends in A, how are you feeling?" he asked.

"Funny how many people keep asking me that question."

"They ask about Aruba? Wow. I didn't realize I was so unoriginal."

"You know what I mean." She kept her voice light.

"Yeah, I know. You have a family full of people who worry about you. Starting with me."

Her brow furrowed a little, but she answered without indicating whatever she'd been thinking. "I'm doing surprisingly well. Before I left, I didn't even lecture Jonquil for half an hour about keeping my baby safe. I managed to keep it to less than a minute—against my inclinations."

Harrison slid his fingers over hers on the table, wishing he could reassure her, but he was going to be very protective of both of them for a while—maybe always, so he understood. "She's going to grow more independent over time, not less."

"Yeah, I'm trying not to think about that, or the things that could happen to her on the street from strangers, never mind someone who should love and protect her. I just can't wrap my head around Mike being behind everything, even though it's been a few days now."

"It's pretty nuts."

She hesitated a little, biting her lip. "I used to wonder if you met my mom, if you saw the kind of person she was, would you think that's how I'd turn out?" She studied him for a moment. "But you don't do you?"

"No. You're nothing like Wanda. You're a pretty incredible mom, you know that? You claim that you can't make commitments, that you're scared that you'll be like her, but you love Cleo so much. You're so good with her and when you jumped in to take her, you put everything into it, from the day you found out. It's impressive."

"Just keep telling me that when I screw up and she hates decisions I make."

"I will." He grinned.

"Why do you put up with me?" Her expression was so confused, uncertain.

"Put up with you? What do you mean?" Where was this coming from?

"I know I'm not exactly Miss America. Why did you pick me when you have so many other options?"

"Because you're you. You're honest and straightforward when it matters most. You've overcome huge odds, and you make me feel like I can do anything, even though I'm no Superman."

Her eyes were a little shiny, but she didn't let any tears fall. "Who wants Superman anyway?"

"Hopefully not you."

"No way."

Her smile warmed him all the way to his toes.

When dinner was over and they lingered over slices of chocolate mousse cake, she noticed the way he fidgeted with his utensils and decided it was now or never. Or rather that it was now and forever. Dinner churned in her stomach, but getting to this place was a major accomplishment and she didn't want to give herself a chance to back out.

"There's something I need to say," she told him when the silence stretched between them for the first time that night.

"Okay, but let me go first. I might lose my nerve if you talk first." He looked anxious and rubbed his hands together a little.

"Unlikely," she denied, but ceded the floor, even though it would be twice as hard to bring it up after a postponement. She really had no idea where to start anyway.

"I've been telling myself for days that I'm pushing you too hard, that I'm going to end up scaring you away when I know how commitment phobic you are. Still, I can't help but think that it's better for you to know what I'm thinking or feeling rather than leaving you to guess."

She nodded, feeling her mouth go dry and her heart start to speed.

"I'm going to lay it out for you, so there's no confusion." He took her hand. "I love you. I want us to get married and make a family, have another a kid or two so Cleo doesn't have to be an only child. I know you're not ready yet, that it might take some time to prove to you that I'm not going to disappear. I'm not pushing for that now, but I wanted you to know that's what I see, what I want so when you're ready you won't be left wondering. When I look at you and Cleo I see my future. There's nothing that means more to me than that."

He didn't get any more words out because she touched her finger to his lips, amazed at how much easier he'd made this for her. Funny that she still felt light-headed. "My turn. I've been fighting the way I felt for you almost from the moment we met. I'm pretty hard headed and I don't always share what I'm thinking or feeling and I know that's going to make me hard to live with sometimes."

"Sometimes?" he asked, teasingly.

"Shush," she smiled, feeling the love in her chest intensify. "I don't know why you'd pick someone as messed up as I am, but after everything we've been through together I can say this much: I love you. I want to marry you too, and there's no one else I'd rather make a family with, grow a family with. It's you and me all the way, and you're not backing out on me now, so don't even think about it. I'd ask Cleo how she feels, but I think she's made it pretty clear that she's good with having you in our family."

He smiled and talked against the finger that still touched his lips. "I asked her last week how she'd feel about me marrying you. She said she'd like that."

Rosemary took her finger away and pressed a kiss to his lips instead. "I guess that explains why she's been so pushy lately." She slid around the edge of the table and he pulled her onto his lap so they could wrap their arms around each other.

"Do you need the big fancy ceremony, or can we do it this spring?" He brushed the hair back from her face, his fingertips teasing her earlobe. "I don't want to wait long. I want you both here every night." He kissed her again, this time a little more urgently than before.

"Sounds good to me." She felt a thrill of mischief go through her. "I don't need a big deal—just a big fancy dress and a thousand flowers and an absolutely perfect ring—you don't happen to have ring already, do you?"

He laughed. "Sounds like a simple ceremony. I kinda hoped it wouldn't take the whole year to get you to see it my way, so I decided to be prepared." He helped her off his lap, then led her into his room, retrieving a black velvet box from his nightstand drawer.

Her heart fluttered. He'd been thinking ahead, hadn't he? This was making things official—which both excited and scared her. When he popped the box open, she sighed. It *was* perfect.

"I thought you would prefer something understated—in complete opposition of everything else that is you. Something that you can wear while you work," he said, passing it to her.

She pulled the ring from the box. It didn't have a large stone, but a row of channel-cut diamonds circled the platinum band instead, creating a smooth surface that wouldn't catch on the gloves she wore with messier mixes and dishes.

"Do you like it?" he asked, as if uncertain.

"Yes."

He smiled and slid it onto her finger and to her surprise, it fit.

"It's perfect." She looked up at him, her heart pounding with excitement. "It's so perfect. You're so perfect for me." She kissed him again.

"I noticed how you changed the wording on that last one," he said when they came up for air. "Only the ring is perfect?"

She laughed. "Well, you're crazy enough to want to marry me so you couldn't possibly be perfect. And really, I just want a fabulous dress and our families at the ceremony. We can keep this a family matter."

"Now *that* sounds utterly perfect." He kissed her again. "I'll talk to Vince about that fairy cottage—maybe he can make it big enough for three of us."

She laughed and felt the echoes of all the bad decisions she'd ever made come back to her. Suddenly they made sense—they brought her here, and there was nowhere she'd rather be.

ACKNOWLEDGEMENTS

Rosemary's story has been so much fun for me to write. She's quirky and brash and covers her pain with a tough exterior, but she's been through tough times and come out stronger for it. It's been so much fun writing her story!

I have to thank the many fans who've anxiously awaited this book—your enthusiasm and support mean more than you can possibly know. And many thanks to Maria Hoagland and Rebecca Blevins who proofed the book for me and helped me make it better. And lots of hugs and kisses (and no-bake cookies) in thanks for my husband, Bill, who loves me, supports me, and is excited to see me succeed at anything. Love you, honey!

ABOUT THE AUTHOR

Heather Tullis has been reading romance for as long as she can remember and has been publishing in the genre since 2009. When she's not dreaming up new stories to write, she runs with the local volunteer ambulance, enjoys gardening, playing with her chickens, geese and ducks, cake decorating and working with her husband in their small business.

Learn more about her at her website at http://heathertullis.blogspot.com/ or her Facebook fan page http://www.facebook.com/HeatherTullisBooks.